Bauer's Run

Bauer's Run

Catherine Curtis

Catherine Curtis

ISBN:10 1497565138
ISBN-13:978-149-7565135

DEDICATION

This is for Bill.
Without his love and encouragement this
book would not exist.

Also for my cheering squad,

Jack and Andrew

ACKNOWLEDGMENTS

No one writes in a vacuum. My circle of friends who read this manuscript in various stages and made valuable suggestions along the way--you know who you are. I couldn't have done it without you.

Any errors in this book are the author's alone.

Catherine Curtis

Prologue

World War II

In the summer of 1944, Allied forces established a beach head in Normandy and turned their faces south to Paris and east to Germany. There were to be many more casualties and hard-fought battles, but in September, the Allies made their first advance onto German soil.

That summer, the tight circle around Hitler began to disintegrate. In July, there was an unsuccessful attempt on his life. Hitler quickly reasserted command and there were wholesale executions of those involved or perceived to be involved in the plot. Even his most loyal officers could see the hand-writing on the wall and began to think of their own skins and a plan for the future. Some envisioned a "Fourth Reich" and sought a way to plan for that day.

In December the Germans, led by General von Rundstedt, launched a counter-attack in the Ardennes Forest of Belgium.

The "Battle of the Bulge" in the Ardennes was to exact a terrible toll on both Allied and German forces, but the Allied march east was inexorable.

Individual German officers began to slip away, many to South America. Few remained to be tried later by the Allies at Nuremberg. Several of the highest ranks, including Hitler, Goebbels and Himmler committed suicide to avoid being tried for war crimes. Goering and eleven others stood trial and were sentenced to death. Goering managed to end his own life before he could be executed.

It was May of 1945 before Germany surrendered to the Allies at Rheims, France. The war that claimed millions of lives would continue to haunt the world for the remainder of the twentieth century and beyond.

Part One
Changeling

Chapter 1

The deep growl of a truck engine in low gear preceded the lorry as it rolled slowly into Berlin's blacked out Friedrichstrasse. Black cloth with just a slit permitted only a narrow beam of light to escape from the headlamps. Fog and misty, light rain swirled in the weak beams as the lorry rolled quietly along the street. The truck drew to a stop near the end of the block. Most of the prosperous-looking houses were boarded up, all were dark. Only an occasional window was seen on the upper floors; there was no light to be seen in any.

No movement came from the truck for several minutes after the engine was shut off. It sat as a great beast, waiting in the dark. The passenger side door opened quietly. A tall man stepped out. His face was not visible in this moonless night, but he carried himself well and moved quickly to the door of the nearest house. He stood for just a moment, turning his face to the sky. It would not clear tonight. The low, heavy cloud layer and rain meant no bombing. Odd that the weather brought respite from the bombs for city dwellers but sheer misery for the troops out in it. Shaking his head, he tore down a paper attached to the door and disappeared inside.

In a partially shuttered window across the street, two men came alert at the appearance of the lorry. Both moved even closer to the window. The older of the two Arabs, an Egyptian, raised a pair of glasses to his eyes and strained to make out a face in the dark street. The fatigue of the long watch showed only in his shoulders. Now the younger man eagerly shifted his weight from foot to foot in anticipation. The boy had no patience. He alternately paced, drank endless cups of coffee and reread the few documents spread out on the table.

A few moments later, the tall man stepped out of the door of the house and motioned to the driver. The driver slipped out of the cab of the truck and walked to the rear, then opened the canvas and climbed up inside. In just a few short seconds, a small, wiry man was rudely shoved out the back, barely landing on his feet. The man looked bewildered in his striped, oversized pajamas that identified him as a prisoner. Laughing, the driver was brought up short by a terse order from the tall officer who stood by the door of the house.

"Silence you idiot! Hurry."

The three men entered the house and closed the door behind them. As the tall man switched on a lamp in the entrance hall, his once handsome face was cast into a caricature of horror. A jagged scar coursed down the side of his face from brow to chin like a wandering country stream. His ice blue eyes dared any to pity him. Close-cropped brown hair and squared shoulders told of a lifetime of discipline. His worn but spotless officer's tunic was tailored for him. An iron cross hung from a silver chain around his neck. The creases in his pants were sharp as a knife, even in the dampness. There was no doubt that he was in charge. The driver took his tongue lashing in silence, eyes down cast, fists clenched.

The officer took a moment then to read the

paper he had torn from the door; this house had been confiscated for the Reich. The penalty for entering was death. A sound somewhere between a snarl and a laugh escaped his mouth as he wadded the paper and threw it to the floor.

Now the driver and his charge, whose family had lived in this beautiful house for generations, made many trips up and down the stairs. Each time they brought up crates as carefully as one would carry a child. Soon the large entry hall was so full of crates it was nearly impossible to turn around. The officer stood silently, cataloging each crate in a small blue book he held in his hand.

On the last trip up the stairs the driver once more risked his superior's wrath. He was tired, and tired of the officer's stony silence. Laughing, he planted his foot into the backside of his charge, sending the old prisoner sprawling to the floor. The crate the man was carrying, the very last one, split open on impact. The officer bent and retrieved the precious Van Gogh that spilled out, now ripped beyond repair. Anger flashed only momentarily in his eyes before they went stone-cold again. Without a word, he snapped off the light and slipped out the door to observe the street.

He stood there a moment in the dark, calming his anger and steadying his nerves. When he stepped back inside, he said, "Quickly now, this is the last, get them loaded."

He once more stood watch as the others did the work. When the last package was secured in the back of the truck, the prisoner walked hesitantly up to the officer.

"Please Sir may I look just one last time at the house?"

The officer gave a twisted smile as he replied, "It's just Horst, Jacob. Of course you can. Do you think we are barbarians? It won't be long now. When this war is over, you and your family will return to live in this house as you always have."

As the man walked past him into the house, the officer gave an abrupt nod to the driver. Moving quickly now, the driver pulled a pistol from his blouse and unceremoniously shot the prisoner in the back of the head. He turned to the officer with brutal satisfaction in his voice, "Well, that ends that."

Horst nodded his head; "It does indeed."

A puzzled look and then terrified comprehension crossed the driver's face in the split second before the officer raised his Luger and shot him in the face.

Horst moved quickly then. He removed the dead man's blouse and exchanged it for his own, put his own watch on the driver's wrist and a silver chain and medallion around the dead man's neck.

Across the street, the man watching nearly dropped his glasses in shock. This was unexpected; his orders were only to watch. He instructed the boy with him to get his bicycle and deliver a message as fast as he could.

"Carefully Hamid, carefully. You must not be seen. Stick to the back streets, but get to the general fast. Tell him 'the prize is moving'."

The boy had just opened the street door a

crack when he heard another shot in the street and quickly closed the door. He leaned his head against the jamb and waited for the pounding of his heart to subside before he slowly opened the door again. Sliding carefully along hugging the wall of the house, he was able to turn the corner without being seen. Only then did he begin to breathe again.

The man who had been watching from the window stowed the glasses in his coat and gathered up the documents strewn on the table. When he was confident there was nothing left behind to identify him, he extinguished the small light and moved toward the door.

Across the street, the officer reached into a small alcove behind the door and returned with a much worn shotgun. *Jacob must have used this for birds.* Using a single shell at point-blank range, he obliterated the driver's face. *I wonder if I will ever feel anything again. I wonder if I will ever care about anything again.*

Bauer's Run

Chapter 2

Horst was exhausted. His scarred face was grey with fatigue. Two days and one night had passed since he left the house in the Friedrichstrasse with the lorry and its precious contents. The trip took pretty much the last bit of will he possessed. His uniform was no longer crisp. His eyes were sunk deeply in his face and red rimmed. The driving was much more difficult now. Spring rains had arrived in earnest. Fortunately there was almost no movement on the roads.

Driving ever southward, he avoided the larger towns unless he needed fuel. Once he obtained a precious tank-full at the point of a gun, but mostly his grim face was enough to get him what he needed.

Food was not as easy. Now that he no longer wore an officer's tunic he'd met with some resistance when he needed food to take along on the road. He was prepared to pay, but that didn't change anything. The army had stripped the countryside of food. No chicken, egg or head of cabbage was safe. Even potatoes were hard to find.

He thought of the last couple he met in his search for food. He hated terrifying them. They were elderly and somewhat frail. He had no doubt he was taking the last of their meager store: a dried-up apple, a small wedge of cheese and two miserable potatoes. The old man stood up to him and was at once shot for his trouble. The woman scurried to wrap what little food they had. As she knelt with tears in her eyes to cradle her dead husband's head to her thin breast, she looked up at the scar-faced man in defiance.

"Leave here," she hissed, "get out of my house."

Horst said, "Thank you, old woman, now you may join your husband." He raised his pistol and shot her in the head. He closed his eyes and leaned his head against the doorframe for a moment before returning to the truck. *I hope she understands the misery I've spared them both. No witnesses, none.*

Eyes fixed on the road ahead, he moved like an unstoppable train through the countryside, finally falling asleep at the wheel. He woke with a start and found the truck headed for a muddy field. Cursing, he wrenched the wheel to bring it back onto the road. Exhaustion dogged him now. Realizing he was near the Czech border, which he wanted to avoid, he decided he needed sleep if he was to keep his wits about him. It would be too easy to make a serious mistake in his condition. He saw what appeared to be a wood ahead perhaps two kilometers. He pulled the lorry into the trees as far as he could, hoping the leaves and moss on the forest floor would keep him from getting stuck in the mud. He could then rest until full dark.

***

The Egyptian found it easy to follow the officer as he left the Friedrichstrasse. He could measure the man's weariness by his erratic driving and he was not surprised when he saw the lorry turn into the woods and stop. Exhausted himself, he dismounted and found a dry place to sit and lean against a tree for a nap.

As he woke two hours later, taking his time in the early evening light, he worked his way to the back of the lorry. He stood quietly by the tailgate and heard the rhythmic snores of an exhausted man. He waited there for several moments without hearing a change in the snoring. He finally decided it was as safe as it was going to get, and reached inside the canvas flap. His fingers felt the shape of an open crate and then— canvas! Risking the light from a small torch inside the flap, he was not disappointed. Row upon row of canvases and several crates holding sculptures as well as a large trunk filled the back of the lorry. He turned off the torch then and stood leaning his head against the truck to calm his pounding heart. He heard a sound then–just rustling, and faded quickly into the trees as he heard the snoring stop. Hoping the boy Mustafa had reached the General, he hurried to return to his motorcycle.

***

Horst slept only three hours and woke without opening his eyes. He thought he heard a soft movement in a nearby bush. Opening his eyes to just a slit, he moved his shaking hand very slowly to the pistol tucked in his belt. *I'm really a sitting duck.* Finally the brush parted. Through the gloom of early evening he made out the beady eyes of a full-grown boar. Horst broke into hysterical laughter.

"You and I, we survive only because no one has the courage to take us on. We must savor life while we can. The end will come soon enough, we can only hope."

He needed to relieve himself but decided he too did not wish to take on the boar. Driving back down the lane, he returned to the small country road on which he had been traveling south. He stopped twice to take out his torch to look at the map, and found it hard to concentrate since he had let down his guard enough to sleep.

The road he was seeking would carry him west a bit to avoid the nearby border. Too many days had passed since he last saw a report about troop movements, and those had probably been stale. He might be in trouble if he came upon a large body of men, but felt confident he could bluff his way through any small group. After all, he had very good papers. Fatigue and solitude were beginning to unhinge his mind.

Barely creeping along, his eyes were glued to the road. *It would be so much easier to travel without the lorry, but the cargo is too precious.* Horst knew he would defend it with his life if need be. Hopefully it would not come to that. It was a measurement of his bone deep weariness that it really did not matter. He just followed orders. This was his chance, his one chance for some sort of a life when the war was over. *Only an idiot could fail to see the end was rapidly approaching. Life will not be good for SS officers when the Allies have won. The future is all we have.*

Chapter 3

A small road became visible on Horst's left, as he drove slowly in the fading light. This was the road he sought. There were no signs, but signs of any kind were scarce in Europe now. He slowed full stop, and turned into the narrow lane. Within a kilometer it started to wind, and he knew he was in the right place. The narrow lane with overhanging trees twisted and turned for several more kilometers. He struggled to maintain a purchase on the muddy surface. Suddenly rounding a bend, he came face to face with a roadblock.

A staff car was slued across the road and two men worked at changing a tire. As soon as the narrow beam of his blacked-out head lamps struck the pair, they both turned and raised their guns. Then he knew there was nothing wrong with the staff car–it was a trap. *How many? Two? Plus one man in the car?* Coming to a stop about ten meters back, he waited and watched to see what would happen. His blouse was suddenly too small for his neck, the cab of the truck terribly confining, his throat dry.

Adrenaline sharpened his senses. He noticed it was a white- haired officer seated in the back of the vehicle, turned slightly to observe the unfolding scene. The face was barely visible in the very dim light but somehow vaguely familiar to Horst. *Who was this? What did they want? Was this trap specifically for him or would anyone serve the purpose?* He drove the truck ever so slowly forward, hands clenched on the wheel. Heart in his throat, he studied the scene in front of him.

The two armed men separated and began to walk toward him on opposite sides of the lane. If he had any advantage in the beginning, he no longer did. As they came closer, he could see the twin lightning strikes on the collar of the tunic worn by the man on his left. *SS! What are they doing here? Who are they?*

The man on the left was even with the truck window and gestured for Horst to open it. Rolling down the glass he said calmly, "I am on official business."

The man outside the window said nothing. As Horst tried to still his pounding heart, he looked the young officer over. *He's definitely young; perhaps too young for the rank he wears to really be his own. Why doesn't he speak?*

"Move the car," he barked. "I am on official business."

The young officer's gun was now leveled at his temple.

"Papers."

The gun hand did not waver as the young officer's other hand reached out for the papers, the hard eyes never shifting. *Perhaps he really is SS. What is this about?*

"They are in my tunic," Horst said as he slowly moved his hand near his chest. The man outside the window did not blink or speak as Horst pulled out the identity papers he had taken off his driver. Papers in hand, the SS officer turned and walked briskly back to the staff car, leaving his partner still standing to the right of the lorry.

Who is the man in the car? What Horst

could see of the battered staff car looked like the type used for the general staff only. *Mein Gott! Is it von Manstein?* He strained to see as the white-haired man stepped out of the staff car. It had to be von Manstein–or the general's twin. *Why is he here? Are the rumors true?* The SS popinjay was now on his way back to the lorry.

"You will now have a passenger."

This did not seem to be open to discussion, so Horst nodded curtly. He would be able to handle "a passenger."

"Ah, so it is Horst Ebberfeld, I had hoped it would be you. All alone too. You always were a lone wolf. I think I shall call you Wolfe, and you may call me Herr . . . Herr Stubben." The general swung himself up into the truck with an energy that belied his age.

"Wolfe. I like it. I thought it a bit of a joke that the men called me that. I think I'll keep it. If you'll get in Herr Stubben, we need to be moving."

Curious, no one is interested in checking the cargo. Could this be because they already know what it is? What was von Manstein's role in this? Is he one of the rogue generals who tried to kill Hitler?

As he started the engine, the staff car pulled off the road for him to pass. He did so and noted in the rear-view mirror that they pulled back onto the road and maintained a discreet distance. Raising his eyebrows, he looked over at the old man. The general spoke softly.

"They are following." It was not a question.

"When I tell you, swerve sharply to the right and then straighten out. Go a few more meters and then stop. They will come to us, I think. I assume you have a gun, you take the one that approaches on your side and I'll get the other."

"You want to tell me what this is about?"

"If you want to live a long life, do as I say . . . NOW!" Horst dutifully swung the wheel, then, his eyes on the rearview mirror he rolled slowly to a stop.

"You were right. Here they come."

Chapter 4

The Egyptian slowed the powerful BMW motorcycle to a crawl. Somewhere in the next kilometer or so would be an ideal place for an ambush. If Hamid reached the general, the old man's staff car was somewhere just ahead. Pushing the bike into the woods, he set off on foot just inside the tree line. After only five minutes of walking, he heard a man speaking. Dropping to the ground, he crept forward. The forest floor was wet and slippery with leaves. He inched his way along. As the voices grew louder, he risked lifting his head to see what was happening. Two men were sitting in the idling staff car watching the lorry stopped in the road ahead, discussing what to do. Where was the general? He wasn't in the staff car, even though the driver looked from the back like the general's aide.

Horst had withdrawn his Luger from the side pocket of the door, and glanced quickly to assure himself the general was watching the right side of the lorry. The same young SS officer came up to the driver's side door. In the split second the young man reached for the door handle, Horst raised the pistol and shot him squarely between the eyes. The report from the gun in the enclosed space left him stunned for a moment, his ears ringing. He shook his head to clear it. As he turned to look at the general, he saw the older man had fired almost simultaneously, and was suffering from the same shock waves.

"Now do you want to tell me what this is about?"

"It's about survival, yours and mine. I

promised your father I would help you if I could."

"My father's been dead for two years, try again."

"I know your father is dead. I was there when they shot him."

Horst's hands grabbed the old man's blouse, but the old general sat perfectly still, waiting. His eyes never left Horst's. Finally Horst released the old man and motioned for him to go on, watching with those cold blue eyes narrowed to slits. He was too tired for games now. He dropped one hand to the pistol in his lap and pointed it at the old man.

"Your father died for the Fatherland. More than that will have to wait. We need to get the bodies and the car out of sight, and quickly. Then we need to get moving. We must cross the border at Lindau. It's a small crossing, only one guard at this time of night."

Horst looked at the general for a long moment, his face a study in distrust. Then without a word, he opened his door and got out. The habit of following the orders of a superior officer was hard to break. Walking back to the staff car, he drove it up alongside the lorry. He dragged the body of the man he had shot into the staff car. Reversing, he repeated the maneuver with the second man. Then, with just a nod to the general, he drove the staff car ahead a few hundred meters and plunged it into the woods.

When he had gone as far as he could, he arranged the two dead men in the front, the SS in the passenger seat. A blanket lay across the back seat. Horst tore it into strips and made a wick for the petrol tank, and using his last match, lit the wick and walked away. Slipping and sliding on the wet ground, fatigue slowing him, he worked his way back to the truck.

Shortly he heard an engine coming up the road and stepped into the brush to wait. Jumping out as the lorry came even with him he didn't even startle the old general. Coming to a stop, the man slid over and waited for him to get in.

Horst had barely put the truck into gear when they saw and heard an explosion up ahead of them. The old general said, "Well done," and closed his eyes to sleep. Horst kept his silence as he drove on through the night.

There is still a long way to go. I need more than ever now to stay alert. What is this old man's game? On one level, the presence of the general unsettled him, but on a deeper, more intuitive level, the man's company comforted him.

Dawn was breaking to his left as his head nodded in sleep. Jerking himself awake, he knew the time had come to find a safe place to sleep until evening if they were to cross the border by night. Besides, he didn't wish to be on the roads in daylight with this cargo.

Ahead was the skeletal form of a burned-out farmhouse. Pulling off the road into a small wooded area, he observed the farm for nearly an hour. It was all he could do not to sleep as the general snored. There did not appear to be a single living thing, not even chickens.

Advancing slowly down the narrow lane to the barn, he was able to drive right up to the sagging structure without sighting anything moving. *Even the land is dead.* Wearily, he got out and dragged open the barn doors. As he drove in, the still silent general re-closed the big doors. Horst climbed to the hayloft to sleep, followed by the general. *Hopefully I'm not so dead tired I won't hear someone driving up the lane.* As soldiers learn to do, he fell into a deep sleep as soon as he put his head down.

***

It had been slow going for the Egyptian. He proceeded very carefully to avoid being surprised by coming up on the lorry. Now that the two men had retreated to the abandoned barn, perhaps he too could rest. His mind was going in circles. It stunned him when the two SS men were shot where they stood and the staff car burned. *The general, his general, participated in the slaughter. What did it mean?* Now it seemed even more important than ever for him to follow the lorry to its destination. But with the General involved, to whom would he be reporting these startling facts? He settled in at the edge of the wood to get some rest.

Chapter 5

Waking in one fluid, continuous motion, Horst came to his feet, opened his eyes and aimed his pistol directly in front of him. He found himself staring down the barrel at the general seated with his back against the wall. The old man was utterly calm. He chuckled sardonically, "I could have killed you at any time in the past few hours. I need you as much as you need me." Horst just shook his head and stretched his aching back.

The light rain was ending and the light was strange–squall light, he thought it was called. Darkness was beginning to fall now with the soft, warm twilight of early summer. A delicate fragrance of lilacs drifted on the light breeze and the song of a bird calling was heard a long way off. *Peace, sweet peace. If I could only stop time right here.*

"Time to move," he said harshly to the old man. Cautiously they pulled open the barn door. Not a movement anywhere. The soft light of early evening did nothing to improve the view of the desolate and empty farm. One tiny yellow tulip blooming beside the barn did nothing to dispel the gloom. Horst drove the lorry out to the road and they turned south once more, the general still a silent passenger. In less than two hours, the narrow, winding road took them to a tiny border post.

Approaching the guard post, Horst stopped the lorry and stepped down from the cab. A young guard, looking like a sleepy child, came stumbling out reaching for his gun: he was not awake enough to realize it was already too late. A single shot rang out, and a red floret blossomed on the startled young man's forehead. His eyes remained wide open in shock as he crumpled to the ground. Horst dragged the boy's body off the road into the brush. He returned wearily to the truck, put it in gear and crossed over into Switzerland.

***

Only a few minutes later the Egyptian approached the border crossing and found the guard post empty. Perhaps the guard had gone into the woods to relieve himself. He shrugged and rolled quietly past and, like the lorry before him, crossed over the border to Switzerland.

***

The old man spoke not a word as the hours went by. Horst found the silence comforting somehow, and began to relax. In neutral territory now, this part of the journey would soon be over. Perhaps having the general with him was something of a good luck charm, he certainly felt safer now. He thought it less likely that he would be stopped and recognized here. Once they arrived in Zurich and disposed of the lorry, he might be able to sleep safely again. Soon he began to discern the outlines of an occasional building on the outskirts of the city. Before long, he saw a dim light here and there, sentinels in the predawn light. *What a luxury, a country with the lights on.* It had been a long time since he had seen an area that was not completely blacked out in fear of the Allied bombing.

He stopped briefly to change into civilian

clothing. An old sweater, some worn trousers completed the look. He woke the general and had him remove his tunic, giving him a blanket to keep warm.

Soon they arrived in the beautiful residential sector of the city where his uncle made his home and found his way easily now. It was almost like coming home. The many happy childhood summers spent here brought it all back to him quickly. The year he turned eighteen had been the last before the war. The family was never to be together again. He assumed his aunt and uncle were still alive, but he knew their son, his cousin, had been killed in the war. *What a loss. That good healthy young man magnified by thousands of families. For what?*

The old man woke when the truck stopped.

"Where are we?"

"About a half kilometer from my contact's home. You stand guard over the lorry. Do you have ammunition? I'll return within an hour or not at all."

"Yes I have ammo. You mean your uncle's house?"

Raising just one questioning eyebrow, Horst said nothing. He eased out of the cab and closed the door softly. Fading swiftly into the trees, he stood perfectly still and watched for several minutes. Finding not a single sound or movement out of place in the early morning light, he began a tortuous trek to his uncle's home. He carefully wound back on his track a few times to make sure he was not followed. *Old habits are hard to break.*

The big stone house soon loomed out of the darkness. He stopped and leaned against a tree as the warm memories of his youth and family threatened to overwhelm him. There was not a hint of light anywhere in this early hour before dawn; his aunt and uncle would, of course, not yet be up and about. They were older now–alone, he assumed, in the big house. Slipping from tree to tree, he made his way to the side of the house. Hugging the stone wall, he made his way around to the back.

Remembering the door that was so easy for him and his cousin to break back into when they were boys, he crossed the brick terrace under the tall linden trees to just outside his uncle's study. He reached for the latch and turned it gently. It did not budge. He patted his pockets for a match then remembered he used the last one to torch the staff car. By touch alone, his fingers puzzled out the lock. It had been changed; a new heavy lock with a stout bar now stood between him and the study.

Cursing silently, he left the terrace and moved to the other side of the house. The beautiful linden still scraped the wall outside the room he slept in as a boy. He climbed up the tree, and found the window lock as easy to defeat as years ago. The room was unchanged except for the musty, unused odor. The breaking dawn just barely defined the two beds and chest in his cousin's childhood room. He crossed the floor quietly. Suddenly, just as he reached for the doorknob, there was a loud creak. *Damn! How could I have forgotten that noisy floorboard?*

He held his breath as he waited to hear the sound of someone moving about in the house. *If I could only take some time, time to crawl into the narrow bed where I slept as a child and wake up in the morning to Tante Marie's pancakes . . .* After several nerve wrenching minutes, he reached for the doorknob and slowly turned it. Then he stepped out quickly into the upstairs hall and straight into the barrel of a shotgun.

"Don't move a centimeter." The voice of his Uncle Fritz.

"It is I, Uncle, Horst." The gun pressed harder into his chest.

"If it is indeed Horst, you know where the switch is for the light, turn it on."

In the dim light of the hallway, the older man gasped and sagged into the wall as he took in the jagged scar on the face of a nephew he had not seen for years.

"God in heaven, it is you, Horst. I was sitting in the study when you tried the door. I don't sleep much these days. I thought you were one of the young ruffians who sometimes burgle homes out here. When you went from there to the linden tree, I hoped against hope it was you."

"You knew? I thought I was so clever back in my younger days."

"The linden has been there for a long time. You were not the first boy to climb down it to freedom for a night."

"Come, Uncle. I have much to tell you and very little time. I'm glad you were up. I was not looking forward to trying to wake you without also waking Tante Marie. Let's go down to the study."

Twenty minutes later, wearing a suit of clothes belonging to his now dead cousin, he left the study by the terrace door and made his way back to the lorry where the old general greeted him with relief.

"I was going to give you only five minutes more."

***

In the hours since he rolled the motorcycle quietly past the border into Switzerland, the Egyptian felt uneasy as he'd seen no sign of the lorry. Stopping the big BMW at a crossroad–he had no idea which way to go. He had lost them, even worse he had no idea of their destination.

The country was small, but not that small. He would have to go back to Berlin, to make contact with the general or at least his assistant. It was becoming more urgent now–the Germans were losing badly. *Who knew what would happen to the general then?* The future of his world and his people could hinge on the next few weeks or months.

Chapter 6

Telling the old general a much abbreviated story took nearly until they reached the financial district of Zurich. They saw almost no one on the streets. Horst drove the lorry carefully into the alley behind the bank his uncle's family had owned for generations. Shutting off the engine, they waited only a short time before seeing his uncle's car pull into the alley behind them. His uncle moved quickly to the only door on the back of the bank.

"We must hurry now," Horst said.

As the old general watched the mouth of the alley and his uncle manned the door, Horst began to unload the crates from the back of the lorry. Although much younger than either of the older men, he was soon winded and drenched with sweat as he carried load after load down the steps to an old vault deep beneath the bank. It was much easier when he had only supervised.

When the job was done the old general said, "I'll leave you now, Godspeed."

"I don't think so. You have some explaining to do."

"We can't very well talk here."

"No, we can't, but I want to hear what you have to say about my father. I know a place where we will be safe for the day. Get back in the truck." The general hesitated. "In the truck!" Horst's tone and expression brooked no debate.

Turning to his uncle, Horst embraced him as if he expected to never see him again. For just a moment, he returned to his childhood, when his father and uncle were the world to him.

"I must go now and get rid of the lorry, and there's much to do after that. It will be weeks before I see you again, more likely not until the autumn. If I don't return, you know what to do."

"You must return, we have no other family left. Take care. Go safely and come back to us. We cannot lose you too."

Nearly two hours later Horst turned the lorry down a farm road well away from the city, and from there to a rutted track barely visible in the spring grass. Obviously no one had been there in a long time. He and the general had spoken little during the trip, only commenting on ordinary sights neither had seen since the beginning of the war. Parking the lorry deep in a stand of trees, Horst stepped wearily down from the truck.

"Just over the hill is a small farm house, we'll be safe there."

"How do you know this place?"

"It belonged to my mother." With that Horst turned and walked east over a small rise. He found the little house much as he remembered it.

It must belong to me now. None of Mama's family is left, except for Uncle Fritz–odd. What happened between my childhood and now? How could I be the last of my family?

The general carried a rucksack with him into the house, and unloaded the contents onto the kitchen table. Seeing the loaf of stale bread and cheese wrapped in gauze made Horst realize how long it had been since he had eaten. His shrunken apple and small chunk of cheese was added to the feast. The men wearily sat and the old man began to talk. His voice was low and weak. As tired as

Horst was, the old man was exhausted.

"I met your father almost ten years ago. You had just gone off to the Wehrmacht. He was so proud of you. He mentioned you every day, always found a way to work his son into the conversation. He was my aide for the next few years and like a younger brother to me. I heard about your every exploit. When you joined the SS something changed and he became very worried about you. I stopped hearing about your exploits from him, but soon began to hear them elsewhere as you rose in rank."

"He became obsessed about the SS, about Goering and Himmler. There were rumors about you and Rosenberg's "Special Action Team"-the Einsatztaub Reichliter Rosenberg. Goering couldn't hold his liquor, and soon word of the art Rosenberg was piling up with your help got to your father. As he was a career officer in the Wehrmacht, the SS unsettled him."

"My father never said any of this to me. I think I would have known if he was your aide for years. He never told me that."

"Do you want to tell the story or should I? The more obsessed he became, the more secretive he was. I tried to talk to him but he just wouldn't listen. He didn't understand how important your work was, how important it was for the fatherland to protect the future."

"You said he became secretive, what did you mean?"

"Twice he forged documents to get into secure areas. We believe he became involved in plots against the Fuhrer. I tried, but I could no longer protect him. Finally he was caught in a trap set for him. I'm sorry to tell you he was executed within the hour, and I could do nothing to stop them."

"You're telling me he plotted against the Fuhrer?"

"Unfortunately it's true. I'm sorry to have you find out this way. I think that toward the end he lost his mind. When I got the report that you had emptied the house on the Friedrichstrasse, I knew where you would be going. Your father told me how close you were to your mother's brother."

"How did you know about the house on the Friedrichstrasse?"

"From your father's papers. I gathered them up immediately when he died. I managed to keep them away from Goering and his friends. Now I can go back and tell the Fuhrer how brilliant you were to hide valuable resources for the future of the Reich not only in a neutral country, but right under their noses!"

"Who else knows of this?"

"No one until you and I return to Berlin."

Horst stood up from the table and began to pace the small kitchen. He stood for a moment, head bowed, looking blindly out the window to the hillside beyond.

"You said 'we' believe he was involved in a plot against the Fuhrer. Who exactly are 'we'?"

"There is no 'we', I said I. I was worried about him. I was—I went to find him. He was my friend."

The cold blue eyes in the scarred face became colder still, as they watched the general, now shifting uneasily in his chair.

"You said he was executed. That's not what I was told. How do you know this? Tell me how you know what happened. Who set a trap for him? Were you there?"

"No, no, I wasn't there! I heard the story at headquarters. I can't tell you what I don't know. Perhaps when we return to Berlin you can find out more about it. After the feat you have just pulled off, none of your father's treason can possibly rub off on you. You'll be a hero."

Sweat broke out on the old man's forehead. Horst continued to pace slowly back and forth in the room, calm on the surface but boiling like a cauldron inside. Finally he came to a stop behind the old man's chair.

"You! You were the one who had my father executed. You said you were there when he was shot. Of course you were. You were the one who shot him!"

The general jumped up from his chair only to find Horst's Luger aimed right at his head.

"Tell me about it," Horst said softly, "and maybe I'll let you live."

Bauer's Run

Chapter 7

For an old man, he moved fast. The general always kept in good shape. He ran in all kinds of weather, his staff questioning his sanity. That insanity served him well now. He kicked the chair over, lifting it with his foot to slam it into the knees of the younger man. Horst fired once, then twice. Nothing! His gun was empty. The general was too fast for him, head-butting him and throwing him to the floor. In a flash the old man was out the door.

Horst cursed and jumped back to his feet, somewhat tangled in his chair. The fatigue of the past week was slowing him, renewed grief for his father clouding his mind. By the time he got to the door, the general was just cresting the hill and was soon out of sight. He started running after him. The next two hours wore both of the men down as the small wood was just large enough for the general to stay out of sight most of the time. After reloading his pistol with a few rounds he kept in his pocket, Horst took several shots at the general. *How many rounds do I have? Two? Three? Only one? Stop. Think. He can't be allowed to get away.* His chest heaving, Horst lay flat out on the ground and quietly pulled some branches over himself. His exhaustion was such that he felt himself slipping into sleep right there on the damp ground, and dug his fingernail into his palm hard enough to draw blood.

The general lay in a hollow a mere twenty meters away. He lost track of the last place he spotted Horst, had he given up? After a wait of nearly half an hour without moving, the general convinced himself Horst was gone. Slowly getting to his feet, he looked around. It appeared to be clear. Horst must have gone back to the truck. He turned and walked in the opposite direction. The shot hit him before he even heard it. Entering high on the left shoulder, the bullet threw him forward and he rolled down a steep embankment, landing half in and half out of a small stream at the bottom. Horst stood up and followed the path the old man took. At the top of the steep ravine, he looked down at the man he had shot. Face down near the water, the general was not moving, blood washed into the stream from his wound. Horst was too tired to climb down, so he just sat on the bank and watched for the next hour. The day was beginning to fade when he stood and walked back to the house. He was aching, tired and wet. Dogs or wolves would take care of what was left of the general; for now, he had work to do. He didn't think anyone other than his uncle might know about the place, but he couldn't take the risk.

Hours later, the old lorry rolled over the edge of a steep mountain ledge, coming to a rest in the thick, dark pines below. Horst set off wearily on foot, needing to separate himself from the truck in case someone found it sooner than he expected.

In the early morning he came to another small, tidy village with a train station. A train arrived from farther up the mountain within just a short time. Buying a ticket for Zurich, he found a seat in the second class car and closed his eyes. The clicking and clacking of the wheels lulled him almost at once into a deep, dreamless sleep, uninterrupted until the train reached the city.

He left the station for a stroll down the beautiful Bahnhofstrasse. As he passed a few small cafes, the delicious aroma of cooking meats and the fragrance of fresh bread wafting around his head made him aware he hadn't eaten a warm meal in days. Sitting with his back to the wall deep in the café, he nursed an ale and wolfed down a bowl of steaming hot stew that actually had some meat in it. The nourishment helped some, even gave new strength to his faltering legs. Later in the day, nerves strained almost to the breaking point, he returned to the station to buy a ticket to another town. Thus he passed the next two days, turning back on his path several times to learn if he was being followed. His only sleep was on the moving trains. If asked, he would not have been able to tell who might be following him, but his paranoia was deeply ingrained. Finally satisfied, he bought one last ticket to a small village high in the mountains. The last station on the line was actually more than a kilometer down the mountain from the tiny village he wanted.

He hoped the surgeon that he sought was still there. If not, he had no idea what he would do next, or where he could run that he would not be found. The evil scar that coursed down his face meant that literally everyone noticed him–even if they did quickly turn away.

Bauer's Run

Chapter 8

The crisp evening air, heavy with the smell of pines, helped to clear his head. *Almost there.* Arriving at a small house on the far side of the village, he knocked quietly at the door. *Be there.* A small, heavily bearded man answered.

"I'm looking for the man who repairs skis," he said.

The thickly bearded man regarded him thoughtfully, pulling on a pipe as he did so.

"I know of no such man, perhaps you might try another village."

"Perhaps I will, these are very special skis."

He turned away from the door and began to walk down the path. The door was closed softly behind him. *He fits; this has to be the right house.* Fading into the nearby wood, he squatted down with his back to a tree to watch the house. *Come on man, what are you waiting for?* He rested against a tree for nearly an hour. It was all he could do to keep his exhausted body from falling asleep. Finally, he was rewarded with the lights going out in the window of the cottage. He sensed, rather than actually saw the door open. Moving swiftly forward to slip inside, he jumped when the door was quickly closed behind him, and he felt a solid object, which had to be a gun, pressed against his ribs.

"You took a great chance, my young friend. No one has come here in a very long time."

"With this face I had no choice," he said. "I was given directions just as I was leaving

Berlin."

"I don't want to hear Berlin or wherever else you have been," the man responded angrily. "Don't tell me. I don't want to know. The stairs are just ahead of you. Go straight up and to the left before I turn on a light."

In the attic room, he waited with ill-concealed impatience for the bearded man to examine his face. It seemed to take hours before the man sat back and said, "I can do this–I can make you a new face. Not in one operation however, it will take more because of all the scar tissue."

"I don't care as long as you can do it."

"I can do it. Can you? It will take time, perhaps several weeks. During that time you will not be able to leave this house, some days not even this room."

What a luxury, nothing to do but rest for weeks.

"Yes, yes. I know. Can we just get on with it?"

"What shall I call you?" the surgeon asked. "Never mind, I'll call you Klaus and you can call me Otto. That will do. I don't want to know your name. Sleep now. There's water to bathe. I am an old man and I must rest before I do such work. I will wake you when I'm ready."

He stared at the door after it closed and locked behind his reluctant host. *I have either made the worst decision of my life, or done the one thing that will actually allow me to have a life. Either way, the course is set.*

Chapter 9

Bored out of his skull, Horst was cataloging in his mind all of the beautiful women he knew. *Those I've met since the scar surely would not be thinking of me right now. With the last surgery behind me, I will soon see if I have a face that will no longer frighten children and turn away women.*

The days of living dangerously had to be behind him now. The life he would lead would be quiet, simple, and above reproach. *I'll be a changeling, from dashing German officer to staid and somewhat boring Swiss banker. The war will soon be over and there will be lots of opportunity for a cautious man to succeed.* After darkness fell, the doctor came into the room with a pair of scissors.

"It is time, my friend, to take a look."

Carefully unwinding and cutting away the gauze that obscured his patient's face, the surgeon slowly revealed his handiwork. When at last the job was done, Horst impatiently reached for the mirror. He was stunned.

"You weren't really expecting to look like yourself, were you? That would not be safe for you."

"But why give me another scar?"

"The scar I have placed across your eyelid will be easy to explain as a childhood accident. A small scar can keep people from looking too closely. I have reshaped your nose, since that is one of the key points of identification. You must not look too much like your old self."

"How soon can I leave here?"

"It will take another two weeks for healing then you can go. Patience, my young friend. Perhaps in that time I will finally be able to beat you in chess!"

Horst thought every day about what had been stored in the deepest basement of his uncle's bank. He had a plan now. It was a risk worth taking. Only a few small, loose ends and a fortune could be his.

A week passed with Horst carefully monitoring his progress in the mirror. On the ninth day he was sitting in the dark by the one tiny window when the doctor knocked before opening the door. As the doctor set up their usual game of chess, Horst casually roamed around the small room. The surgeon had reached a certain comfort level with his patient and no longer paid much attention when he paced.

"Now," he said, "we are ready."

"Yes, we are," Horst said behind him. "We are ready. You have been kind to me. I'm sorry to have to do this."

Too late, the doctor realized something was not right. His patient was not talking about the chess match. Horst's arms swiftly encircled the doctor's throat and snapped his neck. Leaving the attic room, he walked carefully down the stairs to find the man's coat. *There must be no hue and cry for him.* Since the doctor kept to himself so much, it would be a long time before anyone noticed the little cottage was strangely quiet, but this was not a time to take chances. In all the time he spent in the doctor's home, he never heard a visitor. The man was clearly a recluse. The only voices he heard over the past months were from the radio. He could make this work!

Having dressed the doctor in coat, hat and heavy gloves, the man with the new face turned off all the lamps in the cottage and waited in the dark to get his night vision back. Fifteen very quiet minutes later, he carefully opened the door to the cottage. No one was in sight. He picked up the doctor and threw him over his shoulder. Locking the door carefully after himself, he strode easily into the woods. Fortunately for him, the doctor was not too heavy.

Alternately resting and walking for a half hour, he came to a sharp drop, which suited his purpose perfectly. Rolling the man off the ledge, he knew the doctor would likely not be found before spring. *Then it will look like an accident: the man fell and broke his neck. After all, it is beginning to snow.* His frazzled nerves made him laugh insanely; *the staid Swiss banker will have to find a different method of disposing of loose ends.*

Bauer's Run

Chapter 10

It was two nights since the patient killed his doctor. He moved about only at night and stayed out of sight in the daytime, wanting to get as far away from the village as possible before taking any kind of public transportation. Now he walked along the main road and ducked out of sight when he heard a vehicle. Even in this neutral country there did not seem to be a lot of petrol and traffic was light. He hoped to get to his uncle's house without having to show any papers. Getting stopped and asked for papers would be unfortunate since he now had no identification at all.

On the second day he decided it would be safe to hitch a ride. Perhaps a farmer would be a good choice. Soon a truck came along–a truck that appeared to be running on willpower alone. He turned to smile at the driver, who turned out to be a rather plain looking old woman. As the truck stopped for him, his mind scrambled for a story. Explanations unnecessary to a man would be expected by a woman.

"Good morning, Madame. Could I perhaps get a ride with you along this road, as far as you may be going?"

"Where are you going and where did you come from young man?"

Gesturing vaguely behind him he said, "I'm on my way to the city. I've just received word that my mother is ill. Since my father died, she has been living with my Tante Hilda in the city. Now she needs me."

"Why has she not been living with you?"

the old woman asked suspiciously.

"Ah, my house is too small and Mama loves the city." *Leave it to an old woman to rattle on. Can't she just decide whether to give me the ride?* The woman regarded him suspiciously. He made himself stand very still and smile while she decided.

"All right. Come along then, get in. I'm only going to the edge of the city, but I will give you a ride that far."

Over the next hour, the woman asked him questions and Horst made up the answers. He was afraid of making a mistake, but she just kept on. Before long, he felt himself beginning to laugh inside. It was difficult to keep a straight face. *This is too absurd. Will she never shut up?*

"Here we are," she said suddenly as she pulled the truck over to the side of the road. "I must turn here so I will let you out. Goodbye my young friend. Take good care of your mother."

It was with relief that Horst set out on foot, now late enough in the morning that there were people on the street. *Unlike my once lovely Berlin. There is nothing there but ruin now. Put it behind you. You cannot afford German thoughts. You must now be Swiss.*

Shortly he came to a small train station. Buying a ticket to the far side of the city, he practiced the trade craft he knew would protect his life. He doubled back on his track several times to see if he generated any interest at all. It was evening before he found himself near his uncle's house.

He waited patiently in the trees, until

finally he saw the last light go out in the house, and waited another hour before he approached the linden tree. As he reached the window, it slid open carefully. It nearly stopped his heart.

His uncle softly called, "I've waited every evening for you, I knew you would come soon."

"Uncle, you must be quiet. You'll wake Tante. No one must know who I am. It's not safe. I just came about the papers. I'll come to see you tomorrow at the bank."

"It's too late to not wake Tante," a voice from the doorway said dryly. "Is that truly you, Horst?"

A light came on suddenly and both men gasped.

"Turn it off," the uncle snapped.

"You are not Horst. Who are you?"

"Turn off the light!"

"Not until you tell me what is going on here."

In two strides Horst crossed the room and turned off the light. "What now, Uncle?"

"Come my dear, we must all go to the study and I will explain."

She sputtered angrily but to no avail, as her husband took her firmly by the arm and led her downstairs. He closed the heavy velvet curtains and lit a lamp.

"Tante, you must tell no one who I am, otherwise I cannot stay. Please tell her, Uncle."

"Are you truly my darling Horst? What happened to your face? The voice is right but . . ."

"Let me introduce you to Wolfe Bauer, my dear. He is no relation to your nephew Horst who was killed during the war. That is very important for you to remember. Lives are at stake here. Wolfe will be coming to work with me at the bank. You may on occasion meet this man socially, and of course you will be polite to him but not familiar. Wolfe is the son of a man I was at university with. He is a banker who has been abroad during the war."

"Horst is dead? Oh my God, Fritz, why did we not receive notification? Wait a minute, something is not right here. Why does this man sound so much like Horst? And he's the right size. The voice is right . . . what is going on here? You must tell me!"

It took another hour of talking before Horst and his uncle convinced his aunt that she must go along with the plan. Horst was their last living relative, so she finally agreed. She asked several times why he must be someone else, but gave up when he said, "It is just the way it is. If you cannot get used to it, you will never see me again." He waited in silence for her reply.

"All right, I will agree."

"You must do more than agree, you must swear an oath."

"I swear."

Horst let out a deep breath and relaxed for the first time that night. After a few minutes of logistics, the banker gave his nephew money to live on until he could officially come to work at the bank. Horst saw no need to tell him that was not necessary. When he left an hour later, Horst was no more. Wolfe Bauer looked forward to his new life.

Chapter 11

Wolfe soon settled into his new job at the bank. He was introduced as the son of a friend, and fit in with the staff, soon learning what was expected of him. He came to the bank at precisely the same time every day, did what was expected of him, and left at the same time every day. He often volunteered to do extra work, never passing up a chance to learn more about the bank's customers.

He showed up at his uncle's club every Thursday evening, at the theatre every Saturday night, and at church every Sunday morning. Days went into weeks and months. The war was at last over in Europe. A defeated Germany had enough to worry about without anyone noticing or caring about the disappearance of one young SS officer.

The one thing that could still make Wolfe nervous was that once in a while his uncle's secretary (who had been with him many years) seemed to watch him intently. When he mentioned it to his uncle, the man laughed it off.

"She always asks about you. I think she's halfway in love with you."

"What are you thinking? She's old enough to be my mother!"

"No matter--even old women can dream. It's nothing."

That did nothing to calm Wolfe's fears but there appeared nothing could be done about it.

He was entrusted, by this time, to interact on occasion with some of the bank's patrons. On one such afternoon, a young woman with a small boy in tow entered the bank. Her sturdy figure and the freckles across her nose intrigued him. Her clothing was well made and well cared for but clearly old and clearly not European. Her shortly cropped dark hair and clear blue eyes made her very attractive to Wolfe who purposely had not allowed himself to think about women for a long time.

She looked around a bit in confusion, as Wolfe approached her.

"May I be of some assistance, Ma'am?"

"Oh, I'm sorry," she said. "I think I need to see the director, Herr von Erhardt."

"He is not here, Madame. I am Wolfe Bauer. Perhaps I can be of some help."

"I am Renee Wohlberg and wish to review my accounts. I am thinking of returning to America as soon as it is possible for me to do so."

"If your husband will come into the bank, Ma'am, I'd be glad to go over the accounts with him."

"My husband is not in Switzerland, Herr Bauer, and the accounts are my own."

Wolfe bowed in a quick apology. "Please follow me. Now if you have some form of identification, I will be glad to show you the accounts. You have the numbers, of course."

The young woman produced her passport and handed it across the desk to Wolfe.

"This American passport clearly belongs to you Ma'am, as it has your picture, but it says you are Renee Harding." Wolfe regarded her carefully as he waited for her reply.

"The passport was issued before the war, as you can see, and before my marriage. Now that the war is over in Europe, I plan to take my son home to America as soon as my husband returns."

"And your husband is where?" He hears only a mumble, "where?"

She lifted her head and said very clearly, "He is in Germany. I'm sure he will return here to us soon."

"I will look into the state of your accounts– Madame Wohlberg–is it? If you will leave information where you can be reached, I will contact you when I have all the information."

"What, you cannot tell me now?"

"It will only take a few days. I promise to contact you as soon as I have the information."

The young woman appeared close to tears as she took the small boy's hand and stood to leave. "I must know soon," she said with a quivering chin, "please call me soon."

Wolfe watched her leave with her head up, talking cheerfully with the boy. *She certainly has pluck. This could have possibilities.* He followed her with his eyes until she was out of sight. *Let's see what we can find out about the nice American lady.*

Wolfe went directly to the account books. The numbered account she listed had only a small balance in it. There was, however, a sealed envelope tucked into the page with a name on it– the name Harding. For the next two days he searched all the records he could find that might relate to the young woman. Having gathered all the information, he went to the Director.

Wolfe and his uncle, the director, had established a way of dealing with each other inside the bank that would look, to anyone who cared, to be quite normal. They only talked behind closed doors. Even then, they addressed each other formally. There could be no hint of their true relationship.

The director told him, "The young woman is an American from a family of some wealth. She apparently came here to go to school, and fell in love with a German boy, also here for school. When the war started, he was called home suddenly. After a few months, it became obvious to the headmistress of the school that the girl was pregnant. The girl's father was sent for. She claimed she married the boy on a weekend in Berlin and by that time, there was no adequate way to check it out. She refused to leave here, and said her husband would come to her as soon as he could. She was then almost of age and her father seemed to think it would be useless to drag her home. Or perhaps taking her home would have been embarrassing to him. At any rate, he opened an account for her here. We pay her hotel bill out of it. When it gets close to empty, he sends more money. How he knows, I have no idea."

"After the boy was born, he sent that sealed envelope inside another envelope addressed to me. He said if the girl ever came to the bank wanting money to go home, she should have the envelope. That is what I know. I've been able to make some discreet inquiries about the young man. Two years ago he was sent to the Russian front. No one I can find has heard from him since. Even if she can indeed prove she was married to him, I'm sure it would be most unpleasant for her if she went back to America."

Chapter 12

Wolfe waited nearly a week to call the young woman. When he spoke to her, he gave no information but asked for an appointment in two days' time. She nearly wept with frustration, but he was adamant, he would see her in two days. He has been giving the young lady a good deal of thought. She was very young, not quite twenty. The boy had been born just before her seventeenth birthday. *I wonder just how pliable she is. She could be just what I need to round out my new identity. First I must find out if she was ever actually married to the German.*

By the time Wolfe arrived at Madame Wohlberg's hotel, he worked out in his mind a plan to get close to her. Renee opened the door almost before his knuckles touched it.

"Come in. Please sit. Could I take your coat? Would you like some tea?" She rattled on nervously for a few moments before coming to rest on a small chair opposite her visitor. He began to prod her very carefully for information.

"You see, Madame, it is really about correct identity information. The Swiss banker must be very careful to know exactly with whom he is dealing. Now we do have a small account at our bank for Renee Harding, which is what your passport says. But you claim to be Madame Wohlberg. Have you heard from your husband? Do you have some documentation to prove your marriage? Perhaps a marriage certificate? Even an account in another bank? We must be very sure whom we are dealing with before we give out any information that would be confidential."

"No, I don't have my marriage certificate. It has been lost, perhaps in Germany. What is the problem? You say the account is in the name of Renee Harding, as is my passport. Why can you not give me the contents of that account?"

"We might well have done just that had you come to us as Miss Harding, but you say you are Madame Wohlberg. You can see how confusing that is for the bank. For all we know, Renee Harding could be your sister. You look somewhat like the passport photograph, but not exactly."

By now Renee was very close to tears. "I must have the money for passage home for my son and I. Can't you see that?"

"Perhaps after your husband arrives, this little problem will be cleared up."

"Why are you doing this? Are you so thickheaded you cannot figure out there is no husband?" Renee gasped and covered her mouth when she realized what she said. The tears began in earnest now. "I want to go home. It's that simple. I want to take my son home."

"Help me to understand you. Your husband has abandoned you? Has he been killed in action? What happened?"

"There never was a marriage," she said softly.

"Oh. And the boy? What passport does he have?"

"He has no passport."

"But is the boy American–German–Swiss? Can you prove he is your child?"

"I didn't think I would need a passport for

so small a child as long as he is with me."

Renee slumped in the chair, head in her hands.

"And his name, Madame, is it Wohlberg or Harding?"

Renee dissolved into tears and could not speak at all. Wolfe stood up to leave. As he walked past her to the door, she reached out to touch his sleeve.

"Please don't go. You have to help me."

"I must think how to solve this Madame Wohlberg."

"Oh for heaven's sake, call me Renee."

"Renee then and I am Wolfe. Please let me work on this. I will call you soon." *Yes! This does have possibilities!*

After Wolfe left, Renee sat crying quietly. Soon she felt a small hand touch her. Through her tears, she saw her little son try to comfort her.

"This isn't fair to you, darling. I must find a way to work this out. Come let's go for a walk in the park."

Two days passed before Wolfe called her again. This time he asked if she would like to have dinner with him to discuss some possible solutions. Startled, she agreed then asked, "what about Mark?"

"Why bring him, of course."

During the meal, which they took in the hotel's dining room Wolfe kept up a steady stream of light, polite dinner conversation. During the meal, he paid great attention to the boy, tucking a napkin under his chin and cutting his food. The perceptive little boy watched him curiously. He did not know why this man who made Mama cry was paying so much attention to him.

Mama was not quite so perceptive. She and her son usually took dinner on a tray in their room. She only noticed that the man from the bank was very kind, and for once, she was out in public and having a good time.

When he returned them to their room, he squatted down to say goodbye to Mark. He dashed his hand across his eyes and admitted to Renee sheepishly, "I always thought I would someday have a boy of my own, but life has not turned out that way." Renee thanked him for his kind attention and extracted a promise from him to call her as soon as he had news.

Chapter 13

Wolfe began to see Renee every few days. He suggested to her that they first find out what they needed to do to get Mark a passport. She did not notice or care that "she" had become "they." It felt nice to have a man to depend on (even if only temporarily). They took dinner each time in the hotel dining room or in nearby restaurants. They found two or three that managed to procure a better grade of food than most. Every time they went out, the boy was with them. Wolfe seemed to always have time and patience for the boy. He was rewarded by Mark letting down his guard. Sometimes he even took Wolfe's hand as they crossed the street. Wolfe never stayed too long in Renee's rooms; always leaving publicly enough so that the front desk personnel saw that he did not stay in the room.

In spite of himself, Wolfe found himself looking forward to Renee's company. He could not be the devil-may-care man-about-town that he was in Berlin. This was serious. His life might depend on how well he pulled this off. Stories were coming out of Germany about the Allies beginning to try senior officers at Nuremberg. He knew it was only a matter of time before the trial court added his name to the list. He had to steel himself, for he could not afford to be caught up in feelings for a woman–any woman.

The boy was another story. The bright little boy with the startling blue eyes and shock of blond hair captivated him. Mark made Wolfe's emerging plan more palatable. Wolfe could not seem to help the way he felt about the boy. If he had to take the mother to get the child, so be it. At least she was good company, educated and well mannered.

Wolfe had just delivered the latest installment of bad news. Renee sat crushed and slumped on a park bench. He pretended for weeks he was in the process of getting a passport for Mark. Now he told her it did not happen. They had a lovely meal and the weather was so mild they were walking in the park. Mark ran ahead of them, exploring as small boys do. Wolfe explained he was unable to obtain a passport for Mark because of the lack of a birth certificate. He told her the passport office told him the boy's father vouching for his citizenship was a substitute for the missing certificate.

Renee was crushed--so near and yet so far. As she wept under the trees in the big park, Wolfe took her in his arms and patted her back. He murmured words of comfort to her as he held her. Then he kissed her. He never did that before, but somehow it felt natural to Renee. Their friendship grew over the past weeks. For Renee it felt good to have someone take care of her. She had been alone since the boy's father returned to Germany— the rat.

Mark returned to find Wolfe holding his mother. After a moment's observation he decided that was all right. When Wolfe left them at the door of Renee's room, he promised her he would find a solution.

As it happened, his Uncle, the Director asked him one day what resolution had been made with the 'Harding woman'. Wolfe laughed ruefully. "I haven't worked it out yet. That's fortunate or unfortunate as the case may be, since I find I'm quite taken with the woman."

His uncle forgot where he was for a moment as he retorted furiously, "you cannot afford that! Lose her."

"Hush, Uncle. People will notice. I know what I'm doing."

"You know nothing of the kind. She's an American for God's sake."

"Don't bring God into it. He has nothing to do with it. It's under control, I have a plan."

A few days later Wolfe took Renee and Mark to the park again. This time he brought a bag of bread crumbs for Mark to feed the ducks. As he watched the boy happily occupied, Wolfe began to talk about what a difficult life the child would have in America as the bastard son of a German soldier. She reeled as though slapped; she had never seen it that way.

"What can I do? I cannot change his father."

"I think you can," he said. "Here is my plan."

Renee listened in shocked silence. He was proposing to marry her! After that, he would take the boy's birth date to the authorities himself and swear the boy was his son, born in Switzerland. Once they had a birth certificate for him, it would be easy to get both an American and a Swiss passport for him. Wolfe did not tell her that if this didn't work, he would just have the papers forged.

"What is in this for you," she asked?

"You must see how fond I have become of

the boy. He is the child I will never have. I promise you I will treat him as my own. In time he will come to see me as his father. How much better would that be than him wondering why his father cared so little for him that he ran away and never came back."

"And Mark's mother? What of me?"

"I will not lie to you, Renee. I like you, but I don't love you and will never force myself on you. You will have your life and I will have mine. We could certainly both do worse. And don't forget, Mark will also have a life."

"My family in America–what of them?"

"As far as they are concerned, I am the boy's father. They need know nothing else. You go home a married woman."

"You don't know my father. He will not be so easy to fool."

"Does this mean you will do it? You will marry me?"

"I suppose so."

"Well, now that is settled, one more thing."

"What is that?"

"Look happier, tomorrow is your wedding day."

Chapter 14

Wolfe arrived at the hotel for Renee and Mark in early afternoon, wearing his best sharkskin suit with a red rose in his lapel. The hotel staff noted his arrival as unusual and was soon buzzing. As Renee opened the door, she found her groom looking somewhat shy and holding out a small, somewhat glamorous box for her. She opened it to find a small cluster of violets. How had he found them? How had he known they were exactly the right thing, the right choice, instead of something more–more grand? She pinned them to the collar of her pale blue dress. Tucked under the violets was a tiny rosebud for Mark.

All of this conspired to move Renee to tears. These past years had been very hard; she always had to be strong, with no one else to help carry the load. As he held out his arm, Renee slipped her small hand into the crook of his elbow and, closing the door behind her, set out for a new life.

The brief ceremony in the Hotel de Ville was certainly not what she envisioned her wedding day to be, but then, she had not envisioned this groom or her one small attendant either. Wolfe surprised her one more time at the end of the short ceremony when he produced a wide, plain gold band for her hand.

A taxi was waiting when they came out of the building, and the driver quickly opened the door for them. When they were settled in, without a word, the driver pulled away from the curb into the light traffic. Renee raised her eyebrows in an unspoken question to her new groom. "Just wait," he said. *This is going to be much better than I ever dreamed. She is the perfect wife for me. She doesn't question much and she gives up easily.*

In just a few minutes the taxi arrived at the door of the bank where they first met. As he handed her out of the cab and took Mark's small hand in his, he said again, "just wait."

The entourage walked through the main lobby clear to the private elevator at the back. The guard was astonished that Herr Bauer had the temerity to take the Director's elevator without being summoned!

As they came out of the lift on the second floor, a startled secretary rushed to tell him the Director could not see him at this time. "Nonsense," he said as he strode toward the big, hand-carved walnut door and tapping lightly, threw it open.

"Wolfe! What the hell? I'm sorry Ma'am, I didn't see you. What is going on, Wolfe?"

"Herr Director, I came to present my bride, Mme. Renee Bauer and my son Mark Bauer. Renee, the director has been very kind to me. He took me in after I was stuck for years in South America. I respect him as I would respect my own father."

The Director opened and closed his mouth several times. He could think of nothing appropriate to say to Wolfe's audacity that would not embarrass the young lady.

"Congratulations," he finally said. "Wolfe, why did you not tell us? We would have planned an appropriate celebration."

"There will be plenty of time to celebrate. The first thing is to find a suitable house for us to live in. Then it will take some time to settle in and find a school for our son."

Renee regarded her new husband with surprise; she herself had not given thought to these things. "Wolfe, I don't think Mark is quite old enough yet for school."

"Don't worry your pretty head dear. Perhaps we will start with a governess. We will work it out."

By this time, the Director had gathered his wits and invited them to his home for dinner the following evening. Wolfe accepted graciously.

When they left the Director's office, Wolfe took his new family to his office on the lower floor. His assistant was away from her desk and Wolfe settled the boy with paper and pencils, and Renee in an armchair near the window.

"There are some banking details I must attend to while we are here, my dear. I won't be long."

Wolfe moved quickly to the outer vault room where the account books were kept available to bank officers. Selecting the large ledger which contained the Harding account, he removed the letter addressed to Renee, and took it quickly to one of the private booths. Once the door closed behind him, he collapsed into the chair with his head in his hands. *Calm yourself. It went perfectly. Will my uncle let it be? Of course he will, he will have no choice.*

Tearing open the envelope, he was not surprised to find ten thousand dollars in American currency. Briefly he read the note speaking of forgiveness and love for her and the desire for her to come home. With a snort, Wolfe tore the letter in small pieces and threw it in the trash basket. Leaving the small room, he busied himself in several areas in the bank, eventually returning with a stack of papers in his hand.

"Here you are, my dear. I will require your signature in several places on these papers then we can go back to the hotel."

"What papers, Wolfe? What are you doing?"

"I have opened a new account here at the bank in your new name. I have deposited money into the account to very nearly the equivalent of five thousand American dollars. I want you to have the freedom to come and go as you wish and I will deposit more as necessary. I am not the sort of man to tie you to me by keeping you penniless." As he showed her where to sign, she looked up at him with damp eyes.

"You have been so kind to us, Wolfe. I will make sure you don't regret this."

The paperwork disposed of, Wolfe and his new family left the bank and returned temporarily to the hotel.

Chapter 15

When the new family arrived at Wolfe's uncle's handsome estate on the outskirts of Zurich, they were greeted at the door by an elderly servant who took their coats and ushered them into a small library.

"Wolfe, I had no idea we were coming to such a house! This is a mansion by any standards."

"The Director told me the house has been in the family for generations. I think he said only he and his wife live here now, and perhaps a couple of servants live in."

The residents entered and greeted their guests.

"Good evening! I'm so glad you could come. I am Marie and of course you already know Uncle, excuse me, Fritz." The Director paled at his wife's slip of the tongue.

"Welcome to our house, both of you. And this is . . . Mark, I believe?"

Wolfe had taught the child to shake hands when introduced and he did so with great ceremony.

"How do you do, Herr Fritz and Frau Marie?"

"How sweet he is," exclaimed Marie!

Soon the awkwardness of the meeting was past and the adults chatted easily over sherry as they waited for dinner to be served. "...and so in this big house, there are only Fritz and me now. Alas, we have outlived our child. It would be nice to have children in the house once again. What an idea! Fritz, Wolfe and Renee and Mark must come to live here."

White at his wife's babbling, Fritz pretended to hear the housekeeper call that dinner was served. He reached for his wife's arm, which he pinched brutally.

"Come, my dear, Anna has no doubt prepared a veritable feast for our guests."

Dinner passed with polite conversation and no further surprises. Fritz controlled his wife by having his foot firmly planted on hers throughout the meal. After dinner, the men retired to the study for brandy and cigars. The door had barely closed on the two when the Director turned on his nephew.

"What the hell do you think you are doing here? Do you have any idea the danger you have put us all in? Look what is happening in Nuremberg. The word is out that the Americans are searching for many high-ranking officers. One slip of the tongue in the wrong place could put us all at risk."

"Calm yourself, Uncle. I do know what I'm doing. Renee and the boy will only serve to legitimize my identity. By virtue of the marriage, I will soon be able to travel freely about the world as the spouse of an American citizen. The boy will carry my name. Even her family will not know the difference."

"How can you hope to pull that off?"

"Renee herself will pull it off. I have convinced her it will be so much better for the boy to be the son of a Swiss banker she is married to, than the bastard son of a German soldier who never married her."

The older man regarded Wolfe with new respect in his eyes. "I see you have thought this out, but can you control your wife?"

"At least as well as you can control yours. I intend to control her by giving her more freedom than she has ever had--freedom to come and go to America. The boy is the key. She will do anything for him. If she sees me being a father to him, she will not do anything to disturb that. In spite of her awkward circumstances, she is not stupid. She's actually a very practical person."

"How do you expect to set her up in such a way to allow that kind of freedom? It will take a great deal of money."

"Do not make the assumption, Uncle, that the salary you pay me is my only source of funds."

The older man blanched as he was reminded none too subtly that he had much more to lose than his nephew.

"Tante Marie had a very clever idea. We will be moving to this house. It's a simple solution to a complex problem. If I am correct, since there is no one else left in the family, I would in normal circumstances inherit this house eventually. There must be ten bedrooms here. I think I once counted them as a child."

"Wolfe, you can't be serious. It would take so little to make it all come crashing down around us."

"Then we will just have to be careful to make no mistakes. Perhaps when you suggest we live here, you could also suggest we call you Uncle."

Fritz von Erhardt considered his options and found them far too few. He had no illusions about the kind of man his nephew had become. If he did not agree, he very well could find himself a victim of a tragic accident. To say nothing of the fact that if the bank board ever found out what was stored in the basement vaults, he would be forced to resign in disgrace, and could easily go to prison. It would not matter that he was the controlling and primary stockholder of the bank. He would be kept out of there for sure. It would never be made public. That was not the Swiss way of doing things, but it would still be bad for him.

"Very well--we will do it your way."

When the young family left hours later, the plan had been set in motion. The newlyweds would take the north wing of the house. It had several bedrooms, a spacious sitting room, a playroom and a small kitchen which had, a generation before, been for the children of the house. Renee came the very next day to help Marie and the housekeeper open up the rooms and air them out. In a week, everything was laundered, dusted and polished. Wolfe hired a governess for the boy and a housekeeper to help Anna. Adjoining bedrooms were set aside for the governess and her young charge. Two large, side-by-side bedrooms were selected for the bride and groom.

Renee and Mark's meager belongings were moved from the hotel as well as Wolfe's equally few possessions from his bachelor flat. There was an air of celebration in the big house. It had been many years since the house had seen so much activity. Even its rightful owners relaxed. The cheerful, exploring little boy was a joy to them all.

Late on the third night of residence in the big house, a contented, grateful wife slipped into her husband's bed for the first time. He contained his surprise and accepted the gift offered.

Renee had not really planned to go to her husband's room for anything but to talk to him–to thank him for the change in their lives. None-the-less, she selected the one silk nightgown she owned–all the rest looked like they belonged to a schoolgirl. When she slipped into Wolfe's bed, she wasn't sure what to expect. The experience that left her pregnant was her first. Fortunately, Wolfe had a wider experience. It had been a long, dry spell since he left Berlin and he had come to admire the pert young woman who was now his wife.

His hands found her face–his thumb traced her full lower lip. He gently moved himself partly up and over her. Not wanting to frighten her, he kissed her lips softly–then trailed to her neck–then the hollow below her collarbone. His hand slowly slipped the narrow strap of her gown off her shoulder. She gave a small whimper and then a sharp intake of breath as his lips surrounded a nipple. His warm hand slid ever southward, over her hip to cup her buttock in his palm. Cautiously, timorously, her hands slowly found their way to his shoulder–then his waist. He ventured just the tip of his tongue gently circling her nipple as his hand, slowly stroking, moved to the warm and now wet center he sought.

Now he was the one who whimpered

softly. He hadn't realized just how much he missed the feel of a willing woman; his new wife was not pretending. Soon he felt her small hands surround him and her hips lift up to him. He kissed her more urgently, opening her mouth and gliding his tongue across her lips. She was quite lost now–her first taste of truly carnal heat. It was over quickly, that first time. Husband and wife discovered a passion–a heat that could only be cooled by the other. The marriage of convenience found a new dimension.

Chapter 16

Renee and Wolfe had fallen into an easy pattern for their lives. She was happy to leave anything to do with finances to him. With the birth of their stillborn daughter a few years back, Renee retreated from any activity other than caring for her son, helping Marie with the house or traveling to America once or twice a year to spend time with her father. Her mother had died shortly after she and Wolfe made their first trip to Chicago. Wolfe gave her a generous allowance and always paid for her travel. He had been right when he told his uncle he would bind Renee to him by giving her more freedom than she had ever had.

Wolfe's somewhat uneasy relationship with his father-in-law was beginning to stabilize. Mr. Harding loved his grandson deeply and kept a close watch on his development. Renee would bring the boy to Chicago once every summer and her father came to Zurich over the holidays.

Mr. Harding had never quite figured out what the truth was about Mark's father, but since Wolfe claimed him as his own, he could see no-good reason to openly question it? The young family's relationship with the von Erhardts, in whose home they lived, continued to elude him, but he could see his daughter was content. She was well treated and obviously well cared for financially in addition to the trust he set up for her. As far as he could see, she was living at or above the economic level he expected for her even though she had not chosen any of the young wealthy Americans he picked out for her. Immediately after his first meeting with his grandson, he established a substantial trust for the boy also.

***

Wolfe continued to disappear from time to time. No one seemed to know where he went, but no one was willing to question him too closely about it. Renee just assumed he was on business for the bank and his uncle just didn't want to know. Had Herr von Erhardt seen the unsavory looking Arab who met with Wolfe a day or two in advance of one of Wolfe's trips, he would have worried even more.

On one such trip, Wolfe traveled to a small village in the south of Spain. He dined on the terrace of a small tavern, his face in the shadow. Even without the shadow, no one would have recognized the banker from Switzerland. The banker had become a man of many faces. Wolfe enjoyed the little tavern's terrace and the soft sigh of the warm wind off the sea. He could happily have stayed longer to enjoy the peace and solitude, but there was work to do.

Three tables separated him from a dignified old gentleman who took his evening meal daily at the same tavern. This was the third evening he watched the old man but the first time he was this close. The old gent left the tavern at about the same time every night. On this night, Wolfe left the tavern ahead of him and walked quickly up the street. Stepping into a doorway two houses from where the old man lived, he waited. The old man walked slowly but with shoulders erect.   Stepping out into the street behind his quarry, Wolfe followed him softly. As they passed through the darkest part of the lane, he quickly closed the gap.

"Herr General." The old man froze for a moment before turning to see who spoke. His voice was familiar, but the face glimpsed in the dim light was not.

"General von Manstein . . . or is it Herr Stubben?"

The old man's blood ran cold. "Who?"

With his arm around the shoulder and a knife against the old man's throat, Wolfe almost dragged him the last few feet to the general's small home. The man was soon tied to a chair in the middle of his own kitchen. Wolfe asked a lot of questions that night. If he didn't like the answer, he simply opened up a few more inches of skin. In the darkest hours of the night, he finally learned the answers to his two most important questions. The connection the general had to the stash of art, an old friend of Goering's, he was also the uncle of one of Goering's men, name of Daum. Wolfe knew Daum well. This was a very dangerous connection.   The last question concerned who else might know where Wolfe took the art that night long ago. Unfortunately both Daum and one other man knew its resting place.

Wolfe got another piece of information for free. Goering, along with Rommel (the "Desert Fox") made a deal with an Arab prince. Should a homeland be established in Palestine for the Jews, the fortune represented by the art was committed to drive the Jews out. No matter what Wolfe did, the general stuck to his story. Finally even Wolfe could not stomach what he had done to the old man who was once one of Germany's finest.

"This time, Herr General, I'll make sure." A long knife sliced through to the core of the old man's heart. The banker, wearing yet another face, boarded a train a short time later. One more loose end tied up.

Chapter 17

Shortly after returning to the bank from Spain, Wolfe had another angry encounter with his uncle. The meeting came late in the evening, long after the other employees left. Fritz von Erhardt was nearly always frightened of Wolfe these days. He had discovered a large locked trunk in one of the seldom-used vaults in the cellars beneath the bank. He thought he was the only one to have a key to that particular vault door.

"Where did you get the key?"

"You gave it to me, Uncle."

"I did not. What is in the trunk?"

"You do not want to know."

"Wolfe, you cannot keep using the bank this way. You have an opportunity to make a future for yourself here, but the laws are strict for Swiss banks. What is in the trunk?"

"Let's go take a look, Uncle."

Wolfe grabbed his uncle's arm and, none too gently, marched him down the stairs. Upon opening the trunk, he stood aside for the other man to see. The trunk was full of jewels and bars of gold. The Director paled and clutched his chest.

"My God! What have you done?"

"Only what anyone else would have with the same opportunities."

"The stories are true then, about the Jews, about their money and property. You are an animal."

"Don't concern yourself old man," Wolfe sneered, "the Party did this, I've only taken a

small portion of it for myself. What did you think
the night I brought the trunk here and unloaded all
those crates? You knew. Of course you knew.
Don't play the innocent with me. What did you
think then? That the crates contained chocolate?
Or wine? Or perhaps, cheese?" Wolfe was
shaking the old man hard now. The Director's
face became dark purple as he gasped for breath.

"My pills . . . they are in my desk drawer.
Get them for me please."

Wolfe stood back and looked at his uncle.

"I'll get them. You stay here."

Wolfe left the vault, then turned and
slammed the door shut. He heard a muffled shout
from inside and feeble pounding on the door.
Backing up a few steps, he lowered himself to sit
on the stairs. An hour later, having heard no
sound for most of that time, he opened the vault
door. His uncle lay on the floor; he was dead.

"I'm sorry, Uncle. You should have let it
be."

Effortlessly he picked up the old man's
body and carried it up the stairs to the Director's
office. Laying him gently on the beautiful old rug,
he took a seat in his uncle's chair and began to
systematically search the desk. He knew there
was a small safe behind a painting on the wall:
there were few things he didn't know about the
bank. Searching for a key, he found it on a small
ring in the old man's pocket. The safe proved to
have a will and a wad of bearer bonds as well as a
thick pile of large denomination Swiss currency.

*Why you old dog, where did you get all
this? Let's see what the will says. This will never*

do. Fritz had left all his shares in the bank for his wife Marie, with the provision that the bank would guide her. This left her with a substantial income for life with the shares reverting to the bank if she was not living at the time of his death. The will was dated not long after their son died.

It took almost three hours to re-type a will he was satisfied with. He placed the will, a small portion of the bearer bonds, two bundles of currency and some other papers of a miscellaneous nature back in the safe. He arranged some papers and a pen trailing off the desk as if his uncle had been working there when the attack came.

Though well after midnight when he got home, he was surprised to see Renee waiting up for him. She was beautifully dressed and sipped a glass of wine.

"Why are you still up, dear? Is it Mark?"

"No, no," she smiled at him. "I should have told you earlier today I had something planned. Today is our anniversary . . . well, I guess it was yesterday actually. I didn't know you and Fritz would be so late. Marie has gone to bed, where is he?"

"I'm so sorry, Renee. I forgot . . . I've had a lot on my mind. Fritz had me working on some investment possibilities; in fact he was still poring over the papers when I left."

"Poor Fritz, he works so hard. He's getting older now and should be taking some time off to enjoy life while he still can."

"Fritz has always worked hard, I'm sure. Nothing will change that. Come here, my pretty.

What have you cooked up for me? And by the way, I do hope cooking is involved somewhere as I am starving."

Wolfe put his hands on her waist and drew her to him. He kissed her lightly, then again, and again. She laughed at him, then pulled away to look at his face.

"I thought you were hungry?"

"I was," he said, "but just wasn't aware what I was hungry for!" He swung her up into his arms and carried her up the stairs to his bedroom. In a few moments, all thoughts of anything but her husband were driven from Renee's mind.

Chapter 18

Arriving a few minutes late at the bank the following morning, Wolf was whistling as he came through the door. He stopped short as he saw two gendarmes speaking to the assistant head teller. Moving quickly to join the three men, he asked, "What is going on here?"

"Herr von Erhardt is dead. His assistant found him when she came in this morning."

"Who are you?" the older of the gendarmes asked.

"I am Wolfe Bauer. What has happened? Oh no, I should not have left Fritz here alone so late at night."

"What time did you leave?"

"I don't really know . . . quite late. We'd been working on some investments. I'd finished the documents and Fritz wanted to review them so they could be put in the Post this morning."

The older of the two men watched Wolfe closely. "Do you know anyone who might harm him?"

"No . . . are you saying someone broke in? To a bank? Is there anything missing? Fritz...Herr von Erhardt, is he all right?"

"Why would you think someone broke in?"

"I don't know . . . I'm asking you."

"No, Herr von Erhardt appears to have had a heart seizure. The doctor is with him now."

At this juncture, the doctor himself appeared.

"I think Fritz died of heart failure. I really don't understand. His pills were right there in his desk. It must have happened too fast for him to get them. I've made arrangements for his body to be taken away."

Wolfe turned to go. "Dead? Fritz is dead? I must get back home to tell Marie. I'm sure she will want him to be at home until the service."

The younger of the policemen now joined in. "Who is Marie?"

"Marie is his wife. They have been very kind to my family and me. They are family to us, in fact we have lived with them for years, and they are like grandparents to our child. I must go–she should not hear this from a stranger."

As Wolfe turned and walked out of the bank, the younger of the two policemen watched him go. Two days later the autopsy determined Fritz died of natural causes. The service was held in the church Fritz and Marie attended their whole lives. He was well liked in the community and many mourners came to the house. Later, Renee and Wolfe stood with Marie as the last of the mourners left. The very last was Fritz's solicitor.

"Could I speak with you privately Wolfe?"

"Certainly. Let's go to Fritz's study and let the ladies rest."

When seated with a glass of brandy, the barrister broached the subject on his mind. "In the next few days, we must take a look at the will and see what needs to be done."

"Yes, we should. If you would like, you could bring it by to me at the bank. Perhaps we should take a look at it before officially reading it to Marie."

"I don't have it. As far as I know, Fritz always kept important papers at the bank. He said something once about having them in 'safekeeping'."

Wolfe appeared to ponder this and said, "I will ask his assistant. She will know. If they can be found at the bank, I will call you as soon as we find them."

"Also Wolfe, you may not be aware, but I am on the Board of Directors for the bank. We will be having a meeting sometime in the next few days to decide who will be running the bank from now on. I think perhaps you should be there. I know I speak for the rest of the board when I say we would be glad for your input."

"Why thank you," Wolfe replied with a surprised look. *Nice of you to ask since I have absolutely no intention of being left out of that meeting.* The next day, with the help of Fritz's assistant, Wolfe 'found' the safe. Phoning the solicitor in the woman's hearing, Wolfe said, "as soon as we can find the key, you can take possession of the contents of the safe. I will call you immediately."

Wolfe hung up the phone and ignored the quizzical look on the woman's face. "Do you know where he might have kept the key?" She observed him silently for a few seconds. Something about Wolfe Bauer was wrong. She didn't know what it was, but it made her very uncomfortable. She could have sworn she had seen him in the Director's office in the past when the safe was open. If memory served her, Wolfe would have seen Herr von Erhardt lock or unlock the safe with a key from his ring.

"Try his key ring. The police would have given it back to his widow by now." She left the room hurriedly and went back to her own desk. When she had occasion to leave her desk later, she was shocked to see him still at the director's desk, apparently going through everything in it.

Two days later, having acquired the key from Marie, he called the solicitor to come to the bank at his convenience. Wolfe would wait to open the safe until the man arrived. An hour later, Wolfe walked across the bank to his own office and saw Fritz's assistant in a hushed conversation with the barrister. Recovering quickly, he walked directly toward them.

"Here you are. Let's go and open that safe. Madame Werner, please come with us as a witness."

Without further conversation, he led the way back to the Director's office. No one seemed to question the appropriateness of him taking charge. Taking the key from the desk drawer, he went directly to the safe and opened it. As he pulled each item from the safe, he identified it and asked the woman to make a list of the contents. Once the safe was empty, he dismissed her.

Speaking to the barrister he said, "Well, why don't you sit here and read through all these papers. I have some things to do and will be back in about an hour, then you will know what needs to be done next."

He left the room quickly and soon closed

the door of his own office behind him. He paced the floor there for precisely fifty-seven minutes before opening the door and returning to the Director's office.

"Well, did you get through it all? I've called Marie and told her to expect us later." The man was now observing Wolfe closely looking for any sign of deceit. He saw none. Little did he know the man in front of him had nerves of steel and many years of practice as a liar. The man laid things out in front of Wolfe.

"Here is some cash, which should go to Marie. Some bearer bonds, which should also go to her. This is the document for the ownership of the house, which has been in his family for generations, and for a farm he inherited from his uncle. This is a document appraising some jewelry he apparently gave to Marie. Now, this is the will. I think you'd better sit."

Wolfe slowly sat on the edge of the desk.

"The bulk of Fritz's assets consist of bank stock and the family home. The home goes directly to his widow, and seventy-five percent of the bank shares with one caveat: you are to vote the stock. The remainder of the shares goes to you."

Wolfe carefully let a stunned expression cross his face.

"That can't be. Fritz was very kind to our family, but surely he would not have left me that much. Some small token would not surprise me, but not this. Did you know about this?"

"Actually, I did not. This is very strange because he never mentioned any of this to me.

This will is dated over a year ago, but when we went over some other business a couple of months ago, he never mentioned having written a new will."

Wolfe appeared to ponder this. "The only thing I can think of to explain this is the way he felt about his wife. He told me on more than one occasion he feared for Marie when he was gone, as he watched over her since they were both very young. He worried she would have no one to look after her if his heart gave out. She is . . . was . . . his life, especially since their son died. Fritz was very fond of my wife and our son. Perhaps he wished us to remain in his home to look after her. I don't know. This is a shock. I have to think this through. I don't understand."

The barrister remained silent, as did Wolfe, who kept his head down looking at the carpet.

"I have to think . . ." Wolfe's words trailed off as he walked slowly out of the room and out of the bank.

Chapter 19

The day dawned clear and beautiful. Wolfe stood looking out of the windows of his late uncle's study, draining the last of his morning tea. He wore his finest suit. Today was the day of the board meeting at the bank. Fortunately for him he had been invited. Even if they tried to leave him out, the barrister knew he controlled the majority of the shares.

Things went well with Tante Marie. She was terrified of the responsibility of the bank shares: the look on her face as she begged me to take over that duty for her! She and Renee are just alike, as long as nothing disrupts their lives; there's not a lot of reality they wish to know.

The bank's Board of Directors was three hours into the meeting. The discussion was somewhat heated at times. Wealthy and conservative businessmen, two doctors, and two barristers that made up the board were appalled to find out how much influence Wolfe was going to have over the controlling shares of the bank. They were more shocked when he arrived without Marie. He produced instead, a power of attorney for all the family shares.

"Gentlemen, I did not seek out this situation. It came as great a shock to me yesterday as it did to you today. I knew Herr von Erhardt had grown to trust me with more duties in the bank, but it appears he not only trusted me with the bank, but he also entrusted his beloved wife Marie to my care. I wrestled with this all night.

Herr von Erhardt has been so kind to my family and me. I must live up to his expectations. This has been a profound shock to all of us. Perhaps it would be wise for the board to postpone making a decision today and agree to meet again in ten days' time to consider the matter of the bank's new director." Wolfe looked expectantly around the table.

The several board members looked at each other, then one of them said, "I think you might be right, Wolfe, we need to think this through. Another meeting in ten days is exactly what we need."

A brief conversation followed setting the time for the next meeting then all of them rose, gathered up their belongings, and left the bank. The ten days passed quickly for Wolfe. He was very busy visiting the various board members in their homes and offices–even finding one dining alone in a restaurant. It was therefore not a surprise to him when, at the next meeting, one of the men raised Wolfe's name as the next director; there was a quick vote, which appeared to be unanimous.

Chapter 20

Mark Bauer grew up a child of privilege. Although his bond with his mother was strong, he worshiped the man he believed was his father. Wolfe cultivated this relationship from the beginning. A son was more important to him than he liked to admit, and Mark was certainly the epitome of the ideal son.

Wolfe started early including the boy in his daily routine, always looking for Mark at the end of the day to share a few moments and regale the boy with silly stories of people who came into the bank that day. Mark was disappointed if his father was late coming home and downright depressed when Wolfe was out of town. As Mark grew older, he began to follow his father to the bank on days he did not have school. It was not until he was fifteen, and made a new best friend at school, that he began to have a life not tied to Wolfe. From the moment Mark met Claude Depardier, the son of a Paris policeman the young men were fast friends. They even spent a part of each school holiday in the other's family home.

A school term and then summer, followed by school term and yet another summer went by quickly. Before long, his parents discussed university for Mark. Renee wanted him to continue his education in America. Reminding him of his dual citizenship, Renee hoped he would go to school in Chicago, near his Grandfather Harding. With her mother gone, she worried about her father; having Mark nearby would alleviate some of that concern.

Wolfe wanted him to go to University in Zurich and stay at home for a few more years.

Mark proved to have a mind of his own on the subject of higher education. He wished to go to school in Geneve, making the argument that it was far enough away to be somewhat on his own, but he could still come home for holidays. It amused both parents that Mark wanted to go away, but not too far. Unable to deny him anything, they agreed to his choice of school.

Although he was quite young for university life, Mark settled in and became known by his professors as a serious scholar. He was known by his friends as a fun-loving, energetic young man who, despite his wealth, dashing good looks and scholastic aptitude behaved in such a manner as to be thought of first and foremost as a gentleman.

Mark's longtime school chum Claude attended university in Paris, so they kept in touch by post. Claude became more interested in police work and decided to follow in his father's footsteps. Mark meanwhile, was absorbed by art and art history, influenced by exposure to his grandfather's large art collection. David Baruch, his roommate since arriving in Geneve, also influenced him. David was a quiet, serious student several years older than Mark. His thin, bony frame, scholarly glasses and overlong hair were a contrast to Mark's robust, almost American good looks. They made an odd pair–Mark with his six-foot frame, blond hair and startlingly blue eyes the perfect foil for David's slight, dark, quiet self. They soon were fast friends.

David, who was the subject of much ribbing due to his appearance, had some rather nasty encounters with some rowdy students who had teamed up with an unsavory element from the town. He soon noticed he was not bothered when he was with Mark. At first he thought it had to do with his friend's size, but as time went on, he knew that Mark's presence went beyond size. Mark was a natural leader, and respected for his evenhanded approach to everything.

Due to their difference in age and years at school, three years passed before they had a class together, but the coffeehouses of Geneve were their mutual classrooms as well. Several of their professors frequented these same coffeehouses. On one such night near the end of term, the two friends gave up their studies in the library and sought a lighter forum. A less serious tone was not to be found that night.

A professor named Steven Tesla, whom they knew only in passing, was deep in his cups and holding forth on the subject of the German death camps. The students surrounding him seemed to literally inhale his words and the dark eyes of the old man snapped with a spirit denied by his posture.

"The Austrian's quarrel with the Jew was not one of ideology, but of economics. Racial purity was simply the vehicle to round up the Jews and confiscate property."

A student asked, "Professor, surely you don't think Hitler killed all those Jews just for money."

"I do indeed. He was a lazy man in love

with the sound of his own voice. He preyed on the worst fears of the German people at a time when they were most vulnerable. Unemployment, unrest, and poverty are the driving forces behind most wars. You cannot convince a comfortable man that it's in his best interest to fight. Whatever else may be the justification uttered publicly, it always boils down to economics."

"Tesla," spoke a young instructor from across the room, "so the desire for the purity of the race is a smokescreen? You think the Fuhrer did not care about the mongrelization of the race?"

"What race would that be, Sir?"

"The white race."

Tesla rose unsteadily to his feet and turned to face the speaker.

"When will we learn, there is only the human race. Did not Tolstoy say 'the recognition of the sanctity of life of every man is the first and only basis for morality'? War is the time-honored way of redistributing wealth, whatever wealth is seen to be, whether land, or money in banks, or gold or camels. In order for those who covet to convince others to join them to take from those who have it, they must first convince everyone of the inferiority of the nature of the man with the gold. They must first find a way to reduce the very humanity and thus the morality of the man possessing the thing they want.

How simple that is if we can put a face, a race, a creed, a nationality to this man to make him different than we are, and in his difference, inferior. We can then justify our anger that he possesses what we do not. If a man has no money in his pocket to feed his family, no work to go to, no home to call his own, he is more susceptible to this line of thinking. How convenient it is to be able to blame someone else for one's own station in life. This unrest in turn wins peace at home as the result of war abroad, according to Hegel, for now the government is doing something, you see. War is about wealth. It's never about anything else, no matter how you dress it up."

The old professor slumped down in his chair once more, silently contemplating his glass of wine. Several of the students gathered up their things and walked out into the mild, late spring evening. The instructor who taunted Tesla about racial purity stopped by his chair.

"It's not over, old man, just suspended."

Tesla did not even look up. Soon David and Mark prepared to leave the coffeehouse themselves, their light-hearted evening grown somber. Muttering a 'good evening' as they passed his chair, Mark walked only a few steps before he turned back to the professor.

"Sir, what of the Swiss? We don't take sides in war. Does that make us, as a people better or worse? Is there then a morality in being neutral, or is it only to be found in taking sides? Don't we become just like those we take up arms against? I never thought of war as being about money, I thought it was always about ideas."

The old man looked up at him and smiled. "What is your name, son?"

"Mark Bauer."

"It's amazing how much good ideas and high intentions can get all tangled up in money.

Don't take me too seriously tonight. I've had bad news. An old friend who survived the death camps died last night, the victim of a robbery. It's always about the money. Not fighting a war doesn't make one moral–prudent perhaps, but not necessarily moral. Don't you see, there's a danger if you take sides and a danger if you don't. The only side to be on is the side of the angels, and sometimes that's pretty hard to see. We Swiss are hypocrites–safe, but hypocrites just the same. A man has to decide who he is. Sometimes we go through life never asking that question. Who is your Jewish friend?"

Mark looked startled at the question. He looked at David and grinned. "David Baruch, Sir. I guess I never asked myself that question either."

Tesla looked at the young fellow Jew and said, "Keep this man as your friend."

"Yes Sir. I intend to."

"Get out of here now, you two. Don't you have exams coming up?" They hurried out.

"You never noticed, did you?" asked David.

"No, I guess I didn't. It seems there are a number of things I haven't noticed.It's time I did."

"You are a good man, Mark. You see everyone as the same."

"That might not be good enough, David. Remember what the professor said about the comfortable man. Perhaps I've been too comfortable."

His friend looked at him and smiled, "If I didn't know the old man was a Jew, I'd swear he was a Jesuit! Enough for tonight. Let's go home."

Chapter 21

When the last term was over, Mark invited his friend to come home with him for a while. When they stepped off the train in Zurich, Wolfe and Renee were both there to greet them. Wolfe courteously but quickly asked where they could drop David off. Mark responded at once. "Papa, I've asked David to stay with us, I hope it's all right. I know we have lots of room. I'm sorry if I presumed . . ."

"I believe I'll just walk and find something near the station," David said.

"You'll do nothing of the kind," Renee said, of course we have lots of room. You are most welcome, David."

Only David noticed the unpleasant look that crossed Herr Bauer's face, along with the clenched jaw. The next week was very long for all but Renee, who was mostly oblivious to the situation. Mark began to see his father in a new light, and it wasn't very flattering. Wolfe treated David as someone so insignificant as to not be worthy of notice. In fact, he treated Anna, the housekeeper and Dorf, the groundskeeper better than he did David. Mark tried to discuss this with his mother, but Renee simply made excuses for her husband, saying she was sure Mark misunderstood. He knew that was not the case.

Walking along the Bahnhofstrasse one afternoon, both men started to talk at once, "I think we . . ." "Perhaps I should . . ."

Mark stopped and looked at his friend. "I

am so sorry, David. You think you have known someone your whole life and you think you know all about them. It never crossed my mind that my father would . . . He's a German sort of Swiss . . . I didn't know . . ."

"Relax, Mark. It will be just fine. I've been thinking about going back to Geneve, perhaps tomorrow."

"I've been thinking too. Only I've been thinking about going to Paris for a while. I'd like to see Claude. You would like him too, David. He's great. We've been friends since we were boys. I know you'll like him too."

"Mark, I don't know of any other way to say this, I'm sure Claude and I would get along fine, but I simply don't have the money for the train ticket or a room in Paris."

"I will buy your ticket. No, don't argue with me. Money is not something I ever have to worry about, mostly thanks to my American grandfather. It would give me pleasure, as well as make up for putting you in the way of my father's appalling behavior."

"You don't have to make up for anything, but if it will indeed give you pleasure, I'll accept."

The two men were off to Paris the next day. Mark had a long night awake thinking of his father. While he loved him dearly, he was able to see the man had a dark and ugly side to him. Recalling some of the things he had seen and overheard as a child, he ruefully told himself it was time to grow up. Perhaps the whole subject could bear some more thought.

***

The three young men were soon a matched set on the Paris scene. Claude was now finished with his studies and about to officially step into a position with the metropolitan police of Paris. His father had paved the way for him to work under an old friend from the war. This was Claude's last fling, he said, before getting down to work for the next forty years or so. Soon the three were out on the town every evening after Mme. Depardier saw to it that her son and his friends were well fed. The modest household had cheerfully squeezed in both Mark and David and stretched the meals. Mme. Depardier would not hear of Mark and David staying in a hotel. It soon became apparent to Mark that he'd better do some marketing if their appetites were not going to bankrupt the generous family.

Claude's younger sisters had already given up their room to accommodate the two visitors. Mme. Depardier wisely refrained from commenting on their generosity as she watched the girls hang on every word that came from the mouths of their brothers' friends. At least one of the girls was madly in love with Mark, and the youngest had fallen in love with David's dark and mysterious looks. On the last day Claude was to be free, the three young men sat in a sidewalk café late into the night, drinking wine and consuming baguette after baguette and discussing the world in general.

Claude spoke, "David, has Mark told you that when we were children in school, we were very fond of mysteries, always looking for a new one to solve? We must have made our teachers nuts. That love of a puzzle is probably something inherited from my father and no doubt the reason I'm following in his footsteps. By the way, Mark, this may interest you as an art historian. I've been doing some legwork for my father on a case he has been working on. There is a young woman whose parents were German Jews who died in the camps. They had been quite wealthy and sent her, her sister and a trusted housekeeper out of Germany to Paris. A young cousin drove them out early on."

"The older of the sisters, named Inge, was the only one to survive the war. She has told a tale of the truck having paintings and a box of gold under the vegetables. The cousin returned to Germany and she has not heard from him since."

"The girls and the housekeeper lived quietly in a small house on the outskirts of Paris until Paris fell. One day she walked to the green grocer and came back to the house to see soldiers tearing it apart. She was afraid and hid until they left. After dark she crept back into the house. The housekeeper and her sister were gone. She never saw them again. Gone also were the paintings and the box of gold the housekeeper had hidden in a small barn. My father has been able to trace some of her family through the International Red Cross. She did indeed come from a very wealthy family. As far as anyone can tell, she is the sole survivor."

"Now here comes the really interesting part. Taking refuge during the remainder of the war in a convent, she did not speak for several years. After the war the nuns discovered it was not that she could not speak, but that she would not. Such was the horror of what she had seen.

She is recovered now, a happy, useful member of the convent community, now called Sister Michael."

"About a year ago, on a trip to Rome with several other members of the order, she was walking along a street when she saw a painting in a gallery window. She swears it hung in her parent's home when she was small. She questioned the gallery owner who, of course, said he had a bill of sale for the painting and it belonged to him."

"Upon her return to Paris, she went to the head of her order and obtained permission to go to the police about that painting and others she said came with her to France. The case eventually came to my father. He gave it to me. I think to keep me busy.

Interestingly enough, the trail took me back to Rome. I don't know what my father said to his superiors to convince them to buy me a train ticket, but when I got to Rome, I found a very interesting thing. I spoke to the gallery owner, of course, and got the same story the nun did. However, I found another very interesting part of the story."

"On the back of the painting were the first two letters of the nun's family name. I turned over several more paintings before being thrown out by the gallery owner. There was another small piece with the same two letters on the back. Now Sister Michael would like the two paintings returned to her. She would like to give them to the order that gave her refuge during the war. How's that for complicated? Starting with a German Jew who is now a nun!"

"My parents died in the camps," David said almost to himself. "We never had much money, but I'm sure my father had at least some money in the bank. I wonder what became of it?"

"What a horrible story," Mark replied. "When I think of someone like my mother in such circumstances, on her own in an occupied country, not even the country of her birth. What a remarkable woman this nun is. What luck have you had? Have you been able to get the original painting back to her?"

"No, we haven't, Mark. The man who has it now has a bill of sale that says he paid for the painting. The man he bought it from is nowhere to be found. We cannot prove or disprove the validity of his story, at least not to a certainty."

"There actually has been a whole department formed to deal with this problem, but there has been no serious progress made. Unfortunately, it's been over twenty years and many of the people who survived the camps have no way of documenting their losses, to say nothing of the heirs of people who did not survive. As an art historian, how would you approach this?"

Mark thought for a moment. "The real key to knowing anything about a piece of art, especially about paintings, is called provenance. When a piece changes owners, there is usually some kind of a paper that also changes hands, at least there is today. That might not happen if the painting passed through several generations of the same family. So now, a kind of a paper trail is laid. I would think in the case of art looted in the war, the trail completely breaks down. So if the provenance looks strange or disappears altogether from say, 1933 to 1945, you have suspect ownership. But even at that, it would be very difficult to prove the current owner came by it dishonestly. If there could be some kind of registry . . . I just can't believe there isn't already one in existence."

"Actually there is, Mark. There has been, however, no moral imperative to do much more than wring hands and make pious statements about how horrible this is. In fact, there was a top official in the American government who, in 1945, wrote a report suggesting a value of between one hundred and three hundred fifty million Swiss francs in art and more than a billion in gold was sent to banks in Switzerland for safekeeping. One of the more effective organizations to work on the problem was the Monuments, Fine Arts and Archives Commission of the United States Army, but that was a long time ago. In many instances, survivors have been unable to access their family estates for lack of death certificates for those who died in the camps."

"I don't see the situation improving much unless art museums, galleries, and art departments of universities as well as auction houses will get on the side of what is right and just and vigorously search out and question every piece of art that came to them since 1933. So far, no one acts until forced to by a court. Even then, the courts themselves are not much help. It's horrible that these people have suffered so much and still must go back over and over again the most painful details of their lives to try to obtain what is rightly theirs."

The conversation then went off into the area of art theft occurring in present day Paris. As Claude and David laughed over a current case involving the theft of a rather naughty nude from the apartments of a very proper elderly lady, Mark stared off in the distance, lost in thought.

Having just completed his studies, he was well aware that he, now twenty-five, needed to decide a course for his life. Later in this same summer he was scheduled to teach a short course in art history at the Sorbonne. He had been offered an assistantship in Geneve and, of course, his father said he was most welcome at the bank. Grandfather Harding had also written his mother of his hope that Mark would come to the United States.

Certainly he did not need an occupation in order to eat, but he was not a playboy. Over the past year, he had been thinking more of doing something truly worthwhile with his life. He had not said this out loud, not even to David; it just sounded a bit sappy. Perhaps he needed to have a long conversation with his grandfather. He instinctively knew both his father and his mother would be the wrong choice.

Mark knew he didn't even know the questions he wanted to ask. Grandfather Harding was a self-made man therefore he was exactly the right person to ask. He decided to put off thinking about it while he had this short time with his best friends. Claude already had to get serious and go to work. There was little time left for David and him to enjoy the summer in Paris.

Here I am in the world's most romantic city and I haven't managed even an evening with a beautiful girl. What a poor excuse I am! This is a situation that must be remedied!

The next few weeks in Paris found Mark and David seeing as much of the city as they could. Their wanderings took them from Montmartre to the Bastille, from Orleans to Rouen. They saw chorus girls in the Moulin Rouge, painters outside the Louvre, flea markets and flowers in the heart of the old city, and so many museums that even David begged for relief.

It was during this time that Mark heard the full story of David's family. Over the years he heard bits and pieces, but the whole story was grim. It only served to further cement the friendship the two had. They found in each other the brother they didn't have; it was to be both the bond of a lifetime, and a time of unadulterated enjoyment of life.

After David went back to Geneve, Mark wandered the streets near the Sorbonne alone after he taught his class. He usually ended the day sitting in a coffeehouse surrounded by his students. Invariably most of them were girls– beautiful girls, French, Italian, Brits, American and even one lovely dark-eyed lass from Dublin. He enjoyed them all and went back to Claude's alone. When his class was finished, he said goodbye to the Depardier family and sailed to America.

Arranging the trip had presented some difficulties. He wrote his mother from Paris that he intended a trip to see his grandfather and would see his parents again in late fall. His mother was happy about that as she had last been to the States more than a year before. Wolfe weighed in on the subject of the trip, even going as far as seeing Mark in Paris to dissuade him. He reasoned that Mark's dual citizenship could leave him open to conscription with America's involvement in Viet Nam. It took two letters, four phone calls and a promise to return in thirty days to calm his mother's fears.

Chapter 22

When Mark arrived in New York, Grandfather Harding was there to meet him. The elderly gentleman arranged a whirlwind tour for his only grandson. Ensconced in the Harding apartment high above Central Park, the two men made the rounds of the elder man's various enterprises in the city. He was clearly showing off his grandson.

Mark found it fascinating because he had never seriously given thought to the origins of his own very substantial trust fund. In one day alone, they visited a stock brokerage, a publishing house, a medical supply house and an oil exploration firm. On the last day, he was even more surprised when his grandfather told him that the next morning they would drive to La Guardia and take a plane to Chicago.

"The world is changing, Mark. We must change with it or be left in the dust."

At home in the big mansion on Lake Michigan, Mark spoke to his grandfather about his search to do something useful with his life.

"I want to make a difference somewhere. You have given me a great heritage as well as a great advantage with your example and the trust fund you provided for me. I cannot tell you how much I appreciate all you have done for me. It is because of that advantage that I must do something to help others."

Mark went on to speak about his friend David and the death of his family in the camps.

He spoke of the professor who talked about the economics of war.

"It has been twenty years and Europe is still being rebuilt. Some things will never go back the way they were. Families were destroyed, businesses lost, properties which stood for hundreds of years now stand in ruin. Let me tell you a story my friend Claude told me in Paris recently."

In retelling the story of the nun and her lost world, he expanded on that to included tales of lost art he had heard about from Tesla.

"Grandfather the thing that interests me in this, is that art represents the best and the brightest of a culture. Five hundred years from now, how will the world know us? If we lose the remnants of our culture which art represents, how will they know us? By our vast cities? By our leashing the power of the atom? By great armies and navies? By vast commerce? What do we leave behind?"

"Much of Europe has been rebuilt, but in its soul the scars are still fresh. Then, there is a certain element in my country that denies the very event of war. There is a callousness, a disregard for the sufferings of other nations. I think it grows out of our so-called neutrality. If we're not involved, it somehow didn't happen."

"You have a good mind and a kind heart, Mark. As much as I would like to have you close-by, I know you are primarily a European. Your mother also shared with me her deep concern that you could be drafted if the war in Viet Nam goes on much longer. That just cannot happen. At this point I believe you are actually too old for that to happen, but I'm not willing to take the chance. I might feel differently if you had grown up in this country. I think you are on the track of getting something clear in your mind. Keep thinking, Mark: a way will come to you. You and your mother are all I have in the world now. I've been fortunate to be in the right place at the right time several times in my life. I've amassed a great fortune, and there is nothing in life I want to buy. It would please me if, at this time in my life, I can do something useful with it."

"Grandfather, I'm not asking for money."

"I know son, but you'll need it, I'm sure. While your grandmother was alive, she would come to me with a church that needed a new roof, or a school needing a library, or a landmark that needed saving. I haven't had that since she died."

"I miss the projects almost as much as I miss her. I always made it appear she would have to persuade me. Truth to tell, I loved her so much, I would do anything she asked. I know she would approve of spending money on a good cause. When you have this figured out, write me all about it."

"Thank you, Grandfather, for your wisdom. I want you to know how much I value it."

There were tears in the man's eyes as he hugged the young man he loved so much, but at this wintertime of his life, might never see again.

Returning to France on the same ship he had come to America on, (it having made another complete round trip since then) Mark kept to himself. He walked the decks at night and in the daytime alternated between walking, writing in a journal or swimming in the first class pool. The young women on the ship could not take their eyes off the handsome, well-mannered young man. Unfortunately he didn't seem to notice.

***

By the time they docked in Rouen, which was the port for Paris, he had a pretty clear idea in his mind of a plan. As soon as he returned to Paris, he telephoned his friend Claude and made plans for them to meet for a late meal. It was very late indeed by the time they had caught up and Mark laid out his plan for Claude. "...and so you see, my friend, I really do have need of a very good policeman." Claude was silent for a moment while he digested what his friend had laid out.

"This is a masterful stroke, Mark. A foundation whose sole purpose is to locate stolen art and return it to the rightful owner; a foundation willing to coordinate information from any other sources and be kind of a library, to work with the police—this is the kind of effort needed. You are the person who could pull this off. I think you need to meet an inspector I'm working with and soon. He has a wealth of knowledge and I'm sure he can be a great help to you. I hope you know I want a part in this."

Mark laughed, "I'm glad. I didn't know what my next step was going to be if you thought I'd lost my mind."

"Well, you have, but it's a rather refreshing form of dementia. By the way, just how big is that trust fund of yours?"

"I honestly don't know what it is right now. My grandfather funded it with about ten million U.S. dollars when I was a toddler. I haven't used much of it. My parents cannot touch it, though I think the need would never arise. As my grandfather would say, it's a right respectable piece of change. Grandfather also let me know there's more where that came from if I need it."

"You realize, don't you, that this could take many years, perhaps the rest of your life. It could be an insurmountable task."

"If it is, I guess I'd better get started."

In the week and a half that followed, Mark purchased a flat in St-Germain-des-Pre. It was large enough for him to both live and work in: his first appropriation was of the large, formal dining room for an office. He met with Claude's Inspector de la Croix to lay out his plan. Between them they began to give substance to the idea. The inspector knew a lot about Mark from Claude, and he had great admiration for this unspoiled and kind young man. Had Claude not told him, he would never have guessed Mark came from such wealth. He was happy to be able to help in the cause.

Bauer's Run

Chapter 23

Mark's next task was to travel to Zurich to tell his parents. He wasn't sure how his mother would take it, but he knew what his father's reaction would be. He would explode. Mark wasn't wrong, he was, however, totally unprepared. After finding that forbidding his son did no good, Wolfe tried sarcasm.

"Is this the idea of that long-haired sniveling Jew friend of yours? Or did it come from that disgusting drunk Jew Tesla?"

"I won't have you speak of my friends that way, Father. They don't deserve that. This is my idea. I thought you would want to know my plans. I see I was wrong."

"You won't be using a franc from the trust on this. Not after I talk to your grandfather myself."

"I'm sorry, Father. Grandfather himself helped me think my way through this. He not only approves, but also may add money if needed. I've decided on a name for this venture. It will be called the Lillian Harding Archival Trust for my grandmother."

"You are no son of mine. You stupid, stupid, Jew-loving, bastard child. After all I have done for you. I gave you my name; you had every advantage I could give you. I treated you like you were my own . . ."

As Wolfe roared, Mark saw his mother standing in the doorway, her face covered in tears and white as a sheet. "Wolfe, I beg of you, please stop," she cried. Mark's face reflected his shock as his father's words penetrated.

"Get out. I'll handle this Renee, do as I say."

"Mark, I'm so sorry . . ." His mother's tears were more than he could bear. As he went to her and held her in his arms, Mark turned her from the room.

"Don't you walk out on me, I'm not done with you . . . you . . . you little bastard."

Wolfe reached out and yanked Mark back by the collar of his shirt. As Mark struggled to regain his balance, his father struck out and slapped his face. Gathering up the front of his son's shirt, like a maniacal machine, he began to hit the young man over and over in the face. It was a measure of Mark's respect for him that he never raised a hand to his father in his own defense. When he let go, Mark slid to the floor. Barely conscious, his face covered in blood, Mark shook his head to try to clear it. His mother slumped in the doorway, sobbing into her hands.

"I'm so sorry, Mark, I'm so sorry."

Anna heard and came flying down the hall with a wet towel for her mistress. When Renee pointed mutely to her son, Anna went to Mark and gently washed the blood from the face of the young man she had loved since he was a toddler.

Wolfe had subsided and stood muttering and looking out the study window.

"Fools. I am surrounded by fools. You will not do this."

Mark, his arm gently around his mother, helped Anna get her to bed. When Anna left, Mark asked, "What did he mean, Mama?"

By the time Renee finished telling her son the story, the hour was late. When she finally slept, he sat by the bed holding her hand, sleeping himself after a while. He didn't hear Anna or Wolfe open the door to look in. His mother was awake and watching him when he awoke in the morning. His body was stiff from the hours in the chair and the beating he had taken.

"I'm leaving here, Mark. I'm going back to America now while my father is still alive. I've been hiding from reality for a long time. Just closing my eyes if I didn't like what I saw. No more. I'll call your grandfather today. Perhaps this time I will return home by air. Yes, now that decision is made, I don't want a leisurely trip. I want to be home soon."

"I'm sorry, Mama. This is my fault. I should have known better than to try to tell him. I'm sorry you had to go back over such painful memories."

"Don't ever be sorry. I am so proud of the man you have grown up to be. You have to go your own way. I would have had to pay the price at some point. At least now I can go home to Chicago while my father is still alive. I know he's been lonely since my mother died. Don't worry about me, I'll be fine. Take care of yourself. Get your project under way. Now scoot, so I can dress. Please send Anna to me, she will help me pack."

Mark kissed his mother and left her alone. Finding Anna in the kitchen, he didn't have to say a word. Anna saw his grim face and promptly went down the hall to Renee's room.

Mark stood for a time looking out at the garden. When he left there this time, he didn't know if he would ever return. The unbearable sadness of losing the only father he knew, and the memories made in this house would haunt him forever. It would have been easier had Wolfe died.

He no longer remembered the time when he and his mother were alone, but he recalled some of the strange memories of some of the places he had followed Wolfe. He wondered what else churned beneath the surface of the man. *Did any of them know him at all? Did I love him so much I blinded myself to what he was?*

Not knowing how Wolfe would react to his
mother leaving, he resolved to stay until he could put
her on a plane. Since he knew he was going to have to
deal with Wolfe sooner or later, he decided to get it
over with. He found Wolfe in the study, staring out the
window. Wolfe did not move or blink when he came
into the room. Mark began to speak quietly.

"Mama has told me the story. I know you are
bitterly opposed to my plans. I'm sorry about that, but
it is what I must do. I just feel the need to do
something useful with my life. I have been greatly
privileged, and I know that has a lot to do with you.
Whatever goes between us from now on, I will always
be grateful to you for your kindness to my mother
when she was young and alone, and your kindness to
me."

" Whatever you think of me now, you have been
a good father to me. Don't think I don't know that.
Perhaps in time you will realize that I am, at least in
part, the man you raised me to be. I will leave you my
address and telephone in Paris. If you ever need me,
I'll come." Seeing no response, he turned to leave the
room.

"Go. Just go, and leave me alone. I don't need
you. I don't need anyone. I've been alone before. I
know how to survive. I've done it in war and I can do
it now. You don't know. You don't know what it
takes to stay alive. You've been coddled and
pampered, the son of great wealth. Not like me. I had
to kill to stay alive. I did it then and I can do it again.
Just get out of my sight. Leave me alone."

Mark stood still as the shock of Wolfe's words
penetrated.

"What do you mean? What are you talking
about? Whom did you have to kill? I didn't know you
were in the war, you're talking about the war? Papa . .
."

I'm not your Papa. Not now, not ever again. Go away."

Mark's entreaties fell on deaf ears. No matter what he said Wolfe was through talking. Mark finally turned and left the room. Opening the door to the hallway, he found his mother, dressed in a suit, with bags at the end of the corridor.

"My turn," she said with a small smile.

Mark waited in the hallway while she said goodbye to her husband of over twenty years. He heard not a sound from Wolfe, only the quiet murmur of his mother's voice. In less than five minutes she opened the door again.

"I'm leaving now, Mark. Anna is packing my personal things she will ship to me. I'm taking my car to the airport."

"I'll go with you. I'm ready to leave also. Just let me say goodbye to Anna."

Mark found the housekeeper he had known as long as he could remember with tears flowing down her face as she packed his mother's things.

"Anna, I'm sure Mama did not think to ask, would you want to go with her?"

"No, Mark. I'm too old. And your mother did ask, but no, I'll stay here. I have friends and someone will need to look after your father, I'd be out of place in America."

Marked hugged her and wrote his telephone number on a piece of paper for her.

"I'll be back in Paris tomorrow. I'll go with Mama to the plane and then go back to Paris from there. If you need me, if my father needs me, please call."

In a few short minutes, Mark and Renee had the bags loaded into the boot of the car. Mark drove away from the house. At the end of the street, he stopped and looked back at his childhood home. Renee looked resolutely ahead.

"Let's go, Mark."

Mother and son drove to a hotel near the airport to stay for the night. As Renee organized tickets to Paris for them both and to New York and Chicago for herself, Mark arranged to have her car driven back to the house.

The next day Renee went with Mark as far as Paris to board a flight to New York. It was the end of an era. She was going home for good.

Catherine Curtis

Part Two
Discovery

Chapter 24

Mark sat with Claude in the library of his St-Germain-des-Pres apartment, their discussion giving shape to his idea of a trust.

"The problem is that the world, since hearing about the camps nearly thirty years ago, has been focused on the plight of the dead of the camps, and those who survived. So much so that the dead of the Holocaust are reduced by history to insects in amber–an interesting curiosity, but not quite real. The human mind cannot really get its head around the numbers that were slaughtered. While I realize we need to focus on the dead in order that this never happens again, I'm torn by two problems. One, I personally cannot help the dead, but perhaps I can help the survivors. Secondly, as an art historian, I'd like to know how much art was confiscated and where it is now. How much art was destroyed? If we could find that out, we can begin to find rightful owners of the remainder."

"We can't give them back their parents or grandparents, but maybe we can give them back a piece of their heritage in a painting, or a piece of sculpture."

And so Mark, with the help of Claude, his friend Inspector de la Croix, and sometimes David, laid out a map for the trust. Mark kept his hand in the teaching world by continuing to present a class on art history at the Sorbonne. Claude, along with the inspector worked full time with the Paris police and David had come to the Sorbonne to teach full time.

In the early years, they were all overjoyed

if they were able to return one or two paintings to
the rightful owners. As the library of information
they collected grew, so did their successes. David
was spending more time in Mark's office and
often sat with him over his latest find. David
proved to be good legs for the team. Mark's
Lilian Harding Trust was a godsend because it
eventually allowed David to cut back on teaching
and accept a part-time position with the trust.
They were also able to pay for travel to investigate
the sighting of other paintings.

One evening, the three were discussing the
documentation Claude provided about the
"Special Action Team"–the "Einsatzstaub
Reichleiter Rosenberg."

"It amazes me that the Nazis had the balls
to carefully document exactly what families they
stole paintings from. Another guy I found out
about is Haber ... Haber something . . . let me
find my notes here ... Haberstock, Karl
Haberstock."

Mark shook his head. "He looks to be
Hitler and Goering's personal art acquisitions'
officer."

"Where did you find him?" David asked.

"I found his name in connection with a
painting sent out of Holland to a warehouse here
in Paris. Then again in reference to a painting by
Titian traded for a Cranach that had been owned
by a family in Antwerp. If we can tie him more
firmly to the ERR, and can tie even one major art
dealer to him for sure, we can prove a systematic
looting of Jewish assets for the sole purpose of
financial gain."

David replied, "But we know that already."

"Yes, we do. It's just very hard to prove. Leverage we can use on galleries is another thing, and knowledge is that leverage. My last trip to Geneve netted nothing from the bank there, they wouldn't talk to me at all," Mark said. He tipped back in his chair and a frown appeared.

"The Swiss were in a difficult position during the war. Surrounded by the Axis powers, they signed a treaty with Germany in 1940 to keep raw materials flowing in for their manufacturing in exchange for leaving their borders and banks open to the Germans. I wouldn't be surprised if the Swiss system of numbered accounts isn't working in the favor of both the bankers and the Germans who fled Europe for South America."

David said, "Remember the famous 'Jewish Auction' Tesla told us about in Lucerne in, I think, 1939? I believe there are Swiss nationals who benefitted from the confiscated assets and even today are stonewalling efforts to recoup property."

"Mark, is there any possibility your father could be of help to us? He's fairly high up in the Swiss banking system, and of course I remember where his sympathies lie, but if you show him what we have, could we not turn him around?"

"I doubt it. There are things I haven't told you about him. He's a hard man. Though I have considered going to see him now that my mother is permanently in America; I just haven't had it in me. Back to the finding on the ERR, was this Rosenberg by any chance the Alfred Rosenberg of the Nuremberg Trials and wasn't he hanged?"

"I think so, that information would be in those files over there."

"Would that be the files stored on the floor, or the stack about to fall off the chair? Mark, you need someone to organize this mess. Could you have thought when you started this it would get this complicated, or that we would find so many strings to pull on?"

Mark laughed, "Actually, I think it's in the pile about to slide off the table. I have, by the way, been thinking of hiring someone to organize this mess. There are a few older students of mine that appear very interested in the Trust. They are graduate students and I think this would be a good thing for all of us."

"Ha! Are they interested in the Trust or the professor?"

"The professor is getting too old for them, so I'm sure it's the Trust. The very magnitude of the task staggers me sometimes. I lay here at night thinking how many Sister Michaels are out there, to think they are the ones the world considers lucky to have survived. It makes me sick to the core that the world still only pays lip service to this tragedy."

"It's all most of the world can do, Mark. If people were forced to really look at the inhumanity of the Holocaust, they would go mad. Denial is the only path to saving one's sanity."

"The Allies, from the beginning, and even up until today, have an almost studied lack of reaction to the Holocaust. They have even rebuilt Germany. What does that say? What does it take?"

"Mark, you feel things more than most people, and you are very involved in this. Perhaps it takes getting to know a survivor of the camps, someone who has lost everything for it to begin to penetrate. It is just so far beyond comprehension."

"I will tell you something, David. Something I've never told anyone, not even Claude. It has to do with the reason my mother went to America and never returned. The man I have thought all my life was my father, is not. My father was a German soldier. Perhaps that is what drives me."

"What! How long have you known this?"

"I first heard of this the last time I was in Zurich–the time I put my mother on a plane to the States."

"So that's what's been bothering you. I thought perhaps you were unhappy about your parents' separation. Did you find out anything about your real father?"

"No, and oddly enough, it doesn't seem necessary for me to know. This was very painful for my mother. I've never broached the subject in all the five years since she left. My mother will tell me in her own good time. I can only imagine how difficult this must be for her. Wolf Bauer is the only father I have known. You are right, David, I have to go to Zurich someday. I need to give him a chance. He's all alone now, but I'm just not ready."

Bauer's Run

Chapter 25

As the weeks went by, sometimes Mark's work would keep him awake most of the night. He persuaded some of his advanced students to join the Trust for the summer. There was Isabelle, a thin, delicate, scholarly girl and her unlikely roommate, Katya. Katya was the product of a Frenchwoman who fell in love with a Russian artist when she was a student. The artist was long gone, and her mother was married to someone else, but the girl had her father's passion for art. The third student was one of Claude's younger sisters, Colette, who was madly in love with David. An American girl named Julia, Isabelle's former roommate, in Paris for the summer, was the fourth.

The four had been spending as much time as they could to help Mark, who was now "Mark" to them instead of "Professor." Isabelle just wanted to be part of the project and close to David. Colette had resigned herself to the fact that David would never see her as anything but Claude's baby sister. Katya not only wanted to be part of the project, but also a part of Mark's life. Mark was mostly oblivious to them all. At this moment he was madly searching through some stacks of files, muttering to himself.

"What is it, Mark? What are you looking for?" asked Katya.

"I had a file with a list of families who had sent art to a warehouse in Paris for safekeeping. I may have a new name, but I can't find the file."

Timid Isabelle, who never said much of anything, laughed. "I don't know how you find anything in here. Look around you, Mark."

The women laughed as he looked puzzled. "What?"

Then he saw it and began to laugh with them. The room was stacked nearly to the window ledges in most places. Every chair except the one at his desk was piled high with files.

"I just don't have the time," he said.

"You would have more time if this place were organized," said Katya. "I have an idea. Didn't you say you were going to Milan for a few days? If you are going to be out of this room for even a couple days, we could get this place cleaned up and organized. It's the least we can do. Besides, Issi is so organized she even presses and folds her underwear."

Isabelle blushed and said, "Yes, and you need a secretary. I can do that. That is if you will let me."

"I know when I'm licked. You are right. It's very frustrating. The other day I actually yelled at David about a file I had in my hand. Go to it. I will be gone three days."

The young women spent the next three days sifting through the folders and generating a file system. Isabelle, true to her word, made everything neat. When they were finished, they made a key to the filing system, put it in a bright red folder and tied it to the handle of the first filing cabinet. When Mark returned and put his head in the door, they allowed him to come in.

"Amazing! How did you do this? I see you bought more file cabinets."

"Only a couple, mostly we made better use

of the ones you had. Not a single sheet of paper has been thrown out. We've done a very simple filing system, this is the key." Katya held aloft the red folder tied to the file drawer. "Untie this at your peril."

Mark had to laugh. "How can I ever thank you? I will miss you when you start school again."

"You may wish you miss me. I'm going home for a while, but I will be back. I've made a decision to leave school for now. I've been offered a very minor position at the Louvre and I've decided to take it. I want to learn as much as I can. You'll be hearing from me all the time."

He was stunned. Positions at the Louvre were very hard to come by. He considered it an honor they took one of his students.

Bauer's Run

Chapter 26

Over the next few months, romance began to blossom in the Trust office. Isabelle was a very quiet and studious girl, very like David in both appearance and nature. The two "quiet ones," as their friends called them, could usually be found together at the end of the day. David was much older than she, but Isabelle possessed maturity much beyond her years. Mark was the first to notice the warmth in his friend's eyes whenever he looked at her. Soon the evening pairing off became the expected thing–David always walked her home in the warm summer evenings.

Paris in the summer was a collage of sights–beautiful girls, flowers everywhere, tourists with cameras, shops with goods spilled out to the sidewalks and every café gained space by placing tables outside. The scent of baking bread, of tables full of fruit, and blossoms on the balconies filled the air.

David finally asked Isabelle to marry him and they did so in a quiet ceremony with their friends attending; friends being the only family each had.

The wedding seemed to be a catalyst for Mark. For the first time he noticed that all of Paris seemed to be in pairs. He was well past thirty now and wondered if he shouldn't be thinking of a wife. He stood one evening at the window, looking over the late summer streets. Now that it was August, the whole city was on holiday. He sighed when he thought of David and how happy he was with his new bride. *Unfortunately, I don't know any women, nor do I have the time to find and court one. One of these days I need a holiday myself. Soon. But for now* . . . And so Mark spent the remainder of the summer, completely oblivious to both of the women in his office who cared so much for him. Katya flirted outrageously with him, but the object of her efforts might as well have been a stone for all the response she got.

Julia was more pragmatic about him. She knew she would be going home to America soon and she was not as adventurous as Katya. She kept secret the pounding of her heart and the heat that came over her whenever he came near. She knew she wanted to take something of Mark away with her when she went home–and she hung on his every word. She would take all she could learn from him–if he didn't see her as a woman, she would be his student.

Mark was an excellent teacher and he knew when a student was really hooked, and so, ironically, he sought Julia out and taught her as much as he could before she went home. Impulsively, just a few days before she was scheduled to leave, she told him she would be returning the following summer and asked if she might be allowed to come and work with him again. Delighted, he unexpectedly grabbed her up in a hug and swung her around.

"Of course you may! We'd be very pleased to have you back."

When he let go of her and somewhat embarrassed, reached out to shake her hand, she thought she would faint. *He felt so good* . . . *smelled so good* . . . *what am I doing wrong? I wish I was as smart as Issi, or as pretty as Katya.*

Then maybe I would be more to him than just good summer help.

So again that summer ended as summers do, Katya went home to her mother's for a while and Julia returned to America. David and Isabelle had taken a short holiday away, and when September came, everyone went back to work. Mark set new goals for the coming year and was pleased to be able to start the autumn with the return of a small painting to one of the nuns. As usual, when his business was finished at the convent, he sought out Sister Michael for a walk in the courtyard garden.

She had become his dearest friend and he was the brother she never had. He could tell her things he would never tell Claude or David. As they walked in the warm, late afternoon, they spoke of their mutual friends.

"It's wonderful to see David and Isabelle together. They are so happy. I confess I'm a bit jealous sometimes."

"You'll find the right person for you one day, Mark. There is just no way to know when that day will come."

"I just don't meet women . . ."

Sister Michael laughed delightedly. "What would you call that bevy of beauties in your office all summer?"

"What beauties? Oh, you mean the students! Don't you think I'm a bit old for those young girls?"

"From what I hear from Claude, they don't think you're too old."

"You're kidding! Colette is Claude's baby

sister, Julia went home to America and Katya, well, Katya's never serious about anything."

"Oh my goodness, you are even denser than I thought. Dear Mark, you don't have a clue."

"What are you talking about?"

"No, I'm not going to tell you. Open your eyes Mark there's a whole world out there." No matter how he pleaded, she would not elaborate. When he went back to the office, he did so with a lighter heart. Even so, he soon forgot their conversation.

Mark ran into Katya in one of the workrooms of the Louvre a few weeks later. Not sure what possessed him, he asked her to have dinner with him that evening. She accepted graciously and they arranged to meet at a restaurant near the museum. After he left, she let out an exuberant yelp and jumped into the air.

This drew a frown from the matronly curator in charge of the workroom. Leaving work at the earliest possible moment Madame would let her go, she nearly flew to her flat. She hunted furiously through her tiny closet for just the right thing to wear. Brushing her black hair until it shone, she chose a simple black dress and her most flirtatious lipstick.

Mark never knew what hit him. He arrived at the restaurant before her and sat watching people on the sidewalk as he waited. From a block away, his eyes followed a young woman with raven hair and a black dress so short it showed nearly all there was to see of elegant legs. She wore a bright cobalt shawl around her shoulders, walked with joy in her step and seemed to be waving to someone behind him. He turned to see who the lucky man was when it dawned on him–Katya! Katya–of the hair tied up in a bun, with fingers filthy from her work. Katya--of the severe khaki trousers and black tee shirt that was her work uniform. That Katya! He was only able to stammer when she approached. It was the beginning of a romance.

Katya bloomed around him and Mark was more relaxed than he had been at any time since his student days. Soon they were seeing each other every night. For Christmas that year, he gave her a pair of pearl earrings and she gave him a rare book on Titian. When her mother had a stroke and died in late January, it was Mark who drove her home to Lyon. He went with her to see the family plot in the cemetery on the hill, and helped her pack up her mother's house and put it up for sale. It made him think of Wolfe, but he wasn't ready yet. With eyes only for Katya, in another few months, he asked her to marry him. Before long they were happily awaiting their first child.

Bauer's Run

Chapter 27

Quite a few months passed before Mark
was ready to go to Zurich to see his father. In that
time, the Trust became even more active and as a
result, more successful.

Mark had received a letter from Anna once
every quarter about his father, the last one with
regrets. Wolfe had fired the woman who had
cared for him and his family for more than thirty
years. She returned to the village outside Lucerne
where her brother ran a small inn. She reported
that Wolfe had been drinking heavily and she was
afraid for his
health and safety; Mark knew he couldn't put the
trip off any longer.

Not at all sure of the reception he would
get from Wolfe, he took along some of the lists of
art he was working on. He'd not completely
forgotten the Wolfe he had tagged around after as
a child, but he was no longer a child and he meant
to ask some hard questions and he expected to get
answers.

***

The man sat in a chair in a darkened study,
light was fading outside but he made no move to
turn on the lamp on the desk. This was his usual
spot in the evening; the house was empty now
except for him. The housekeeper had been the last
to leave; gone a few weeks now, the house was
beginning to reflect her absence. There were few
clean dishes in the kitchen and almost nothing in
the pantry. The whole house smelled musty. The
man didn't eat most nights; he only sat in the
study drinking and staring out into the night.

They'd all left him, but he didn't need them. He didn't need them. He did not need them. Weeks ago he wrote his wife in America and ordered her to come home but he'd had no reply. His son, dear God, his son . . . how could you leave me? Don't you see I've lived my whole life for you? You are the reason I married your spoiled, empty-headed mother. Since the day I met you, everything I've done was for you.

The pattern was the same night after night. He could take the days-it was always busy at the bank. But the nights–the nights were the same. Alone in the house he drank himself into a deep melancholy that ended in pain. So far, he had been able to compartmentalize his life; no one at the bank knew his family was gone. He had given out the story that Renee was ill and no longer wished to socialize. Not even his assistant knew she was gone. He would not have them pitying him. *I don't need you–you'll see, you are the ones who need me. You'll come back–you'll beg me to take you back.*

A tapping on the glass startled him. He jumped out of his chair, tipping it over in his haste. Feeling his way in the dark, he opened the desk drawer to find the pistol he kept there. The tapping came again.

"Papa! Papa, are you in there?"

Wolfe rushed to the French door. "I knew you'd come back." He tripped and fell into the door, shattering the glass and discharging the pistol. Fortunately the gun was pointed downward and the bullet smashed harmlessly into a planter box of long dead flowers beside the door. Mark put his hand carefully through the glass to reach the door latch.

Upon opening the door, he said cautiously, "Papa, it's Mark. What happened?" Only groans sounded from the floor. He felt his way to the desk and turned on the lamp.

What he saw then was Wolfe passed out on the floor, the room reeked of whiskey. He very carefully slid the pistol out of his father's hand and unloaded it. Placing the bullets in his pocket and the gun in the desk drawer, he began to set the room to rights as he waited for Wolfe to come around. It was a long wait.

Mark picked up the glass, set the chairs back upright and secured the door. Wolfe was out cold. There didn't appear to be much he could do to help the inebriated man so Mark got a pillow and a blanket to cover Wolfe. He sat back in the chair to rest. *For sure I can't move him.* No point even trying to lift Wolfe. Tall as Mark was, Wolfe outweighed him by a lot. He couldn't begin to carry the man upstairs to bed. Mark took one turn around the house after he covered Wolfe and was dismayed to see the condition of the place. Soon Mark slept in the chair, even the drunken snores didn't keep him awake.

"What? What happened?" Wolfe sat up with a shout just about dawn.

Mark opened his eyes and beheld the spectacle of the disheveled man trying to stand. "What happened, Papa, is you were stinking drunk, and you passed out."

"You! You, how did you get in here?"

"You opened the door by falling through it.

You're fortunate you didn't cut yourself up badly. What is going on here?"

"What's going on here is none of your business. I knew you'd come back–you need me."

"No, Papa. One of the reasons I came back is I thought you might need me."

"Need you! Ha!" Wolfe tried to stand and nearly fell through the window again had it not been for Mark's swift movement to steady him.

"We need to get you to the shower. I'll help you up to your room."

"I don't need your help and I don't need you."

With a sigh Mark turned to the door.

"All right, Papa. Have it your way."

"Don't go, please don't go." A low whisper, almost unheard, but Mark turned back.

"What did you say?"

"I said, don't go. Please don't go, Mark."

Without a word, Mark got under his father's shoulder and steadied him up the stairs. He ran the shower and helped Wolfe undress, then steered him into the water. By the time the hot water ran out, Wolfe was feeling almost normal. Mark prepared a light meal for them with the meager contents of the pantry. By then he was getting a clear idea of how far things had slipped since Anna was last here. His father was not easy in the best of times; soon there was nothing to fill the silence. As Mark gathered up the few dishes, he asked, "Where is Anna? The house looks like she has not been here for a while."

"She left. After all the years I paid her well and took care of her, she left. There isn't any loyalty anymore."

"You can't buy loyalty, Papa, it has to be earned. Besides, didn't you fire her?"

"That's why you're here, that old woman was spying on me."

Mark looked at his father carefully. He always thought of him as indestructible. The past years had aged him badly–his hair was all white and in need of a haircut. There was sadness in the fading blue eyes. The shirt he put on after his shower was clearly worn before. A wave of pity washed over him. This was a sad, lonely old man, and Mark owed him. There was no way around that. Wolfe was nearing seventy and showing every day of it now.

"Papa, why don't you come to Paris with me for a while? I'm sure the bank could do without you: you certainly haven't taken many holidays over the years."

"Why don't you come back here? Leave that nonsense in Paris, and come back where you belong? I'll give you a job in the bank. In time you can take over from me."

"You just don't get it, do you? That nonsense in Paris is my life. My wife and my work are there."

"Your wife? When did that happen? Come back here, this is a great house for a family–you are going to have a family?"

"This happened months ago. Katya and I were married very quietly. We're going to have a family, soon, in fact. She's expecting."

"That's wonderful, now you really must come back here!" Wolfe stopped suddenly and looked at Mark suspiciously. "Katya, that sounds Russian. Tell me she's not a Russian Jew."

"She's a lovely girl who is half French and half Russian, and who happens to be Jewish."

"My God, what have you done? You can get out of it. That's it. We'll get you out of it. She won't be able to say that Jew bastard baby is yours."

"Where does this hatred come from, Papa? It doesn't make any sense. You have people on the board of the bank that you work with who are Jewish. Anna is Jewish, did you know that? Mama is Catholic. My wife is Jewish. We are all just people who are trying to live our lives."

"My God, if you only knew the atrocities perpetrated on the Jewish people! But you have to know–you're the right age. Even here in Switzerland, you couldn't possibly be so isolated you didn't know about the camps. You had to know. All the Swiss banks were open to the Germans through the war. How could you turn a blind eye?"

"You have no idea what you are talking about."

"I don't? Then tell me, Papa. Tell me how you see it."

"Those people will take over everything. They always do. They almost took Germany down and would take us all down if it hadn't been for Germany."

"What are you saying? You can't possibly think . . ."

"I can't possibly think what? That the Nazis were right? Of course they were right.

They just made some stupid mistakes. The Fuhrer was a babbling fool. If his top generals had contained him, the face of Europe would be different today. You would speak German instead of French, and the abomination that is the State of Israel would not exist."

"You can't believe it's that simple. What of Nuremberg? What of crimes against humanity?"

"Someone had to do what had to be done. It wasn't easy, some of it was very unpleasant and some people with twisted minds did some hideous things. But the cause was just. The Aryan race must be kept pure. Look at America–they are a nation of mongrels."

Mark rubbed his eyes and shook his head. He couldn't believe what he was hearing. He jumped up from his chair and moved away from Wolfe as though he had never seen him before in his life, and maybe he hadn't.

"How do you think you've lived this privileged life? I made it happen. I did what I had to in order to survive. That's what it's about–survival of the fittest."

"I don't know you. I can see I never knew you. You were good to Mama and me. Who is this monster?"

"Monster, am I? I took good care of you both, and this is how you repay me?" Wolfe's voice rose to a shout.

He came at Mark who was frozen to the spot. Even though a part of him knew what was coming, he still couldn't hit the man back. Wolfe's fist swung through the air with all he could muster behind it. Mark tried to dodge it but was too close to the wall. When it connected with Mark's jaw, he sank to the floor.

Shaking his head to clear it, he saw Wolfe leave the room through the terrace doors, leaving them standing open like a gaping wound. As he got to his feet, he heard Wolfe shout from the lawn, "Get out of my house. You are not my son." The sound faded off into the distance as Wolfe walked away from the house and down the street.

Mark started wandering around the house like a ghost of himself, somewhat in shock. He went through the rooms in a daze, opening every door and closet. He pulled out every drawer and stared blankly at its contents, but he didn't know what he was looking for. Perhaps his life–perhaps his childhood.

There were too many blanks in what he knew, or thought he knew about Wolfe. He found nothing unusual in his search. At the back of a desk drawer he found a set of keys and remembered the safe he had seen as a boy. A short search and he found it again. Empty except for some currency, it was anticlimactic. Throwing the keys on the desk, and leaving the safe wide open, he walked out of the house.

Chapter 28

Mark arrived back at his own apartment in Paris late at night. He let himself in noisily as he always did so Katya would not be startled. He reached their bedroom just as she was getting out of bed. Enfolding her in his arms, he began to weep. Before long, the whole experience poured out of him like a cresting wave. Katya rocked him as she would a child, and finally tucked him, clothes and all into bed beside her. She woke the next morning to find him propped on one elbow, staring down at her.

"You are so good. I just never realized how great the distance between good and evil. I will always take care of you dear, I promise you that."

"I know that, Mark. I have always known that. But I know also that the distance between good and evil can be just a hair's breadth. Someone said that the only thing needed for evil to flourish is for good men to do nothing. That's what happened."

"A lot of normally good men and women stood by and did nothing. What's worse, they pretended not to see. You are a good man, dear, and what you are doing is certainly not nothing."

The days passed and he went back to work with a vengeance. He demanded results from Claude and David. One day Claude started to say something back to him in anger, but Katya touched his arm and shook her head. Later, Claude asked her what that was about.

"Leave him alone for now, he saw the face of evil and it shook his world. He'll come back to himself. We just have to give him time."

As the weeks went by, work kept Mark up late at night. The only way Katya ever saw him, was to come sit in the room with him. Her presence seemed to calm him and he always took time to talk to her.

"You are beautiful today, Katya, I mean even more beautiful than usual. Pregnancy seems to agree with you."

"I'm feeling well–I do get tired though."

"You have to rest. It's not a whole lot longer now."

She laughed and said, "Easy for you to say!"

She stayed in the room when he went back to his papers and would sit and read or sew while he worked. Eventually he would rise, take her hand, turn off the light and go to bed. He never seemed to notice he needed rest, but he worried about her and in this way, she saw to it that he rested also.

***

When Wolfe came back to his house to find it searched, he knew at once who did it. He tried to remember if he left anything incriminating at home. He didn't think so, but it bothered him. All his work–it would be for nothing if Mark got it in his head to do some investigating. There were no other loose ends–he'd seen to that. Of course there was always the possibility that he could have missed something. Perhaps Mark still knew the student whose father had been with the Surete. It was weeks later when he was able to contact the detective he had used before; they met in the usual place in the dark of night.

The detective had done many jobs for the banker, though none in the past few years. He knew far more than he ever reported, even about the banker–this man who did not seem to be on the face of the earth before 1945. He suspected that his employer would not hesitate to remove anyone he perceived as a threat, so he was very careful to appear nonthreatening.

"Here is a picture of the man I want you to follow. I want to know everything you can find out about him; his address is here. I want to know whom he works for, who his friends are, what his interests are. Do what you have to do, you will be well paid as usual."

The man waited until the banker was gone and he himself returned to his office before looking into the envelope. It contained the usual generous amount of cash for expenses as well as a photo of the man he knew was the banker's son.

What was the old man up to now? He wants me to spy on his son? He made the usual copy of everything in the envelope and listed the serial numbers on the bills. Before he left town, he would mail it to himself in care of a friend from long ago. So far it had never been necessary for his friend to open any of the envelopes.

He waited until the subject boarded a plane with a man he had identified as Surete. That night he easily let himself into Mark's apartment through a window on the fire escape. He was quietly working his way through the files when he heard a sound in the hallway.

"Mark, are you back already? Why don't

you turn on a light?"

Katya came through the door and found a stranger with a torch looking through the files. She started screaming and couldn't stop. In a panic, he ran to her and grabbed her around the neck. She had to be quiet! He shook her. He tried to make her stop. Soon she did. He dropped her to the floor and rushed to the window. Looking out, he saw a light come on in the apartment below, but he had to risk it. Racing down the fire escape, he was soon out on the busy street. Fortunately for him, Paris is a city that never sleeps. Even here in St-Germain-des-Pres, there was foot traffic as well as cars on the street. That was a close one. He wondered if he killed her, if not, could she identify him? Maybe not, since the room had been pretty dark.

It wasn't the first time he'd had to hurt someone in order to protect himself but he hated that it was a pregnant woman. She made a lot of noise for a slip of a girl. He was terrified that she could be Bauer's wife. The banker told him nothing about a wife. *The banker! If the banker wanted him to investigate his son, they were clearly not on speaking terms. If she could not identify him, it could be just unfortunate she came across a burglar. Too bad he hadn't thought to take her jewelry–maybe he should go back . . . right!*

Chapter 29

The pounding on the door finally wakened the family housekeeper. As she hurried down the hall in the dark she called out, "I'm coming, I'm coming. Give an old woman time!"

In the dim light from the street, she saw her mistress crumpled on the floor just a split second before tripping over her.

"Oh my God. Oh dear God. Madame Bauer." The pounding on the front door continued. She ran to open it to find the downstairs neighbor standing there in a robe.

"Call a doctor! Oh, please call a doctor- Madame is unconscious."

As the housekeeper ran back to Katya, the neighbor ran to call the gendarmes and an ambulance. With the lights on now, both of the women could see the marks on Katya's neck.

"Someone has tried to kill Madame."

"Didn't you hear her screaming? I heard it downstairs. Why couldn't you hear it?"

"What? I can't hear you. I don't have my earphones on."

The emergency personnel came through the door and knelt by Katya's side.

"There's still a pulse. We have to get her to a hospital. What happened here? When is the baby due?"

The neighbor told what she knew in the short time it took to load Katya's still unconscious body into the ambulance. Soon they were racing to the hospital, the medics trying vainly to revive her.

With the help of Isabelle, who was called

by the housekeeper, Mark had been found and he and Claude were on their way back to Paris. Hours later, both men came rushing through the door to the emergency room. A white-faced Isabelle sat waiting for them.

"Oh, Mark! This is so horrible. It looks like someone broke into your apartment, and Katya surprised them. The doctors won't tell me anything–I don't know how she is."

Mark made a beeline for the nearest nurse, who quickly led him to the door of a nearby room, and tapped lightly. An elderly man in a white lab coat came out of the room to greet Mark. There was a deep sadness in his eyes as he told Mark he had a son, but his wife was dead.

"I need to see her," Mark said quietly. "She's young and strong how could she possibly be dead?" He was led to Katya's bedside where he saw her pale face and bruised neck. He put his head in his hands and wept.

Mark took his wife's small hand in both of his own, and slowly sank into a chair. Speaking softly, the doctor told him everything they tried to save her. "I'm so sorry, sometimes all we know is simply not enough. I don't know what else to tell you." The doctor left him alone in his grief.

Out in the hall, Claude was grilling the waiting gendarme.

"How did he get in? What did he take? Was any other apartment broken into?"

"It looks like he came in through the fire escape. The latches were so old I don't think it presented much of a challenge. We don't know if anything is missing. He was apparently in the room used as an office when Madame surprised him. At least that's what we think happened. The housekeeper is deaf as a post without her hearing aids. It doesn't appear that he broke in any place else."

"Why this apartment? I want the whole place dusted for prints, especially the office; get the file cabinets and every surface. I want this bastard."

Claude turned just as Mark came out of the room, and in a wordless gesture, he opened his arms for his boyhood friend.

"We will find the bastard–I swear to you. Apparently Katya caught him going through the files. Do you have any idea what this could be about? Is there something going on I don't know about? It's not as if your work is a secret, but you don't exactly advertise. Why now? What's different now?"

"I don't know. There's nothing unusual going on, nothing major. I'm going to leave that to you, right now, I just don't care. Nothing will bring Katya back. Don't tell me anything until you have him safely locked up. Right now I could tear him apart with my bare hands, but I can't afford the luxury, I have a motherless son. I'm going to go see him then I will have to make some arrangements for Katya and call my mother."

"When you get ready to leave the hospital, my driver is right outside the door to the emergency room. He is now your driver."

"You can't do that, you need him. Besides, I'll be fine."

"I can do that and you will take him. He'll

be replaced every shift until we find out what this is about."

"All right, Claude. Thank you. It means a lot to have you here. I'm going to find my son now. I'll talk with you later."

Claude watched him go with pain in his eyes. He turned to find Isabelle and David walking toward him. The couple promised that after they had something to eat, they would go to Mark's office to determine if anything had been taken. It was a grim day for all of them.

Chapter 30

Mark found his very small son in the arms of a nurse who rocked him gently. She stood at once and put the tiny bundle in his arms. He raised a questioning look, "Is he really going to be all right?" He didn't know anything about babies.

"Well, we think so, but he'll be here for quite a while yet. We'll know better after he gets through the next few days; we're all so sorry about his mother."

"Thank you. Can I just sit here and hold him for a while?"

"You may, for a while anyway. We have a neonatal specialist coming in shortly to look at your son. By the way, does he have a name?"

"Not yet, I'll have to work on that."

When he arrived at his apartment later, Claude's technicians were gone and his grief-stricken housekeeper was waiting for him.

He tried to comfort her then went to his room to rest for a while. Everything about the room reminded him of Katya. *How stupid am I, to have left her alone here? I've never felt unsafe here . . . was this random? If it wasn't--why? Why now? I have to call Mother, what in God's name will I tell her? She never even got to meet Katya, how can I tell her she's gone? That our son is going to grow up without a mother?*

Renee's response to her son's tearful phone call was to take the first plane she could get to Paris. She arrived in a taxi the next day.

"Oh Mama, I hate that you had to come all this way, but I won't pretend for a moment we don't need you."

"Darling, what else could I do? I can't believe she's gone. How is the baby? Will he live?"

"They seem to think so but he's very tiny; they told me they'd know better in a few days."

"What are you going to name him?"

I think I'd like to name him for his great-grandfathers. That would make him Samuel Harding Bauer. I guess I will call him Sam."

"Sam, it is. When do I get to see my grandson?"

"We can go after the memorial service, which, by the way, is in two hours. Let's get your things into the guest bedroom, Isabelle will be here soon and will go to the service with us."

Mark was amazed at the number of people who came to pay their respects. From the police who knew Mark through Claude, Claude's family, even many of the shopkeepers in the neighborhood came. Sister Michael and several of the nuns from the convent came. Mark was numb.

The funeral behind them, Claude and David soon pushed Mark to busy himself with work. Claude's men made no progress in the case, and he couldn't bear to tell his childhood friend that their efforts so far had been in vain.

By the time Sam came home a few weeks later, Renee had completed the job Katya started in preparing the nursery. The housekeeper had a young niece, Bella, who wanted a job in the city to get away from the farm. At nineteen, she had just enough experience taking care of her six younger siblings to be a good choice to care for Sam.

It was getting rather crowded in the Bauer household by then. Mark had a hard time believing how much paraphernalia a baby needed, but he was happy to see his mother so involved. He hadn't seen her so content in a long time. One evening as they ate their dinner in a favorite corner overlooking the street, she said she had a surprise for him.

"Mark, I have something to tell you. I wanted to wait until I was sure it would work out, and it has. I sublet an apartment in the building next door. It belongs to an archeologist who will be gone for six months."

"Mama, you didn't have to do that."

Renee laughed. "Yes, I did. I have no intention of going home just yet and we're getting very crowded here. Bella should be in the room next to the nursery where I am now, and besides, I'll be better off also with some space for myself."

"What about Grandfather?"

"I talked to him recently, he's doing fine. As a matter of fact, he mentioned he hadn't been to Paris in years, and was thinking of coming to see his great-grandson."

"Well, I'm impressed. He must be eighty now, isn't he?"

"Eighty-four actually, and he's in good health. For a while after my mother died, I thought he was going to go downhill fast, but he pulled out of that. In case you're wondering, if he does come, I'll have room for him in my flat."

"Is it furnished well? Do you have what you need?"

"It's actually very beautiful, Mark. You

can walk over with me tonight and see for yourself."

"I'll do just that. I can't thank you enough for staying. I'm sort of out of my element here."

"For the time being, it seems to be the best solution all around. Not that this is a hardship for me. I get to enjoy being around my first grandchild for a while."

So they all settled into a routine and baby Sam grew and thrived. Isabelle ran the office; Julia came to help in the summer. Mark was mainly distant and silent, making an effort only for his mother. He forced himself to go to the nursery–Sam looked so much like Katya it broke his heart. Renee waited and prayed he would come out the other side of his deep grief.

Chapter 31

Wolfe paced the floor of his study. He was never long on patience in the first place and that resource had been sorely tried. He received a report in the post from the man he had sent to Paris, but the man had disappeared. He tried all the usual means of contacting the man, but none worked, and he began to think something had gone very wrong. In light of the report and the absence of the detective, he decided he himself would go to Paris. It had been a long time since he had done any investigating on his own, but he was afraid to trust anyone else.

What did that damn fool detective do? Did he really think I would just let it go because he sent a detailed report of Mark's files? I'll have to be very careful if I'm going right into Mark's neighborhood. It would be very dangerous if his son recognized him. He would have to go in disguise. *I'm too old for this.*

***

Mark found himself going to see Sister Michael more often. At first it was because he was working on locating a painting for one of the nuns, but after a while it was that he found a need to spend time walking the peaceful grounds of the convent.

The convent courtyard drew him when he could not contain his grief, and sometimes Sister Michael came to walk with him. Occasionally they would talk–her quiet faith seemed to calm his soul. She was the one person he could say anything to; she never got angry, only listened patiently as he railed against God. She was the one who got him through the first months without Katya.

***

Renee sat in the sun that streamed through the large window in her Paris apartment. The bright room was painted a rich gold, which reminded her of the fields of sunflowers in Provence in late summer. She was leaving very soon, in fact the archeologist she sublet from expected momentarily. It had been a good time for her. Spending time with Mark and Sam was not something she expected, but in time the tragedy of Katya's death was mitigated by the presence of a happy, gurgling baby. Sam was turning out to be a sunny and active child; even though he was early, he was rapidly catching up. Bella was proving to be a very capable nurse, and Isabelle was the perfect assistant for Mark. Between his friends and his efficient staff, her son stayed very busy.

It was time for her to go home to Chicago; perhaps try to figure out what she was going to do with herself. She seemed to have more energy now and she was still far too young to, as Mark said, 'rust'. He said goodbye this morning as he left to board a plane to Geneve. She shuddered when she thought about going back to Switzerland. She supposed she owed Wolfe the courtesy of telling him she had divorced him. Mark talked her out of making any contact without telling her what had transpired when he had last visited the family home in Zurich.

Renee was roused from her reverie by a knock at the door. It was her landlord and after saying goodbye to him, and one last time to the baby, she was off to America once more.

***

The old man was sitting at the same table in the sidewalk café where he had taken a light lunch for the past two days. Old and bent over, he shuffled into the café and wheezed his way to a table where he had been camping out now for well over an hour at a very light meal. He irritated the waiter, but the young student let it go because they were not busy this time of day. Soon he would have to get the old bird moving in order to get the dining areas clean for the evening crowds.

Wolfe sat in the sun like the very elderly gentleman he was portraying. Across the street and down one building was the place where his son lived. From this spot he could just see the doorway without craning his neck or looking suspicious. He'd seen Mark come and go several times now, as well as that policeman and the Jew. There was a lot of coming and going from that building. Yesterday, in this same spot, he'd seem more than thirty people enter or leave that one building. Like the woman who came out of the building directly across from where he now sat, they all looked fairly well to do.

The woman across the street . . . *it couldn't be!* As the taxi driver loaded her bags in the back of the taxi, the woman was clearly visible to him. He turned his head quickly, forgetting he was in disguise. *How could she be here? She said she was going to America, could she be visiting Mark? Why that building, not the one where Mark lives? What a catastrophe to have gone to all this trouble only to be recognized by his own wife. Calm down fool. What does the luggage mean? Think! Could she be going to the airport to go home? How long had she been here?*

He realized a shadow had fallen across the table; the waiter was standing over him saying something.

"What?"

"I asked if you were ready for your check, Sir."

"Of course I'm not, you fool. Can't you see I still have tea in my cup?"

The young waiter sighed and moved away from the table. *Crotchety old man.*

Wolfe dared not move until the taxi bearing his wife drove out of sight. Then he called the waiter.

"Where is my check?"

He was sure the boy would recognize him again if he saw him. The next time he came he would have to look and dress differently. This was a lot harder now than when he was younger. *Damn Mark anyway. Why couldn't he just come home to work at the bank?* He hated to admit the thing that hurt most was the absence of his son. Mark's mind had been poisoned. *I have to get out of here.*

Chapter 32

Wolfe climbed the back steps from the big vault room in the basement of the bank; this was the last load. Every few weeks he moved more of his stash out of the bank vault to his home. In every instance he stayed late after the bank closed. Given his position, no one would question his right to do so. Putting a small box in the trunk of his dark blue Mercedes parked in the alley, he went back inside to reset the alarm. Pulling out of the alley, he nodded as he drove past the policeman who walked his beat in front of the bank.

It's done. Now I have to stay alive long enough for the next step. I'll not allow Mark to give back one painting–not one. I will make him see what's right.

When Wolfe returned from Paris the last time, his drinking began again in earnest. He often prowled the halls late at night when he couldn't sleep. He was getting older now and some things were beginning to bother him. He had a small stroke, and then another. The drinking led to a further deterioration of his mind. One night as he made his way down the cellar steps for another bottle of wine, he leaned on the wall about half way down in order to catch his breath. He felt something move under his hand. Peering closely at the rock wall his hand had shifted, he saw nothing out of the ordinary in the dim light. Shaking his head, he continued down the stairs. Later that night, he recalled the moving stone as he wandered the hall bottle in hand. Urgently searching for a torch, he dropped the wine bottle, not even noticing in his haste. As he shined the torch down the side of the stairwell, he searched for a place where his hand may have disturbed some dust. Soon he found the spot and pushed hard against the stone. Nothing. He moved his hand over and pushed again. Nothing. In frustration he pounded both fists against the wall. As he turned away, his elbow brushed the wall gently and he heard a sound like a sigh.

He turned back in astonishment to see not only a single stone, but a whole door sliding inward. The fetid air that poured out sent him reeling back. Covering his mouth and nose with his shirt, he shined the torch around the door and into the previously unseen part of the cellar. Fritz had never told him of this place. Afraid to enter the vault and leave the door open behind him, Wolfe experimented to find the way to close the door. Once he understood how it worked, he found a length of wood and jammed it in the opening to prevent the door closing.

Cautiously, he stepped inside the room and tried to orient himself as to just where the room lay in reference to the main floor of the house. He suddenly realized the reason the room did not call attention to itself was that it was outside of the main footprint of the house and under the terrace. He could walk about ten paces in one direction and six in another—a rather large room. Several trunks sat gathering dust at one end. There was nothing of note on the shelves except a crate of Lafitte Rothschild 1931. Certainly worth hiding, he thought. A close inspection of the room netted no more than family mementos of the past century. He knew the house had been built in the late eighteenth century, but it must have been Fritz who put the wine there. Did Fritz come to own the house in the mid-twenties?

Wolfe remembered being here as a small child, but his memories were fading now. He sat there feeling confused for a while, then went upstairs to bed without closing the newfound room. The next day before leaving for the bank, just as he was locking the door, he remembered the vault room. He went back into the house and down the stairs to see if he had dreamed it–he dreamed a lot lately.

His dreams often woke him to a cold sweat. One night he dreamed vividly of his neighbor Jacob in Berlin . . . the man seemed to be calling to him. Wolfe struggled to sit up, but by the time he did, Jacob was gone. Sometimes the dreams were worse and sometimes they didn't completely go away when he awoke.

Wolfe Bauer was a man undergoing a very visible change in his life. He soon began to move all his treasures to the hidden room. His appearance deteriorated so badly that two members of the bank board visited him in his home one evening to ask him to retire. His presence at the bank became even more erratic, but the men were even more alarmed to see the condition of the house. They had both been invited there in years past, and it had been immaculate under the care of Bauer's wife and housekeeper, neither of whom seemed to be present now. They inquired gently about Frau Bauer, but got an incoherent answer that seemed to indicate she left years ago. They extracted a promise from him that he would clean out his desk and retire sometime in the next few weeks. He didn't seem to care.

He wandered the halls now. If anyone had asked the nearest neighbors, they would have found his condition rather bizarre. Sometimes they could hear him shouting. With the windows open during the warm summer evenings, they could hear a lot. The desertion of his wife and son broke the old man's spirit and the nightmares became worse as time went on. He only dreamed of the war now. It became his war to the exclusion of anyone else. The men he killed peopled his dreams. They frightened him. One old man shouted at him in a language he didn't understand and pointed his finger just under Wolfe's nose. There was a young woman with a child in her arms, who fell on the road and cried out for someone to save her child. His old neighbor Jacob came nearly every night to ask if he could see the house just one more time. The old general followed him in the streets in a cruel parody of when their situations had been reversed. The old man stabbed him over and over, night after night, as Wolfe had stabbed him. He rarely shaved now, even more rarely, bathed. Often his clothing bore the stains of wine he spilled down the front of his shirt.

He wrote in a journal daily. He carefully listed his crimes as if to do so made penance for them. It brought him no peace. In his mind, if he could just explain himself to Mark, then maybe he could get his son back. It was Mark he missed,

Mark he talked to in the night. He spoke of his hopes and dreams, of the horror of war and the things he'd seen done and done himself, things done in the pursuit of a madman's dream. He only turned thief to protect himself, to have a future. The leaders gambled away a whole country's future. They were all to be left with nothing. It wasn't his fault. Ever since he met the small, blue-eyed boy named Mark, he claimed him for his own. Besides, hadn't the boy's father been a soldier for the Reich? How could it happen that Mark got hung up on morality? Why did he care what had been taken from the Jews? They were only Jews, what did it matter?

He went down the steps every night now to look at his treasures. He uncrated paintings and opened boxes of gold. One such night he carefully lined up the bars of gold on the shelves. In one of the boxes he found a diamond necklace and wore it around his shrinking neck for the rest of the night. Days later when he remembered to shave, he was startled to see it hanging there in the white hair of his chest. For some reason unknown even to him, he no longer left the house and the grounds. He wanted to see Mark but couldn't seem to remember where he was or how to contact him. He had one shouting conversation after another with the international operator, but couldn't get through to the stupid woman that he just wanted to talk to his son.

The wine no longer helped him—it used to dull the pain, but now left him sobbing in his cups. He wrote day and night in the journal. It was the only way he could have the talk with Mark he wanted to have. He had to explain–Mark is the future.

Sitting in the chair behind the big desk in the study one night, he pawed through the drawers. He pulled out keys for the house and looked at them. One by one, he emptied all the drawers. In the last, he found the revolver, which resided there for many years. He rolled it around in his hands, examining it as though he had never seen it before. Then, in the first moment of clarity in many months, he pointed the gun into his mouth and pulled the trigger.

Chapter 33

Mark flew into Zurich days after his father's death. Odd, after all the years, he still thought of Wolfe as his father. It was a member of the bank's board who finally reached him in Paris. With a great deal of dread he prepared himself for the trip. He was somehow not surprised Wolfe killed himself. Mark made all the arrangements, and on one gray, misting afternoon, he laid to rest the only man he had ever known as a father. A small island of gray and black umbrellas huddled together under the dripping pines–only a handful of people from the bank were at the grave side. He called his mother, but she declined to come and couldn't find it in his heart to blame her.

When he went back to the house after the short service, just a walk through it depressed him beyond belief. Thankfully, some kind soul had cleaned up the mess from the fatal wound. There was a pile of journals, account books and a letter arranged on the desk blotter. The letter had his name on it.

He put them all into a soft-sided leather satchel he found next to the desk and left it by the door to take with him. He checked the safe, which was empty and took a last walk through the house; he would have to deal with it another time.

The family who lived next door was happy to close the house for him and keep an eye on it. He gave them a generous check to cover the cost of having the house cleaned and closed up and gave them his Paris address. He mentally made himself a note to come back in the spring and put the house up for sale. He was not to know how much time would pass before he returned.

***

Shortly after he got back to his Paris home, he received a telegram from his mother. Her father had passed away in his sleep. Mark packed up Sam and the nanny and flew to Chicago. He couldn't help but compare the two funerals. Grandfather Harding's was an overflow crowd in a large and grand cathedral. Hundreds came to the grave-side; flowers spilled like rivers of light around the grave and at the mansion where more than fifty stately black limousines lined the curved drive.

The housekeeper, butler and several members of their families, pressed into service for the day, took coats and circulated with plates of food. Mr. Harding's lifelong friend and attorney informed Renee that he had her father's will with him. There were no surprises.

The attorney stayed after everyone else left and that business was concluded quickly. Mr. Harding had been a precise and orderly man. Renee, as his only child, inherited the house and all its furnishings, a huge trust in addition to the one she already had, and all of her mother's jewelry. He left a large block of stock to further fund the Trust named for his late wife. To Mark directly, he left a large portfolio of stock as well as some very valuable paintings. A trust was established for Sam to have when he reached twenty-five. He remembered everyone who worked for him up to and including the gardener.

Properties he owned around the country and around the globe he left to Mark with no restrictions on what he did with them. All the rest, which was considerable, went to charity. Renee and Mark found themselves unable to truly mourn for a man who had lived such a full life. The day ended with them sitting in the rose and green living room, telling "grandpa" stories.

Finally Renee asked about her former husband's death.

"Thank you for handling all that yourself, dear. I just couldn't go back there."

"No reason you should have to, you divorced him long ago. I didn't deal with the house. I guess I will have to at some point. I'm sure you're still his heir, Mama, since he never recognized the divorce."

"I really don't care. I couldn't go back to that house, besides, Mark, it's just as possible you are his heir."

"I'll contact his solicitor and see if anything needs to be done. He should know if there is a will and where it is."

When everyone else went upstairs, Mark stood at the window looking south and east across the lake to the bright lights of the city. He began to realize there was a darkness in him that had nothing to do with the deaths of his father and grandfather.

It was the funeral that turned his thoughts inward. Not the funeral itself, but all the friends his grandfather had. It was not hard for him to see he was really more like Wolfe than he cared to admit. The number of people he called friends was very small, and he had isolated himself even more since Katya died. His world had shrunk over the years rather than grown. He wondered if he would die like Wolfe–alone.

He missed Katya. Sometimes, no matter how hard he tried, he couldn't bring her face up in his mind. She was with him such a short time. He even thought sometimes it was a whole different man who had been married to her. Only Sam really touched him. As close as he was to David and Isabelle, he ended most of his days feeling alone, but not interested in doing anything about it. Except for his work, there was no passion in his life. His black mood lasted all the way back to Paris.

***

A few days after his return, Mark found himself at the convent telling Sister Michael about the stark contrast of the two funerals.

"It's a sad fact, Mark, but most of us die as we live. Wolfe was a loner, you've said that yourself. He was a deeply troubled man. Your grandfather was a man who loved life, with many friends and colleagues. Both are gone now just the same."

"Sometimes I feel that I failed as a son. I never really got to know him, or maybe I was afraid to."

"You didn't fail, Mark. From what you've told me, you tried more than once. Perhaps no one, not even Wolfe, understood Wolfe. He clearly had his demons, we all do, some of them are just bigger than others. Only God knows our hearts, even better than we know our own. Forgive yourself–Mark;   it's   over–he's   gone."

"You're right, of course. I don't know what I would do without your wise counsel; sometimes I just can't see the light. Thank you for being there for me, as always."

"As I always will be, Mark."

Bauer's Run

Chapter 34

Mark was once again standing and looking out the big window of the main drawing room of the Lake Michigan house waiting for his mother to join him. She told him she needed his help to wind up her father's estate, but he thought she was just really lonely in the big house all by herself. She aged a lot in the year since he saw her last; he still didn't think of her as old, like his grandfather was, but definitely no longer young. *For that matter, neither are you.* His fortieth birthday was behind him now; it was only Sam who kept him young. *The boy is getting so tall! He looks more like his mother every day; in fact, it is only in looking at Sam that I can remember Katya's face.* Her dark hair springing from a pronounced widow's peak comes alive around Sam's head, and her dark eyes look out from his face.

Renee swept into the room on a cloud of perfume, interrupting his reverie. As always, she was well groomed and smiling to see her son.

"There you are, dear. Hannie has dinner well in hand, would you like a drink? A scotch, perhaps?"

"Mother, you know I never really got the hang of that. I will take a glass of wine though."

"I've been meaning to tell you, Mark, I've received a letter from your father."

"From my father? How could you?"

"I didn't mean recently, dear. I think it came about the time Dad died. I came across it the other day when I was cleaning out Dad's desk. Wolfe must have written it very close to when he died."

"Well, what did it say?"

"Actually, I haven't opened it, Mark. I was wondering if you would."

"Oh for heaven's sake, Mama, he's gone. He can't do anything to hurt any of us now. I'll read it for you later if you want, but why bother?"

"Thank you dear. I know I probably should just throw it out, but somehow, it just doesn't seem right. In fact, if he were still alive, I don't think I'd bother opening it, but . . ."

"All right, Mama, I get the picture. I'll open and read it later this evening, but not before Hannie's wonderful meal."

Later that evening after Renee went up to bed, he eyed the letter she left on the side table. *Might as well get it over with.* He slit open the envelope.

As he read the first of several pages, he realized Wolfe was either quite drunk or impaired in some way when he wrote the letter. It had indeed been written the very day he took his own life. He spoke of a secret room and of documents he put aside for Mark, asking Renee to make sure Mark read the papers and acted on their contents. None of it made any sense, except that it was Mark who was Wolfe's heir. He resolved to tell his mother the general contents only and deal with it when he got back to Paris.

As the day neared for him to go home, it became obvious Renee was going to have a hard time in Chicago by herself. Two days before he was to leave, upon hearing for the fifteenth time how much she would miss him he said, "Mama, why don't you just come home with me?"

"Oh, I couldn't."

"What's to hold you?"

"Well, Hannie would be left with . . . "

"I don't know if you've noticed but Hannie's been managing this house for a long time. Come with me, it's beautiful in Paris this time of year."

"Darling you always say that about Paris."

"Only because it's true. Please come."

Renee quickly decided to go with him, and the decision seemed to lighten not only her spirits but his as well.

Soon they were at home again in St-Germain-des-Pre. Isabelle quickly saw Renee needed a purpose, so she enlisted her in a project she was working on.

Three small paintings had surfaced in a tiny gallery shop on the outskirts of Chartres. An employee of the shop had a connection to Claude through one of his sisters. Madame du Foy saw her employer bring in paintings before with somewhat dubious provenance. There was no way to prove the man's complicity in moving stolen goods, but this was too much! Three paintings at one time!

David visited the shop as the prospective buyer. No one but David had the special knack of examining the paintings in detail while seeming to observe them only casually. When he returned to his car, his notebook was soon filled with the tiniest details about the three canvasses. Details, which taken together, will not only identify the painter, but help to find the owner. Years of research had netted extensive files in Mark's office. Over time, many survivors of the camps had found their way to him by letter or in person. There was excitement in the air whenever the team realized they were hot on the trail of ill-gotten goods. For a while, even Mark forgot his loneliness. One of the paintings proved to be a tiny Van Gogh, and wonder of wonders, it appeared on one of their lists.

The woman who told Mark of the painting said it belonged to her parents. Her mother was a Jewess, and as such was sent to Treblinka in Poland. Her father, a young Wehrmacht officer, died in the siege of Stalingrad. The woman was quite old now, and in poor health. She long since given up any thought of the Van Gogh or that any other of the family's precious heirlooms would ever be found. It was Mark's pleasure to tell her the painting had surfaced and informed her of their efforts to return it to her.

The three-headed sword of Claude, Mark and David worked on the current owner of the painting. Mark was the good cop, Claude, the bad cop, and David, something in the way of a father confessor. Only rarely did they ever go so far as to ransom a painting. Most people truly wanted to do the right thing when faced with the facts. The few who did not were subjected to a delicate but unending campaign of what Isabelle referred to as Chinese water torture. This particular gallery owner was most angered by the "bad cop", leading them all to believe the man knew the painting was stolen.

On the day Mark returned the painting, he

stopped on the way home again to visit Sister Michael. She always liked to hear about his successes, but dealing with this particular man had truly depressed him.

"I get so discouraged dealing with bottom-feeders like this."

"There will always be bottom-feeders, Mark, just as there will always be people like you who spend their lives trying to right a massive wrong. As banal as it sounds, in light of my life and yours, I truly do believe in the long run, good will triumph. The wrong and bad things of the world cannot stand against men of good will."

"You are good for what ails me, Sister. For a while, I am almost persuaded."

Mark delivered his usual parting line to her. "What is a nice Jewish girl like you doing in a place like this?"

Bauer's Run

Chapter 35

The light faded from the soft summer night as Mark walked slowing along the Quai d'Orsay. Oblivious to the tourists clogging the path all around him, his head was in another time and place. He had successfully avoided a trip back to Zurich since Wolfe's death a few years ago. *How like my mother I am-avoiding the unpleasant. I guess I can't avoid it any longer–this is probably as good or as bad a time as ever.*

The day before, Mark had heard from the neighbors who were the caretakers of his father's house in Zurich. The man had died and his widow felt she could no longer manage the job and her son was not interested. Perhaps the time had come to put the house up for sale. He didn't want it, and he knew full well his mother didn't either. He could save it for Sam, but that didn't seem to make sense. He had to go to Zurich. There was no getting around it.

Last night he reread the last letter Wolfe sent to Renee. He told Renee she must make sure that Mark read the journals. It was the only completely coherent sentence in the letter.

He read the letter several times, the ramblings of an old man's broken mind. He failed to understand what Wolfe was saying. This morning he had asked Isabelle if she knew where he might have put a briefcase he brought home after Wolfe's death. She went directly to a large drawer in one of the desks and retrieved it for him.

"I knew someday you would be ready to deal with this," was all she said. She'd left him alone then.

He started with the envelope with his name on it.

My dear Mark,

If you are reading this, I am dead. I know I don't have much time left. The nightmares are bad now and they're even coming in the daylight. I'm not saying this to make you feel sorry for me. Sometimes I think I must be losing my mind or maybe I lost it long ago. At any rate, I want to tell you something before it is too late.

I want you to understand my life. You have been angry with me for some time now. There is so much you don't know, actually, no one knows.

You first entered my life when you were just a small boy. I think I began to love you as my own from the first day I saw you with your mother. The war was just ending and I like many others, had fled for my life. I just did it differently than most.

You see, just like the father that deserted you, I too was a German officer. But I didn't desert you. You were the very embodiment of what I and millions of others fought for. You are a walking example of the new German. The picture of an Aryan of pure blood. I have left for you a legacy, which could just as well have come from your natural father had he lived. You see, I know who he was. I didn't at first, but I was able, in time, to learn his identity. He was a fine soldier who gave his life for the Reich.

Your inheritance is hidden in the house. I'm sure you will be able to find it if you think hard. As a small boy you were very good at solving mysteries–here is one last one for you to work on.

A vast fortune is hidden deeper than you might think. You must push on, until you find what seems not to be there. Push gently, if you push too hard, you will be stonewalled in your efforts. Read of our history, it will help you. The oldest book will lead you to the next step.

I'm ready to go, I'm tired. Someday you will understand. From the day I first met you, everything I have done has been for you. I know you followed me as a child, I always knew you were there. The places I took you, the things you saw, were not accidents. It's your turn now.

I am truly sorry about your wife. That was not supposed to happen but it is better that you are free. It's your turn now. The time is coming to rise up again, watch the signs, it's coming. Papa

Oh my God. What is he saying? What could he have been talking about? Is he really saying he had Katya killed? How could that be? He couldn't have been there . . . ,did he send someone? How could this monster have harmed my lovely Katya? Papa, what have you done? A vast fortune hidden in the house? I always thought the family wealth had been Mama's. Could Wolfe's family have had money? Did Wolfe even have family? Katya, my lovely Katya, you were killed because of me!

Mark's head whirled with the implications found in the letter. He could not remember having ever heard of family on Wolfe's side. His mother never mentioned it. If there were anyone, wouldn't he have heard about it over the years? This had to be the rambling of a drunken old man. Even if Papa had bank stock, and surely he did, that probably wouldn't amount to anything that could be called a "vast" fortune.

Katya–Katya, you died so young–I miss you–Sam misses you and he never knew you. How could you, Papa? How could you even know a person who would harm an innocent? What happened to you?

Mark walked and walked for several evenings mulling the letter over in his mind before he was willing to even think about going back to Zurich, to his childhood home.

It was always Katya who brought him back: he had to know, to reconcile in his own mind the two Wolfes. Who was he really? The one who raised him? Or the one who . . . he could not even finish the thought. When he finally made up his mind to go, he mentioned it to David and Isabelle. Showing them the letter was farther than he was willing to go, but he told them briefly about the situation with the house. Possibly while he was there, he might be able to figure out what Wolfe had been trying to tell him. He decided to take the train. Perhaps by the time he arrived in Zurich, he would be ready to be there.

Chapter 36

When Mark stepped off the train in Zurich, dread came along like a stow-away passenger in the pit of his stomach. It had been years since his last visit to the city of his birth, and even longer since he had faced down the monster. Somehow, even though the man was dead, it felt like he had to do it again.

Striding across the station carrying only a small leather bag in his hand, he stepped through the door to find himself on the busy Bahnhofstrasse. The weak, late-day sunshine feebly lit the piles of spring snow on the sidewalks. Spring came here later than to Paris. Bracing himself, he stepped forward and waved for a taxi. The driver heard a terse address and nothing more. With a shrug of his shoulders, he put the car in motion. Foreigners were odd sometimes.

Mark slumped down in his seat: even taking the train instead of flying did not give him adequate time to prepare, but then again, maybe there just wasn't that much time. He had only brief flashes of memories now of the time he had been alone with his mother as a small child. For nearly all of his memory, Wolfe was his father. His mother never told him Wolfe had been a soldier, had she even known? As he settled back in the taxi, he told himself this would only take two or three days. If he found out what Wolfe was talking about, fine, if not, if not . . . he couldn't seem to finish the thought.

He would first open up the house and find someone to clean it for him; then he would go through and pick out anything his mother might want, as well as anything he might save for Sam.

That doesn't make any sense; if Mama wanted anything, she could have asked me to retrieve it long before now. Sam was another story, but Sam had never known the man. I guess all I'm doing is complicating this. Two days, two days it is.

The taxi pulled up in front of the house where he spent his childhood. The widow next door was watching for him, and came outside as he stood for a moment looking at the house. She immediately began to give him reasons she could no longer care for the house.

He told her gently, "Madame, you have been so kind to do it this long, I am very grateful to you. I'll be selling the house now–I don't know why I didn't do it long ago."

"Monsieur Bauer, your father was not well at the end of his life. He sent away anyone who tried to help him, and several of us in the neighborhood did try."

"I have no doubt of that. That he died alone in the world was the fault of no one but himself. I'll sell the house now, perhaps you will have a family here again after all these years."

He couldn't put it off any longer. Picking up his small suitcase, he walked quickly up to the house. By the time he had his key in the lock, the widow had disappeared into her own home. Opening the door, he braced himself for what the house looked like after the years of neglect. Much to his surprise, the house was as spotless as when his mother and Anna had been there. Obviously the neighbor had taken her responsibility for the house seriously. No wonder she couldn't do it anymore, she didn't merely close the house, she kept it up. Now he felt truly bad. The tables were waxed and shining, the floors spotless, and even the sheets covering the furniture were white and clean.

Walking through the house, he opened all the shutters to let the sun in. The last room was the study. As he stepped into the room, he felt all the memories of all the years come back to him. He rushed to the doors to open them so he could breathe.

The lindens still shaded the stone terrace as they had for a century. He looked up into their branches and sucked air into his lungs. The grass was neatly cut and the terrace was swept. The only difference was that his mother's flower beds were gone. He sat for a while on the low wall separating the terrace from the broad lawns, his thoughts rambled through time in his memory. Fresh mown grass. The scent of beeswax . . .

What a beautiful place. It looks as if it has stood here for centuries. I wonder how old the house really is. I wonder if Mama would know. Haven't you procrastinated enough? Time to address the problem at hand. I'll spend an hour or two trying to figure out Papa's letter. Funny, I guess he will always be Papa to me.

Back in the study, he pulled out the letter. *"A vast fortune is hidden deeper than you might think."* The cellar–it had to be the cellar. He hurried down the back steps to the old cellar beneath the house. He remembered going down there when he was a child to retrieve potatoes or a jar of preserves for his mother or the housekeeper. Nothing much had changed over the years. It looked about the same except the larder was now empty. Looking the room over carefully, he saw no sign of a hidden door or compartment. There was a large trunk in the corner-perhaps that held Wolfe's fortune. It took him a while to jimmy the lock, but once opened, the trunk proved to belong to his mother. It contained some clothing, a few journals, and a small bunch of dried violets which, when pressed to his nose, brought back a ghost of a memory that almost, but not quite came back to him.

There was nothing there. *"You must push on, until you find what seems not to be there." What seems not to be there is easy, there's nothing there. What did he mean?* Taking off his coat, Mark once more walked the length and breadth of the cellar.

He found nothing out of the ordinary. Running his hands over the stone wall, he looked for a notch or abnormality that would suggest a hidden space. *"Stonewall,"* what was that about? He hurriedly grabbed up the letter and read. *"Push gently. If you push too hard, you will be stonewalled in your efforts." Stone wall, he's trying to tell me about the stone walls. He carefully and slowly covered every bit of the wall again and found nothing. I'm stonewalled, all right.* He was now covered in dust and sweat from the effort. With a groan he got to his feet.

That's it. That's enough. The man was crazy,
doesn't mean you have to act like a lunatic too.

Taking a bottle of wine from one of the
shelves, he wearily climbed the steps to the
kitchen. While looking for a glass, he realized he
was hearing the sounds of refrigeration running.
When he opened the door, he saw the widow had
stocked the basics for him–he couldn't believe it.
With a groan he realized what a prize jerk he had
been for walking away from the house and
dumping his problem on someone else. He would
have to find a way to make it up to the widow.

After downing the first glass in a gulp, he
now sipped from the glass as he paced around the
study and out through the terrace doors. What had
Wolfe meant? Mark was stonewalled, all right.
He went to take another drink from the glass that
was now empty; when reaching for the bottle, he
found it empty also.

That's stupid, and you're going to feel
even more stupid in the morning, with the
hangover you are going to have.

He fixed himself something to eat in the
kitchen and went back to the study to eat.
Stonewalled . . . stonewalled, what was next?
"Read of our history, it will help you." Our
history? What history? Swiss? German? Family
. . . family history? Where would family history
be? "The oldest book will lead you to the next
step." ... the oldest book . . . the oldest book . . .
family history . . . what would be the oldest book
of family history? His eyes roamed the
bookshelves. *The oldest book of family history . .*
. oh, dammit–the old man meant the Bible! That's

where Mama wrote family history—births, deaths, their marriage.

Lunging to the wall of books, he looked for the old family Bible, where was it? Here! Taking it to the desk, he turned on the lamp and cleared a space in front of him. Opening the book, he turned to the pages in the center with family history.

He traced his own birth date in his mother's hand. The day she married Wolfe was duly recorded. Under that, in what looked like his own hand, Wolfe had entered the date of his own death.

It took Mark's breath away. This was the book, 'read the family history'. He tried to make some sense of the simple entries, but none of it enlightened him. His head soon drooped and he slept in the chair. In the middle of the night, a brisk shower woke him. He went upstairs to his old room and without even turning on the light, he felt for the bed and dropped on it. He was asleep before he could form a thought.

Chapter 37

Mark bolted awake. The sun was already streaming in the windows of his childhood room. *The oldest book will lead you to the next step.* Maybe there was a note somewhere in the Bible. He hadn't thought of that. Racing down the stairs, he picked up the book and held it upside down to see if anything fell out. Nothing.

The oldest book will lead you. Mark sat at the desk and started at the beginning to look for a note. In the book of Job he found the first faint pencil tic. *"For now thou numberest my steps: dust thou watch over my sin? My transgression is sealed up in a bag and thou sewest up mine iniquity. And surely the mountain falling cometh to naught, and the rock is moved out of his place."* What did it mean? *"Thou numberest my steps"*—*"If you push too hard, you will be stonewalled."* Was something to be found a certain distance from the stone wall? Mark took the book down the cellar steps with him. *"My transgression is sealed up in a bag"*— there was no bag, or anything that could be loosely called a bag except for an old suitcase, which was clearly empty. *'And the rock is moved out of his place,' a rock that moves . . . that makes sense . . . a wait . . . 'Thou numberest my steps'* the steps he just came down . . . but what was the number? He put the book down and carefully scrutinized each step and the stones around them for anything that looked out of place. Nothing. *"And the rock is moved,"* the rock was the key—the keystone! Carefully, and ever so slowly he made his way step by step looking for the stone that was the key to the mystery. Three more times painstakingly crawling up and down the steps made him excruciatingly aware of his knees, as well as his stomach. Looking at his watch, he found it was getting late in the afternoon. Groaning, he picked up the Bible and climbed back up the stairs to the kitchen to find something to eat. Armed with a thick ham sandwich and a small pot of coffee, he once more retreated to the study.

The soft afternoon light through the lindens drew him to open the doors. He sat on the low terrace wall rolling the words around in his mind. *Numberest my steps . . . stone walled . . . transgressions sealed in a bag . . . what transgressions . . . what bag . . . the rock is moved . . .* Somehow he felt the secret was staring him right in the face. He knew he should quit now, list the house, go home, and get on with his life. *It had to have something to do with a rock that moved. Somewhere in the numbered steps . . . numbered steps . . . the oldest book will lead you . . . maybe it was still in the book!*

Seating himself at the desk with the light pulled close, he slowly began to examine every page. He started again at the beginning, what if he missed something? He absentmindedly rubbed his hand over his rapidly thickening beard. Hours later, he leaned back in the chair. If a message was there, he missed it. It had to be there; otherwise, the clue didn't make sense. If he started again, he must to look more closely. His mother's magnifying glass! She used it when she did fine embroidery. Where had she kept it? A half-hour's search brought him back to the study. *I have to call the estate broker and get on with putting the house up for sale.* Still looking for the glass, he opened the drawers of the desk and found it in the back of the top center drawer. Wolfe must have placed it there. His mother never went into Wolfe's study. Now he was getting somewhere, he was sure of it. Beginning again with the first page, he carefully moved the glass over the page, looking for the slightest mark.

After a couple hours passed, he still found nothing. It was dark out now. He got up from the desk and walked through the house, closing the draperies and locking the doors. It wasn't for the privacy; rather that he had to move about before he got so stiff that he couldn't. When he seated himself at the desk once more, he noted he was on page 1101. How many pages did this Bible have? To his dismay, the number was 1322.

He went back to his task, 1150 . . . 1200 . . . 1250 . . . 1300 . . . 1319 . . . *wait* . . . *What was that? Where was it?* He slowly backtracked and there he found it—page 1309, the tiniest pencil mark—really only a tic, at the very bottom of the page, the last line, under the word *seventh.*

He sat back in the chair. It was very late, and he was very tired. Though he thought he had it now, there was no way to be sure until the secret opened itself to him. Though he might have the correct elements for the answer, he would still have to be able to put them together properly.

Gathering up the letter and the Bible, he

once more headed for the cellar. It had to be something about the steps. *"Numberest my steps . . . the seventh . . . Was it seven from the top? Did one count the top level, which was the floor, or start with the first step down?* He slowly counted as he placed his foot carefully on each step. The seventh . . . he was there, now what? Seated on the step above, he carefully ran his hands over the stone, looking for some sort of an indentation, a notch, anything. *"Don't push too hard, you'll be stonewalled."* Gently—ever so gently.

As he ran his hand lightly down the wall, there . . . he felt something. What was it? There . . . a gentle pressure on the corner of the stone, and with a faint sigh, a door swung open in the wall. Mark sat slowly on the step. He could tell there was a void, but it was too dark to see in. He went back up the stairs for a torch, and sitting once more on the step, aimed the torch into the dark and switched it on. The color left his face like blood leaving a corpse as he shined the light around the room. *"Ohhhh . . . my . . . GOD!"*

Chapter 38

Claude joined David and Isabelle for dinner at Mark's apartment, expecting that Mark would also be there, but the main topic of conversation was the fact that no one had even heard from Mark. He had expected to be gone a couple of days, but now at the end of the fourth day no one had spoken to him. David and Isabelle were hoping he would call this evening.

"I'm not really surprised. I always thought Wolfe Bauer was a man with a lot to hide. Did you know he was not actually Mark's father?"

"Yes," David replied. "I only met the man once, but let's just say we were not destined to be friends."

"I've always suspected he was at least a Nazi sympathizer if not worse. There were a few things I heard from Mark about him when we were children that made me think he was not as he seemed. Once after Mark's mother had gone back to the States to live, I tried to find out what I could about Wolfe Bauer. I could never find any record of him before 1944, and I certainly have plenty of resources within the Surete. I've never told anyone about it, my father would have been very upset with me, to say the least, if he knew I used my position for private reasons."

Isabelle queried them both. "How have I never heard any of this? Why have you not told me, David?"

"I didn't really have anything to tell, just more of a negative–nothing to tell. Mark has been putting off this trip to close the house and sell it for years now. I couldn't tell if that was because he really doesn't want to get rid of the house, or something else. We're bound to hear from him soon though. He's usually pretty good at checking in."

"Yes, he is," Isabelle said. "But did either of you know he took with him a satchel of documents he initially brought home here after Wolfe's funeral?"

"What documents? What was in them?"

"I really don't know as I never looked. When he went off almost immediately to his grandfather's funeral, I put them in a drawer. This past week was the first time he asked about them" Isabelle recounted. Claude and David's conversation went off in another direction while Isabelle mulled over what might have been in the satchel she had stored for so long. The men were discussing a report David found recently.

"The Russians had marched west into Berlin, and much territory that had been in the hands of the Nazis fell to Russia. On that march west, it is now known that hundreds, if not thousands, of pieces of art had fallen into Russian hands. The cold war ensured that the West was not going to hear about them, let alone see them. With things opening up in the old Soviet Union, there is hope that someday inquiries might actually generate a response on the subject," David said.

The lists that the Harding Trust built over the years of artworks that disappeared were still growing every year. David ran his hands through his unruly dark hair, "It's so frustrating. I talked to a man in New York last week. His family was Dutch. His parents were interned during the war and all their property was confiscated. His mother died in the last week before the Allies arrived to free the camp. The father was a broken man. He could not even claim a small property his wife owned because he didn't have a death certificate for her. He apparently tried for the rest of his life to recover two paintings of great value. His children didn't know about this until after his death. The son, who now lives in Colorado—in the States, inherited his father's old trunk, which was shipped to him from Holland. Inside was forty years of correspondence from his father's efforts to locate the paintings. This past week we added them to our lists."

Claude spoke, "It is still the dirty little secret of the war. We are just now starting to see some loosening up of governments. Going back, so many paper trails end in the early 1940s. My big contribution for the past year has been to get one museum, only one to scrutinize their records for anything acquired since 1933. Who knows what they will find? Or if we will hear anything about it if they do. The curator of this particular museum is a Jew. Imagine if we could get every museum to audit the provenance of every single piece. It would be a giant job, no doubt about it, but what progress could be made!"

The friends talked late into the evening but there was no call from Mark, even after the housekeeper left for home.

Bauer's Run

Chapter 39

Mark shined the torch around the chamber he opened. Just a few feet from the door was a stack of crates, on top of which was a black leather bag decorated with a swastika. He remembered the words *"My transgression is sealed up in a bag."* He shuddered to think what horrors lie inside. To the left was a row of shelves completely covered in hundreds of small packages wrapped in brown paper. To the right, more shelves holding many small leather and cloth bags of varying size and shape. Beyond the stack of crates were many canvases leaning against the wall like a macabre gallery of the dead. There appeared to be almost no dust, and the temperature of the room was comfortable. *How long had this been here? For that matter, who put it here? Was it Wolfe? And if so, how?*

Moving very carefully, so as not even to touch the door, he stepped over the sill. *Exactly what did this represent? Obviously, this is the vast fortune Wolfe had referred to.* Fatigue overwhelmed him. The enormity of the cache swept through him like a flash flood in a canyon. Almost afraid to touch it, he picked up the black bag.

Looking inside, he found three journals, one embossed with a swastika, one with the swastika and the letters ERR, the third a simple brown leather volume, and one tiny blue notebook. He picked up the bag, then, changing his mind, set it down again and took out only the brown leather book. Making his way up the stairs to his old room, he dropped to the bed and swung his feet up. It was about all the strength he had left. Reaching up to turn on the reading light, he opened the book at the beginning. Written in Wolfe's handwriting and completely in German, it was the last straw, and more than he could handle right then. His childhood German was rusty at best, if he could just close his eyes for a minute . . .

Sun streaming in the window woke him. He looked at his watch and knew he had slept for hours. The weight of the leather volume on his chest reminded him his nightmare was real. Downstairs he made a pot of coffee and prepared himself to go back down the cellar steps. A quick look at the other two journals revealed they also were written in German–of course. He wasn't ready to find out what was in the crates, so he began to go through the canvasses against the wall. He was looking at a huge fortune in paintings alone. He opened one small cloth bag on one of the shelves. It contained a single strand of perfect pearls. He suddenly felt he could not continue alone. Going back up to the study and to the telephone, which he realized would not, of course, be working, he went next door to ask the widow if he could use her telephone. Ringing his own office in Paris, he was relieved to hear David's voice.

"David, I need you here."

"What is it, Mark, are you ill?"

"I guess in a way, I am. I need you here. Take the next flight."

"I can do that, but what's the matter?"

"Not on the phone. Come quickly."

Now David was alarmed, "I'm on my way."

Mark quietly said "Thank you," but David had already hung up the phone.

While he waited for David, he went back down the stairs to explore the rest of the hidden room. The more he found out, the more his sick at heart feeling was replaced by what was becoming cold, hard anger. He didn't have to read German well to know what he had found. He now knew what Wolfe was. Mark resolved then and there that his mother must never know. It would kill her. As for Wolfe, he knew in his heart that the man now had to occupy a very special place at the very bottom reaches of Hell.

David's tap on the front door was answered so quickly, he knew his friend had been watching for him. The taxi had not even turned around in the street before Mark pulled him inside. David didn't find it necessary to ask any questions, one look at his friend's face and he knew it was bad. Following Mark down the cellar steps, he wasn't sure what to expect. He didn't have a high opinion of Wolfe Bauer, so he was bracing himself for even a body. It was worse–the ghost of millions.

Mark still had not uttered a single word. David looked at his friend in horror as he quickly made a turn around the room, coming back to the black bag. One after another, he pulled the books from the bag. Flipping through them quickly, he knew he had to get his friend out of there, right now. Taking Mark by the arm, he almost pushed him up the stairs.

"Have you eaten? How long ago did you find this? Have you slept? How much of that could you read? Talk to me, Mark."

"I found it last night," Mark said in a voice little better than a whisper. They were now in the study. The brown leather journal lay on the desk where he dropped it before making the phone-call to Paris. Mark pulled a crystal decanter and two glasses from a compartment of the desk.

"This one seems to be addressed directly to me."

Taking a glass of the cognac from Mark, David sat and opened the book. Looking up only occasionally, he read the book from cover to cover. When he finally put it down, he looked up at Mark and asked, "Do you want me to summarize?" Mark nodded.

"First of all, this is not the only such cache. Wolfe says there are five more men with equal 'assets.' All worked for Rosenberg's ERR, you know about that. Apparently the six men could read the handwriting on the wall even before the Allied invasion of Normandy. There is a great deal about the mismanagement of the war by the general staff. They call themselves the 'council.' They were preparing to lose the war, this time, not the next. The council chose to prepare to fund the Fourth Reich. What you found is one sixth of the total banked for that purpose. There follows a very precise accounting of where everything in the room came from. Interestingly enough, Wolfe's theatre of operation seems to have been France. Every single 'entry' indicates something 'collected' from a French citizen. I don't know if that will make this easier or more difficult to deal with, I mean the fact that it all came from one country. Have you looked at the brown paper-wrapped packages on the shelves?" Mark shook his head.

"Brace yourself, they are gold bars."

"Oh my God."

"Wolfe's estimate of the value, this would have been shortly before his death, is one hundred to one hundred twenty-million francs."

Mark sat back in his chair stunned. All color drained from his face.

"I don't know what to do. I can't begin to think . . . This exceeds anything we have ever come across."

"I agree. We have to think this through carefully. We may need Claude, but first of all, let's take care of you. Go clean up, we're going out to get something to eat."

"We can't leave, not with all that in the cellar."

"Of course we can, it's been here for years, just close the door."

"I guess I'm not really thinking. You're right, of course."

The two men spent the next few minutes fiddling with the door to find out how it worked and then just left it closed.

Bauer's Run

Chapter 40

From a back corner booth in one of Zurich's leading restaurants, the two friends looked out on the Bahnhofstrasse and watched the evening pedestrians. Mark wanted to delve right into the subject of the hour, but David stopped him.   "We're not discussing this until you have something to eat. It's been there a long time now. Another hour will make no difference."

When they had ordered their meal and were able to relax over a bottle of wine, David began to catch Mark up with what was going on in his absence. Finally, their meal out of the way, they returned to the house and sat in the study over brandy.

"This may sound bizarre, but bear with me. When I was a child, maybe from say seven or eight until I went away to university I actually had a relationship with Wolfe. I vaguely remember when he married my mother, but only vaguely. I guess when I got older I just thought he and my mother were together before the war and he had to go away. I'm not sure what I thought. I was so happy at that time to have a father that I followed him around like a puppy. It probably made him nuts. But there was an attachment on his part also, because I remember when he came home at night, he came first to see me and then, and only then, to find my mother. If he was late or out of the city on business, I would sit by my window at night to watch for him."

"By the time I was eleven or twelve, Claude and I really became best friends, and by fifteen, we were into mysteries. Claude wanted more than anything to be an inspector like his father, so we had great fun 'detecting.' We could make a mystery out of almost anything. There was always a certain amount of competition, in a very friendly way, between us. At one point, I got the idea that if I were to follow Wolfe, who was a very glamorous fellow, I could probably come up with a better mystery than Claude.

One time I followed him all the way to the train station, very late at night. He always walked, so I could follow him easily. On this particular night, he met a man in a long dark coat on the platform of the station. There was no one else around. I couldn't see the man's face; he was wearing a snap-brim hat. They talked for a few minutes and a train came and went."

"Another train was arriving from the opposite direction just as it appeared Wolfe was getting ready to leave. As he reached out to shake the man's hand, it looked to me like he pushed him off the platform and under the wheels of the incoming train. I was so shaken; I didn't know what to do. I think I repressed that part of that memory until yesterday, the part about him pushing the man. Wolfe just turned and walked away. I got out of there as fast as I could without running headlong into Wolfe. The next day, there was a picture in the newspaper about an unidentified man who was killed by falling under the train. It showed a covered body with a hat rolled off to the side. I tried, ever so cleverly, to question Wolfe about it, saying it was being discussed at school, but I got nowhere."

"My God, Mark, what a thing for a child to

have seen! Did you tell Claude about this?"

"No, it scared me too much. I followed the story in the newspaper, and the man was never identified as far as I knew, nor was the death ever seen as a murder. The paper just said the death was an accident. I think I must have decided to believe I did not see what I saw, but I know about that time, some part of me began to be aware that Wolfe could be a dangerous man. I kept that pretty hidden though, even from myself."

"Did that mean you stopped following him?"

"Not entirely, but I was a lot more cautious. I think it might have been about then that I stopped following him in the middle of the night."

"What a horrible thing for a boy that age to see."

"It gets worse."

"How could it possibly?"

"Wolfe was always on foot when I followed him. Do you know what that means? He wanted me to follow him."

"Mark, he couldn't have known."

"But he did."

Mark went on to tell his friend of the line in Wolfe's letter that said Wolfe knew he had been followed, and was trying to teach him.

"It gets even worse. I think I have known what he was for a very long time. I've just been very successful at hiding it, even from myself. That's a little of my mother in me, I think. If it's unpleasant, it just ceases to exist. I think there is a strong possibility that he was involved in Katya's death. No that's not right, a strong probability is more like it."

By the time he finished the story of what he knew and suspected, as well as the last conversation he had with Wolfe, even David's face was gray. "So, you see, this was planned out for me. I was the German child, being raised for a new Germany. That 'pure' Aryan blood flows in my veins. When I rejected him by rejecting that way of thinking during my university days he and I came to words—blows even."

"He was furious when he found out I had married Katya without telling anyone. Not quite true, actually, I told my mother, but they were separated by then. He was even more furious that she was pregnant with my child. He killed her. That Sam lived was a mistake. It's the only thing that makes sense; nothing was taken, why else would someone just happen to break into our home?"

"Mark, I think you're reaching here. You're making more of this than there could possibly be."

"How can you think that? You saw it! All of that stolen property- from all those people . . . most of them dead by now. How in God's name could you say that's an exaggeration?" Mark's voice was beginning to rise.

"I know, I know. We have to think this out. I think the first thing we have to do is call Claude."

"No."

"We have to."

"Not yet, we don't. Calling him might just put him in an impossible situation with the Surete.

More importantly, I have to figure out how to protect Sam."

"What do you mean, protect him, from what?"

"Think about it. There are five more out there just like me. This represents an international conspiracy the scale of which I'm not sure anyone could comprehend. My reputation would never survive, and the person who would take the brunt of that is Sam. I need time to think, and take inventory."

Bauer's Run

Chapter 41

Mark and David called home that night to let Isabelle know they were fine. David let his wife know they would be staying on for a few days to work out some problems with the estate. The following morning the two men went down the stairs to open the vault room and began a precise inventory of the contents. David proposed that they first make their own inventory then, they sat down and carefully cross-referenced it to the inventory in Wolfe's book.

"He clearly didn't take much out of here for himself," David observed. "It looks like what he did take out, which sometimes was a lot, he invested and returned the original amount later, and that just appears to be the case with gold. He kept very good records. Can you believe it? How very German of him. I think we can safely say the entire contents of this room came from France. It boggles the mind."

"This represents the largest cache found since Goering. In fact, this makes the Goering stash look restrained. Imagine that somewhere there are five more of these. How can I protect Sam from this?"

"I'm not sure just where your thinking is going on that, Mark. What do you want to protect Sam from, the publicity?"

"There will be no publicity! If I can't figure out how to do something with this without hurting Sam, I'll lock up this vault for all time."

"You can't be serious!"

"I'm deadly serious. This either doesn't touch Sam or it stays gone for all time."

"It's bound to touch Sam in some way. Mark, you aren't going to be able to help that. There will be a lot of publicity. If we even succeed in returning a small portion of the art, it's bound to get out. What's more, you know the harder you try to keep something like this under wraps, the more likely it is to leak."

"Sit down and listen to me David. It is pretty clear everything in here came from France. What if I return it to France, to our area of operation?"

"Are you talking legally here?"

"I'm talking whatever it takes."

"That's it, I'm calling Claude."

"Sit down. We'll talk to Claude, but in France, not on the phone. We can take all our lists from here and cross-reference them to our own files. Because our files are so heavily French, we should find some matches right off. First, let's just see how that goes. We can't talk to Claude from here. I won't compromise him. This is a personal problem, and as such, I'm asking one of my oldest and dearest friends to help me. Will you?"

"Let me see if I'm following you here. You want to return everything surreptitiously to France and once it's there, begin to do the tracking to return things to their rightful owners. Is that it?"

"That's it."

"You have lost your mind. How could you possibly ever find the owners of the gold, the jewelry? What of the government taxes and fees and . . . and . . . the Swiss government and the border, not that it's regulated much these days. Can you honestly say you can do that without publicity? Who will raise Sam once you have gone to jail? How about that publicity hurting him?"

"If I go to jail, which is not going to happen, you and Isabelle will be there for him just as you have always been. You may not have noticed, but Isabelle is, in all reality, Sam's mother. The gold and the money I haven't figured out yet, but I have no intention of going to jail. Don't you see? The only way this can be done at all is secretly? What would happen if one of the other five should hear what I'm doing? You think Sam would be safe then?"

"I'm beginning to see your point, but it's very dangerous. You don't know where, or for that matter, who the other five are. They could be anywhere from Germany to living next door, to Argentina, or even the States. They could be sitting on their cache waiting for the Second Coming, or they could have spent it by now or all be as dead as Wolfe. They may know each other, or only know there is someone else out there. I'm not so worried about the second generation, like you, but about the original conspirators.

They were fanatics; anyone in this generation could be just like you. The problem will always be that you don't know. I repeat. It's very dangerous."

"But doable, I think. Will you help?"

"I don't know yet. I'll have to think about this and have a better idea of just how you plan to go about it."

"Well, thank you for that. And I don't know just how I will go about this. I wasn't sure I was going to be able to get you to do that much. Sam must never know his grandfather was a war criminal who should have been hanged. Or that he was probably the person responsible for his mother's death. Not if I can help it. I'm asking for your silence, your absolute silence until I say. That includes if anything happens to me. If I die before I get this done, it dies with me. You must promise."

"What about Claude?"

"I honestly don't know yet, but for right now, you can't tell him. Nor Isabelle either. Swear."

"I swear. All the years you have given to this, I guess you are entitled to do this one your way. I have just discovered there is something more painful than having your parents die as martyrs. This one will be your call."

Mark winced; he knew exactly what his friend meant. They went back to their cataloging. He would have preferred to have a photograph of everything, but right now they couldn't take the chance.

They created a simple substitution code for their inventory. If anyone knew, they'd be dead anyway. Mark didn't know where he was going from here but, for the first time in a long time, he felt a purpose for his life. He and David agreed to take the books back to Paris when they went for David to begin a translation. Mark dreaded the moment. He had a strong suspicion he really didn't want to know.

Chapter 42

The two friends had continued to brainstorm on the flight home to Paris, careful to keep their voices low. By the time they landed, they felt they had a game plan of sorts. First David would do the translations and Mark would cross reference the paintings. The gold and jewelry would have to wait, their archives on those items being very sketchy.

As they came through the door of Mark's apartment, he vaguely noticed that Isabelle was in the front parlor with some guests, but such was his preoccupation that he didn't stop but continued down the hallway to his office. Arriving at his desk, he found he was talking to himself since David was not right behind him. Walking out into the hallway again, he realized David had gone to greet the wife he had been away from for several days. Feeling like an idiot, he too went back down the hall to the drawing room.

Nearing the door, he thought the voice he heard sounded familiar, but he couldn't quite place it. As he entered the room, he stopped short in surprise. The creature who was talking with Isabelle was nothing short of glorious. Tall and slim, the Titian-haired beauty wore a trim sheath of lime green linen with her hair caught up in a tumble of curls, escaping here and there about her face. Mark could not take his eyes off of her, and only when David cleared his throat, did he realize the beauty was actually talking to him.

"I don't think Mark remembers me, do you?" she asked.

"I'm thinking the man's in shock,"

commented David.

"I do remember you, I think, except you've really grown up, I mean, I don't know what I mean. Julia? It's really Julia?"

She laughed and walked toward him with her hand out, "a whole bunch older and a mom too, as you can see." Only then he noticed the matched set of twins seated beside Isabelle on the floor. Isabelle was amused because this was the exact affect her old Sorbonne roommate had on men back in their university days, at least men other than Mark. Nothing had changed. Julia stopped men right in their tracks. The best thing about it was that she was totally unaware of her effect.

Stumbling over his words, Mark first shook her hand and then hugged her before greeting the young twins. The conversation soon got going again and before long Sam came in to get the youngsters for dinner in the kitchen, as the adults sat down with wine near Mark's favorite window looking out over the Rue de Seine.

Julia was not quite as unaware of her effect on Mark for she was having the same reaction to him; she was just concealing it better. She hadn't experienced this gut wrenching physical attraction to a man since a much younger Mark. Not even her late husband, whom she adored, had this physical effect on her. She only hoped she was actually making sense when she spoke. *His blue eyes only got better with age, the square jaw . . . you're an idiot . . . the long legs, gray in his hair . . . Where did all this come from? You're a grown woman for goodness sake!* Somehow she got through it and when Sam came back in with the twins she was able to see Katya in his face, and risked a swift look at Mark. She recognized the sadness at the back of his eyes; she knew it was there whenever she looked at her daughter and saw her late husband.

It was a pleasant evening for all of them. The twins wound down and were sitting side by side on the sofa talking politely to Isabelle, but their eyes were beginning to glaze over. David stood first and said he needed to get his wife home. It had been a long day. Julia stood also and kissed her friend's cheek and agreed to meet the next day.

Somehow Mark worked it out so that Sam walked the twins back to the pension where they were staying just around the corner-he would walk Julia back in a few minutes.

When the two of them were alone, some of the stress went out of them. They sat across from each other and talked of their lives since they last met more than ten years ago. They talked as old friends would, of the sadness of raising children alone, each speaking in turn of the partner they had lost. Julia felt the same powerful attraction now that she felt earlier, but it was somehow more comfortable now, not a threat. Mark treated her with a warm courtesy and sat back casually in his chair. He was giving her a lot of physical space, but that wasn't just for her sake. It was all he could do to stay away from her.

It took all his control not to have an embarrassing and obvious reaction to her. For a few hours she took him out of himself. He'd all but forgotten the horror of Zurich, and the job that was beginning to outline itself in his head. All too soon, she stood and said she needed to get back to the pension. As he walked her slowly back to her hotel, he knew he had to see her again before she left.

Standing in the tiny lobby, he asked if she would have dinner with him the next night, which was to be her last night in Paris. She hesitated briefly, "You do remember I come with twins. I'll ask Issi."

He gently touched her shoulders and leaned forward to kiss her on both cheeks. As she turned and disappeared around the corner of the hallway, he stood waiting for Sam. For the first time in years, for Mark, the emptiness of his life, the restlessness, was lifted.

The next evening, the twins, worn out from their one last sightseeing venture around Paris, were left in Isabelle's care. Julia took a short nap and a long bath in preparation for her dinner date with Mark. She felt a bit giddy, and scolded herself mentally. He was just an old friend. She heard a soft knock on her door and took one last look in the mirror. She wore a periwinkle blue silk dress with a scoop neck and a long flowing skirt. The color of the dress was echoed in the ribbon that tied back her hair. Not bad, she thought as she opened the door.

"Not bad" was not the phrase that went through Mark's head when she stood before him. When he found his tongue, he asked if she were up to a stroll.

"Of course."

The night was lovely, the lights along the Seine twinkling in the misty air which tonight, had a slight breeze. They walked a few blocks down to the beautiful Champs Elysees and turned the corner past the Grand Palais to a restaurant across the street. The maitre d' recognized Mark at once and led them to a small, somewhat private alcove.

"This is impressive," she said. "Are you a regular here?"

"Not quite," Mark laughed. The maitre d' is married to one of Claude's sisters, otherwise, we would not have been able to get in here tonight."

"Ah, in that case, thank you Claude."

It was a quiet and leisurely meal, almost as if they had done it before, and often. At a point when she spoke of losing her husband, he reached across the table and lightly touched her hand. She didn't pull away and he left it there.

She was beautiful in the candlelight, and he couldn't believe his good fortune. He also couldn't believe she was going home in the morning. After indulging themselves over dessert, they decided to walk back instead of taking a taxi.

They paused for a while and leaned on a wall overlooking the Seine. The light breeze gently lifted the curls of her hair and her green eyes sparkled in the streetlights. He stopped in mid-sentence and just looked at her, before slowly and softly bringing his lips down to meet hers.

She was startled at first, but only for a moment, and then began to return his kiss. He sighed and with his arm around her shoulder tucked her close into his chest. She reached up then to initiate another kiss.

When they finally parted, he looked down at her and said, "I can't believe you are going home in the morning. I don't know what I'm doing, I only know it feels right."

"It does, doesn't it?"

"I want you," he said softly, "but not just for tonight."

She reached her hand up to cover his lips, "Shhh, tonight is all we have, it's all we ever have."

They walked and kissed, and looked at the Seine, and kissed some more, as lovers have done in Paris for centuries. As they came to the doorway of the pension, he stopped and looked at her. She smiled at him and didn't move. He wanted more, suddenly—he needed more. He pulled her to his chest one more time, and reached behind her to pull the ribbon from her hair. As the curls spilled down over her shoulders, he ran his hands through them and pulled her face up to his once more.

"I don't quite know what to say to you."

"You don't have to say anything, Mark."

"But I do. This is not casual, not just for tonight. I have a lot on my plate right now—that's not in any way an excuse. I just don't know what happens next. Will you promise to call me the minute you get in your door at home, please?"

"Of course I will."

He looked at his watch, "It's going to kill me to not take you to the airport. I don't think I could let you get on the plane. I will be talking to you as soon as you get home."

"Goodbye Mark." She smiled up at him and turned away.

"Not goodbye, it's au revoir." He watched her walk inside.

Bauer's Run

Chapter 43

In the morning Isabelle returned the twins and helped Julia load the suitcases and they were off to the airport. Isabelle, the usually very quiet and shy Isabelle, turned into something else behind the wheel. Julia just hung on as the twins roared with laughter as "Aunt Issi" deftly negotiated the teeming Paris streets on the way to Charles de Gaulle airport. They had enough time for the two friends to have one last small visit.

"How was your evening with Mark?"

"It was lovely. I had a wonderful time."

"That's it? That's all I get? Where did you go? What did you do?"

"He took me to dinner at Lasserre, and we walked and talked and walked some more."

"Oh, Julia, I see now. He is a very complicated man, dear. He has not been the same since Katya was killed. There's sadness in him that goes very deep. Be very careful, sweet Julia. He has a hard edge to him. Don't misunderstand me. He is a good man, just angry. Angry that Katya died, angry at every project that comes to a dead end. David and I both love him and Sam very much, they are our family."

"I know. It was a lovely time. Sometimes that's all we get. I'm not sad, Issi."

A loudspeaker over their heads announced boarding for their flight. "Call me when you get home."

"I will, write me soon, and Issi, please think about coming. Au revoir, darling, it was so good to see you again. Come on kids, time for us to go home."

The twins gave their newfound aunt hugs and kisses and were soon scrambling down the aisles of the big jet looking for their seats and got settled in. Not even Isabelle saw the tall man in sunglasses standing by the window in the departure lounge, watching the plane push back from the gate.

***

Both David and Claude were sitting in his office when Mark came through the door.

"There he is. Are you up early or late?"

Mark just smiled at them and asked, "What's up?"

"I guess that means he's not going to tell us about dinner with the lovely lady," David said.

"You're a fine one to talk. You didn't tell me a thing."

Claude laughed, "Well this sounds interesting, what would you have told him about Julia, provided, of course, you told him anything at all?"

"Well, maybe I would have told him she's gone from pretty- college-girl to drop-dead gorgeous, but then he could see that for himself."

Claude did an exaggerated double take, "Drop dead gorgeous, our Julia? Cute, redheaded, gangly, somewhat shy, Sorbonne roommate, and best friend of Isabelle, Julia?"

"The very same!"

"Oh oh! And I missed it!"

Mark changed the subject at once and asked what Claude had come for. Knowing he wasn't going to get any farther with his old friend, Claude was asking if he could take Sam on an outing he was chaperoning that included two of his sister's sons. Mark gave his permission and soon Claude was on his way with promises to grill his friend later.

Once Claude had left the office, Mark sat in the chair behind his desk and looked at David, who was looking rather uncomfortable.

"Out with it, David."

"I don't feel very good keeping Claude out of the loop on this, it could backfire on us."

"I understand, but it's only temporary. As soon as I am able to get things sorted out in my head and you finish with the translations, we can talk about bringing him in. Not before. I just don't want to put him in an awkward position before I have a clear idea of how I want to proceed."

"You're sure about that?" David asked.

"Yes, I am.   How's the translation coming?"

"Not bad. I'm about one-third of the way through the first book. It's going to take me several days more, I think. I could go faster with the translation program, but I really don't want anything put in the computer at this point."

"I agree. Sorry it's the hard way, but I don't think we can be too paranoid about this."

"You're right. I am planning to work on the documents in this office only, and I want them in the back vault at night. Given what I have read so far, I don't want Isabelle in on this for now."

"I didn't think of that, but you are absolutely right. For that matter, I don't want her to ever see the actual documents. It would be awful for her; we'll keep this between us for now.

By the end of the week we should have a clearer idea of what we've got here."

"Was there anything else you wanted to tell me before I hit the book again?"

Mark smiled at him, "Not yet, but we'll talk."

The two men got down to work, Mark comparing the list of paintings against their lost list and David continuing to work on the translation. Mark noticed that from time to time, David's face lost all color, and he knew what he was reading was taking a terrible toll on his dear friend. When Isabelle came into the office, he addressed her at once.

"Isabelle, come sit and talk with me for a few minutes." When she was seated across from him, he plunged right in. "David and I are working on a project now that requires some security. For your sake and for your safety, we both agree that you need to be kept out of this for now. We've done this before, so you know the drill. There's just one other wrinkle in this thing, for right now, Claude is also out."

"You're working on something with that much need for security and you're leaving Claude out? That's very unlike you, Mark. Does this have anything to do with your father?"

"Trust me when I tell you at this point I'm trying to keep Claude out of a possibly very bad spot. Right now, this is the way it has to be."

Isabelle noticed he completely sidestepped the subject of his father. Clearly, it did have something to do with Wolfe. This worried her though she had never met the man, but her

husband had told her of his one experience with
him. "If this is a high-security thing, and I can
understand that, can't Claude provide you with
some level of safety?"

"Not this time."

"You know I trust you both absolutely.
What can I do?"

"I think it might be best if you were out of
here for a few days. You haven't had a good long
visit with Sister Michael in a while, have you?"

"Now you're scaring me. The only times
you have asked me to go to the convent was when
you were working with some very dangerous
people. David, husband of mine, don't you have
anything to add to this conversation?"

"Isabelle, I'm not very happy with this
myself, but Mark is the boss, and in this one thing
anyway, I completely agree. You need to go to
the convent."

"For how long?"

"Not more than a week or ten days. I'll
take you myself." Isabelle said nothing more, but
it was clear to both men she was very unhappy
about the situation. Over the years the men had
dealt with some very unsavory characters.
Usually there were no problems, just threats
sometimes, however, one time it went beyond
threats. A year or so after Katya died, they found
a painting that was on their "lost" list and tried to
get the current owner to return it. The man
reacted badly and in addition to shouting and
calling the police, he showed up at the apartment
one night, very drunk and abusive. It scared both
Mark and David enough that they adopted a policy

of getting Isabelle out of there. They would not even let her stay at home alone; thus, the idea of sending her to the convent became a reality.

David took Isabelle immediately to their home to pack, and then to the convent. As he kissed his wife goodbye, David said, "Everything will be all right."

"Does this have to do with Wolfe?"

"I can't answer that."

"You just did, dear. How can a dead man hurt anyone?"

"I just can't answer Isabelle. I'll call you every evening after prayers when Sister Michael is back in her office."

As David turned away, she asked, "What about Sam?"

"Mark sent him with the housekeeper to her mother in the country for a few days."

"This is related to what happened to Katya, isn't it?"

"I'll talk to you tonight, dear."

As he drove back to the office, he wished he could say without a doubt that they were being absurdly cautious, but at this point, he actually knew more than Mark did about the situation they were in, since he was doing the translations. This was a lot worse than Mark's worst fears. He was going to have to bring in some of his old friends from Israel. People who knew how to deal with this kind of nightmare.

Chapter 44

The two men labored long into the evening, taking a break only to go to the kitchen to prepare some food. David was giving out no previews of the translation, and though it was all Mark could do, he didn't ask.

Late in the evening on the eighth day, David sat back in his chair. Scratching his head and rubbing his bearded face, he announced, "I stink. I'm going to use Sam's room for a shower and a nap, and then we'll talk." Hours later, when both men were showered and rested, they sat at the table in the kitchen eating sandwiches made of thick slabs of cheese and washing them down with a bottle of wine. Mark waited patiently for David to start in his own way and time.

"You're going to want another bottle of that wine. We might as well be comfortable."

Mark followed his friend down the hall to the drawing room where they both picked a comfortable chair. Food and a nap revived them somewhat, but the strain of the last few days showed in both their faces.

"Where to begin." David balanced the three books on his knee and began to speak. "The first book was indeed very personal and mostly written to you, although sometimes it's just Wolfe trying to justify his actions in his own mind. Toward the end, he was losing his grip rather badly. He had some lucid days, but he was slowly losing his mind, and what's more, in his lucid moments, he knew it."

"I could just read your translation, you know. You don't have to do this."

"No, you will sit and listen. I've done this all your way, now we're doing this my way." Mark nodded his assent.

"First of all, you were right about Katya. Wolfe did not intend for her to die. He sent someone to look at your files. Katya must have surprised him. According to Wolfe, he never saw the man again. He followed everything you have done since you went off to university. You were right to be paranoid about this. He was having you watched. He had, like many old Nazis, some very unsavory friends, including some from the Middle East. There is an Egyptian he seems to have had very close ties with. Nothing in the journal suggests the watch on you ended with his death. The 'council' I told you about, consists of six men. Are you ready for this? One of them was Goering."

Mark looked stunned, "Then who was Wolfe Bauer?"

"That, my friend is the one thing he didn't tell us. Of the six, there was Goering, Wolfe, a Haussman, Daum, and Herter. There is every indication that Daum died on the eastern front; Haussman he assumed fled to Argentina. We know what happened to Goering. The sixth man does not have a name, though there is some indication he could be fairly highly placed in the Belgian government. I'm not sure I'm reading that right. Herter was never mentioned after the first time. I will have to create a diagram or chart of the group to make sure I have it right. I could be confusing them in my mind right now. The big question is if any of these men are still alive today.

They would have to be very old."

"If they aren't, this could be into the second generation." Mark observed.

"True. All five besides Goering worked in the shadows of the ERR. Goering actually may have been the ringleader, or even completely uninvolved."

"That's a pretty big difference."

"It's hard to tell if Wolfe is using Goering as a sort of protective coloring. Suggesting the 'council' for the Fourth Reich was authorized at the highest levels of the Fuhrer's general staff. Nowhere in the journals do we get to know who Wolfe Bauer was before 1944. Of course we already know, and have since 1945, about the warehouse full of art that made up the so-called 'Goering Collection.'"

"So you're thinking there could actually only be five, but they were attempting to give themselves some cover by naming Goering, since they would be in a position to know how much art he was skimming off for himself . . . just in case they ever needed cover."

"It's possible." David said. "There is a sort of braggadocio about it. Like little kids claiming they are a part of big kids' gang. But if the other caches are anything like this one, it's a big kid's gang all by itself. We could be looking at half a trillion francs in today's market. That could start a lot of trouble in today's world. With the attitudes surfacing in Germany now, this could fund a whole new war. Now that the wall is gone, and the country tries to cope with things like unemployment, there are old grudges coming to the surface."

"Well, there is some good news in this."

"And that would be?"

"And that would be?"

"I have been able to match nineteen canvases with our lost list, plus a couple more maybes."

"Only nineteen in that whole pile?"

"That's just on the face of things. There's no indication of where Wolfe came from in there?"

"None-that was a secret he just wasn't sharing," David said.

"Claude told me once that he tried to get a line on Wolfe, but as far as he could tell he was hatched fully grown in 1945. His face doesn't show up in any of the archives of German officers either, so you may be right about it being a new face. At any rate, there's really no way to find that out now. It no longer matters at all to me. I just want to protect my mother as much as possible and shield Sam from any fallout."

"So what now? Have you made a decision of how to deal with this?"

"I think so. I'm going to start with bringing it all to France."

"Mark, you know you can't do that. The Swiss will never let it out of the country."

"Then I guess I just won't ask them."

"You're crazy. If you're caught, you'll spend the next twenty years in jail, and there's no way you won't get caught."

"Maybe there is. If it is packed along with the rest of the household goods and then shipped as household goods, the chance of it being caught would be very small. I don't intend to ask the Swiss. I don't believe Wolfe ran that bank in a vacuum. The Swiss government had to know what was going on. They have sand-bagged any of our efforts over the years. They are up to their very courteous asses in collaboration."

"Interesting point Mark, but you have always gone overboard on the side of the law. That's why you have had so much cooperation from people like Claude. Are you sure you want to go out on a limb like this? What about Claude?"

"Actually, I've been thinking about Claude. It's almost time to bring him in on this."

"Well, I certainly agree with you on that."

"Here's what I'm thinking . . ." By the time he finished talking nearly an hour later, he had his friend and colleague's full participation and grudging agreement.

***

The phone rang by the side of Mark's bed late that night after David left. He reached for it with a smile, as he knew who it would be.

"I was wondering if you would call."

"I'm sorry for the odd hour. I've been very busy, but wanted to talk to you."

"Me too, on both counts."

"I must confess I'm thinking of you much too much."

"Something happened between us that night, Julia. I know it and you know it."

"Something did. I guess I can admit that much at this distance. My life is complicated though. Remember I do have those two young twins . . . I have to do some thinking."

"Don't get too nuts about it just yet. I have a somewhat complicated project I have just begun. If it's all right for me to call you, I will do so from wherever I am over the next few weeks. I'm sorry, most of the time you won't be able to call me."

"Sounds like a rather large project."

"I'm not at liberty to say just yet. When I am done though, you and I will have to talk at great length about this thing that has happened to us."

"That's fair. It will also give me a chance to think. I wasn't expecting this, Mark."

"Nor was I. That's what is so nice about it."

They talked for a few minutes more and when he hung up the phone, Mark knew he had come to a major crossroad in his life.

Part Three
Restitution

Bauer's Run

Chapter 45

On the far side of the city from St-Germain des-Pre, a man with tousled black hair leaned against a tree in the soft dawn light and fed the pigeons gathered around his feet. Before long, an old man came and sat on a bench a few feet away and opened the morning newspaper.

"Good morning, Ben, how are you?" The pigeon feeder spoke softly, even though there was no one nearby.

"I'm doing well, David, but somewhat puzzled. It has been a very long while since we last talked."

"I have some names for you to check out with our friends in Tel Aviv."

"Then I suppose I will have to ask you for a cigarette."

He turned his head then, as if the old man had just spoken to him. Taking a pack of cigarettes out of his shirt pocket, he advanced toward the old man with the pack out. The man took a cigarette and a tiny sheet of onion skin paper from under the box. The pigeon feeder went back to his birds and after three or four more minutes, moved off down the path. Hoping he was being completely ridiculous, David felt in his soul that Mark had stepped in a bear-trap this time.

***

The old woman noticed that Monsieur Bauer's son had arrived again in a taxi. She had been looking for a sign that the house had been put up for sale, but had not seen so much as an estate agent looking at it. Perhaps young Mark would not sell the house at all.

Nearly two hours later, a small van pulled up in front of the house. A young man started unloading what looked to be flattened boxes, and took them to the front door. When he was admitted, the woman decided the house would be for sale after all. She wanted her son-in-law to buy the house so her daughter and the grandchildren would be right next door. After all, he was a wealthy barrister and could well afford to buy the house.

As Mark stood aside and let the man from the moving company come farther into the house, he said, "I thought perhaps you could take a look around? You will have an idea about how much space will be needed in your truck. I will pack most of the things that belonged to my mother. I should be ready for you by the end of the week."

The young man took a look around at the furnishings. He then promised to return at the end of the week. Once the man left, Mark went up to his old room and put on some clothes he found there. After going out to a nearby delicatessen in order to stock the refrigerator, he got down to the task at hand.

Starting in the study, he began to pack box after box. About every third box, he would create a pocket in the very center of the box for a special cargo he brought up the stairs. Even working consistently for four hours on, resting for four hours, it took him days to finish the job. He thought he was going to have some serious problems with the largest of the canvasses, but he solved the problem by gently rolling them to fit loosely among the clothes in the wardrobe boxes.

When he was done, he took a walk through the house to examine his handiwork.

There was nothing sinister about it. Leaving everything as it was, he went down the stairs to his next project. He brought with him, in the small bag that also held his clothing, a special kind of aging material that was usually used in the art world to age and enhance a forgery. He obtained it from a young forger he caught and turned over to Claude. He used it to make the vault room disappear. After cementing the keystone back into place, he used the aging medium to make it look as old as the rest. After sweeping up and redistributing some dust, the cellar steps appeared to have had only sparse traffic in recent times.

***

On a back street in Tel Aviv, an old woman shuffled down the steps to a cellar door of an even older house. The watcher saw her go in and called softly to his partner to come and take his place. When the boy came, the first watcher moved on down the street to a café and selected a sidewalk table. The old woman puzzled him. He'd never seen her before, and strangers did not usually come to that particular house. He'd been told to watch for a man, an old man. Could the old woman be a man in disguise? She was about the right size. He decided to play it safe and call it in. If it were the man he watched for, his superiors would not thank him for losing the man.

After a cup of coffee arrived at his table, he took a few sips and then left the table as if he were headed for the men's room. He walked past it instead, to the far back of the restaurant to a pay phone that hung on the wall in deep shadow.

Dialing a number he said only, "He's inside."

He quickly ducked into the restroom and soon came back out wiping his hands on a towel. Taking his time over his coffee, he didn't go back to his post for a few more minutes. When he arrived at his post in the courtyard out of sight from where the old woman disappeared, there was another man waiting in the shadows of late day. They were able to discuss the development at great length before they were to see the old woman appear again just at dusk.

"I believe you are right—it is the old man—he looks very different, but it's his eyes, I think … yes, it's him."

"It's been years since he has surfaced here. What can this be about?"

"I don't know. I was only told he left France and entered the country here."

The two men discussed the possibilities for just a moment more before the older of the two sauntered out on the street to discreetly follow the old man dressed as an old woman. She wandered along the street until she came to a busy market corner. Taking a string bag out of her apron, she began to haggle for produce and a chicken as she worked her way deeper into the crowded stalls. The man following her began to tighten up the distance so he would not lose her. Abdul would beat him if he allowed that to happen. He hurried now as the old woman disappeared around the corner near a rug merchant. Turning the corner, as he stepped into the deep shade, he knew he had made a serious mistake. It was his last thought as a sharp knife cut his throat from ear to ear. The old woman vanished.

Bauer's Run

Chapter 46

When the young man with the moving van came back at the end of the week, Mark had already listed the house with an estate agent and everything was ready to go.

The mover was surprised that the man was actually finished packing. His usual experience was that the customer under-estimated both the time and the effort needed to pack a whole household of belongings, so he would have quite a bit of packing still to go when he came with the truck. This man was ready for him to load and go. It took only a few hours to load the truck and the driver was anxious to be on his way. It wasn't often he got to go to Paris, and this way, he could have an extra night in the city without his wife knowing—if he got on the road right away.

Mark agreed to meet him at the storage warehouse in two days. The man wished him a good flight. Mark didn't correct him. The car he hired was parked on the next street.

It was simple for him to find the truck, as there were only so many roads out of the city in the direction of Paris. Wearing a ball cap, American blue jeans, and sunglasses, the truck driver was unlikely to recognize Mark even if he drove directly alongside the truck. Mark, however, stayed well back, and only passed once the driver had committed to the highway.

The four-minute stop at the border of France exceeded Mark's wildest dreams for simplicity. The back of the truck had been briefly opened to show average looking household goods and then rolled down and the truck was on its way.

Mark's own entry into France five minutes later was just as simple.

***

This time it was the pigeon feeder who came strolling into the gardens and sat near the old man reading the paper. As he tossed crumbs to the birds, the old man gave him a report on the three names. One died on the Russian front in the last days of the war. One was still living in Argentina, a wheelchair-bound old man. The third it seemed would take some time to find. Would he like to tell his friends now why he wanted to know about these men?

"Not yet, but soon."

"We owe you a great deal, my friend, and would not like to lose you. One man has died since you asked the question. It would serve no one to lose you. Please be careful."

"Was it one of ours?"

"No, this time one of theirs who followed me too closely, but it's not a good thing."

"I will take care, my friend, and hopefully we will talk soon."

***

Mark was watching from the roof of a building across the street when the moving truck arrived. The driver was early; he was going to have to wait while he scanned the street behind and all around for any sign that the truck had been followed. After ten minutes, Mark ran lightly down several flights of steps and out the back door of the building on whose roof he spent the last hour. His car was several blocks away and he reached it shortly. He drove the few blocks and pulled to a stop in back of the moving truck.

"I see you were able to find the place. Have you been here long?"

"Only a few minutes. Where do I need to park to unload?"

"We'll just ring the bell for the watchman to open the overhead door and you can drive right in. There's an elevator to the floor where the cargo will be stored."

Soon the truck was driven inside and the door closed again. The large freight elevator would hold a lot, so the driver, who enlisted the help of the watchman to operate it, soon was moving boxes and furniture quickly. This was the night he would get to spend in Montmartre without his wife being the wiser. When he was finished, the man whose household goods he moved tipped and thanked him. Neither the tip nor the thanks were lavish enough to be remembered the next day.

The watchman, an old retired Surete man, who had known Mark for years, helped him set the alarms and lock up. Mark now had other arrangements to look after. Over the next ten days, the household goods moved into the loft of this old warehouse building would be moved three more times. Each time, different sets of people were involved.

The third and final time, they were brought to a cellar many levels below the street. An elderly man met the truck and opened the large doors into the courtyard and closed the doors behind the truck. The truck was unloaded into the courtyard and the driver left, happy to not have to carry everything up or down stairs into what was obviously a very old building.

Mark was the next person to arrive. He carefully unpacked several boxes and crates and each new treasure was carried very carefully down the stairs to a temperature-controlled room where several people were working over canvasses of many sizes and ages. Before long, the attention of most of the staff members drifted away from their own work to what was just coming in.

The staff had been there a long time and was very trusted. None who had not proven himself over and over again ever got to see this part of the museum. One who could not be trusted to keep his mouth shut ever even heard of the cellar projects. The curator was a friend of Mark's for many years. There had been many times that he came to the old curator for help with stolen art. The man, whose sister was married to a Jew who was arrested and taken away from his home and never heard from again, was very sympathetic to Mark's efforts to return property. It was he who taught the young Mark the accepted ways to establish provenance. The elderly man walked slowly, and with a cane now, as he looked over the collection the younger man brought him.

"This is a great thing you are doing, Mark. The museum will keep the works safe as you look for their owners. I suppose you are still not ready to tell me where you found them?"

"No my friend-not now, not ever. I care too much for your safety."

"I am an old man, Mark. Safety means much less to me than satisfying my curiosity."

Mark laughed, "Even so, my old friend, you will have to stay curious this time."

***

It was in the early hours of morning that a man dressed solely in black slipped around the side of a large home in the best residential district of Zurich. It was not his first time here. Using a key he made several years ago, he let himself in through the terrace doors, as he had done at least four times a year for the past few years. In the early days, he and several of his confederates had the task of searching the house top to bottom after the old man died. He didn't know what they were looking for—he was told he would know it when he found it. Well, he'd never found it. His task now was to carefully note any changes—anything moved in the house. He took the time to carefully search the house himself at least once a year. He found nothing of interest. This intrigued him because all his boss told him was that "it" had to be still there. He was an intelligent man and things he could not figure out made him nervous. Now he pulled the heavy draperies shut behind him and switched on the torch. The room was empty!

He moved quickly through the house—completely empty. He slipped back out the door, locking it behind himself. As he moved around the side of the house to the street, he saw something he missed—an estate agent's sign. The boss was going to be angry and he wasn't looking forward to it. He would have to come back in the daytime, perhaps as a prospective buyer of the house, to see what he could learn of interest.

Bauer's Run

Chapter 47

Mark, Claude, and David agreed to meet that evening at the St-Germain-des-Pres apartment.

"All right, you two, this had better be good. Not only am I missing dinner with a beautiful woman, but it has been a very long week."

David and Mark alternated telling the story, from the finding of the stash to the complete translation of the books.

"The names in the books are: Goering, we know about him, Haussman, Daum, Herter, and one nameless man. By the way, I prepared a complete transcript of the books for you, Claude."

"Wait a minute, are you telling me each of these men had a stash like Wolfe's?"

"It would appear so. Of course we all know what happened to the Goering collection. It was restored, as much as possible, to its rightful owners after Nuremberg. Actually, I'm not sure the Goering collection was for anyone but Goering. The mention in Wolfe's journals was so off-hand, I think it may have been a red herring. Like a little kid wanting to be part of his big brother's gang, so he says he is. David was able to learn that Daum died on the Russian front as they moved to take Berlin. Who knows where his cache is? Maybe now that the East is starting to open, we might someday hear about it."

David laid it out for Claude. "Haussman escaped to South America. We don't have any indication of how he lived there, although he is apparently still alive. Herter we have nothing on. The sixth man is still a mystery," Mark said.

"So what now, Mark? How can the Surete help?"

"We've found some indications that Herter could be somewhat highly placed in the Belgian government. Is there any way you could tap into your files for a face and maybe match it somehow against the current Belgian government?"

"That's doable. If the face is there, the computers can match it up sooner or later, especially if we access the Interpol files. Any clues on the sixth man?"

"None. David is doing some research in the Nuremberg files for the mention of a possible candidate."

"Let me know if you come across a name you want me to run."

"For right now, David's friends are also looking."

"I don't want to know what David's friends might be doing. So what about the rest of the stash? You said Wolfe kept records. Does that mean you have a pretty good idea who all the various properties belong to?"

"I wish! We just have to see how many of them are still alive."

"Will you have to work out of Zurich to finish the project?"

"No, Wolfe's area of operation was France. The bulk of the stash we know for sure belongs in France. It was my intention to return it here and work out of Paris."

"Good luck. The government of Switzerland will never let you take property of that magnitude out of the country. The best you can hope for is one at a time as you are able to prove ownership. That could take you the rest of your life."

"You didn't hear what I said. I said it *was* my intention."

"Oh. Well, I'm glad you thought better of it. The Swiss have always stonewalled at the highest level whenever we have tried to get any cooperation out of them regarding French assets seized and transported to Switzerland."

"You aren't listening. I was speaking in the past tense. Going on the theory that it's always easier to get forgiveness than permission, I didn't ask them. It's already here."

"What!" Claude came up out of his chair. "How did you get the Swiss government to agree to that? Oh, no . . . tell me you didn't . . . you smuggled a fortune into France? How did you do that?"

"I really don't think it would serve any purpose to tell you that. You'd just have a stroke. Then I'd have to deal with all the lovely ladies of Paris who are trying to wed you."

"Where is it and what do you intend to do with it?"

"I'm not going to tell you where it is. What I'm going to do is return it, as much as possible, to the people of France. You have known me nearly all my life. You know I will do what I say I will do. What I will not do is give this 'council' for the 'Fourth Reich' any publicity at all. Can you imagine if word of this got out? It would be a worldwide feeding frenzy looking for the other men and their loot. We are talking trillions of francs here."

"How can you hope to keep something like this quiet?"

"I not only can, I will. I have cooperation at the highest levels of the Jewish community. The silence will hold. This is the one way I can protect Sam from any fallout over this. His life would be forfeit if it were publicly known I was sitting on a fortune this size. What I need from you is some cover if things go awry."

"What could possibly go wrong? Obviously you've covered all the bases, and accounted for the only hundreds of French laws you are going to break or have broken already. To say nothing of the risk to you and David, and incidentally to Isabelle and Sam, no matter how you do it. You have lost your mind."

"Maybe, but you know what it has been like over the years since we started this, I'm tired of governments playing fast and loose with people's property. People they didn't protect in the first place. I'm tired of governments being as big an obstacle as the crooks. I'm angry. The scope of this is unconscionable. Governments had to know. Believe it or not, I have thought of Sam and Isabelle and David. If the stolen property can be seen publicly to have come from me, Sam gets hurt. There's no way it wouldn't get out somehow that it came to me through Wolfe. It didn't take you long to find out that Wolfe Bauer didn't exist before 1945, how long do you think it would take some enterprising young paparazzi to unearth that? Sam's grandfather a Nazi? I won't take the chance."

"I see your point. How can you know there can be trillions of francs involved?"

"Tell him, David."

"Wolfe's records. I would guess the one book was intended as a sort of insurance for him. It bothers me that the sixth man is never named. To my mind that could be saying the sixth man is a name the whole world would recognize. In that case, what we don't know can hurt us."

"Wait a moment. Didn't you say something about gold?"

"Now you're beginning to see the picture, so to speak. A canvass is very traceable; gold is without provenance. Gold is something to kill for. If the canvasses surface publicly, someone, somewhere, knows there is also gold in the same cache."

"How can you possibly return the gold to its owners then?"

"I can't. Quite simply, the owners of the gold are no longer alive-any of them. The gold was melted down from teeth and wedding rings and necklaces of the dead of the gas chambers. It can only be returned to the Jewish people. I will do so."

"How?"

"Three words: Jewish banks-privately."

Claude was, by this time tensely pacing the floor. While Mark sat quietly and David's head turned back and forth between his two friends, he cracked his knuckles, scratched his head, and paced. Finally he stopped in front of his boyhood friend.

"What is your intention about finding the remaining men of the 'council' and their stolen goods?"

"I leave them to you and David and God. I want no part of it. When this project is finished, so am I. I'm too old for this. I intend to have a normal life."

"Are you serious?"

"I couldn't be more so. The Lillian Harding Archival Trust will be handed over to the people of Israel. I'm sure there are lots of people there with lots of ideas how the money could be used." Claude and David both roared with laughter.

"I don't know what's so funny. It wasn't an insignificant amount of money in the first place, but it is very serious money now. It can go to a good cause or two."

David was still laughing, "By the time they get through taking a poll and getting a consensus from Israelis', it'll be a lot bigger!"

"If you're serious," Claude said to Mark, "I can keep this under wraps. When you're done, you're done."

"That's the way it's going to be, Claude. I mean every word."

"Are you sure you don't want to tell me where it is?"

"I'm sure."

Claude nodded his head, gripped his friend's shoulder with emotion, and turned and left the apartment.

Chapter 48

After the three friends went their separate ways that night, Mark's friends seemed to accidentally run into each other on the street; in that very brief moment, a meeting was arranged.

Much later the policeman leaned against a tree in his own back garden smoking a cigar. He heard a slight sound and turned to see his friend slip through the back gate. Putting the cigar out, he moved toward the house and a side door. There were no lights showing either inside or outside and the only sign the two men entered the door to the cellar was a slight darkening of the already dark night.

"I think you'd better fill me in on what I'm not supposed to know. Have your friends in Tel Aviv told you anything you're not saying in front of Mark?"

"Very astute of you. The most worrisome thing is that two of the names have a connection to the Bekka'a Valley. It seems the people who would like to wipe out the State of Israel today have something in common with the folks who tried very hard to wipe out the Jewish people in WWII. Both the Haussman and Daum caches found their way to the Bekka'a."

"I suppose it would be useless for me to ask just how you know that?"

"I've always said you were a very smart man."

"Mark cannot afford to run afoul of these people. He's an innocent compared to them."

"As long as he sticks to dealing just with what he found at Wolfe's, he'll be okay. I think between us, we can protect him. Besides, he's not into taking risks these days."

"How do you know that?"

"He hasn't said anything yet, but I would guess that our friend is very serious about getting out of the business. I think a certain lady knocked him out of his socks."

"And that would be the beauteous Julia?"

"Exactly. I don't think he's aware that I know, but he calls her nearly every day."

The two men continued their conversation for another hour, working out the details of how to keep the operation under wraps and keep Mark safe. Their biggest concern was the unnamed sixth man, as well as the connection to the Bekka'a Valley, home of the world's finest terrorist training camps.

The sixth man was also the topic of conversation in that back street in Tel Aviv. The difference was, in Tel Aviv, they knew who he was. They had known the identity of this man for many years; the unknown link they were searching for was unexpectedly dropped in their laps when their man in Paris came to them with the story of the cache found in Zurich. Wolfe Bauer was just about the last piece of the puzzle.

They were very close to being able to put a stop to a very well- funded operation. The purloined copy of Wolfe Bauer's little insurance document gave them the last piece they needed.

***

Mark hung up the phone and sat back in his chair and reflected on the relationship with Julia that was developing over the telephone. She said to him as their conversation came to an end, "I can't wait to see you again either, Mark, I want to know where this is going." He wanted to know the very same thing. Just where is this going? He could not afford the distraction right now, but it was that very distraction that kept him going. He'd never felt like this in his entire life, not even with Katya. This was more like a drug, one taste and he was completely hooked.

Catherine Curtis

Occasionally she wrote him so she could put thoughts down on paper that she would have been able to say to his face but were difficult for her on the telephone. He knew she was just a little bit embarrassed about the heat of that night in Paris, even though they hadn't made love as they both clearly wanted. He smiled as he remembered how she looked that night. He saw her face in his mind's eye, huge green eyes and wisps of red hair curling about her temples in the misty spring night air. *It would take a better man than you to resist that!* Now he only wondered how he did.

He was beginning to form a plan in his mind to include Julia if things continued the way they were. For the first time in years, he felt his life had a purpose beyond raising Sam. As much as he loved Sam, being alone since Katya died had taken its toll on him. Not only had his work weighed on his soul, but without dumping everything on David and Isabelle, he had no one to share it with. No one, that is, except Sister Michael. His friends deserved a life of their own; they gave so much to the cause he laid out for them all those many years ago. To say nothing of what they had done to help him raise Sam. The one person who really understood him was Sister Michael. Oh the burdens he lay on her over the years! She was a true friend. When darkness shadowed his soul, she was his true light, pointing the way out of the depths.

Tonight he was planning to do some work in the cellars of the museum, but had waited for the call he knew would come. Sam was away on a school trip and David and Isabelle had gone home at a reasonable hour for a change. He would meet Claude for a late supper, but he might as well get some work done before then. The sooner he got done, the sooner he could begin to have a life.

Bauer's Run

Chapter 49

When the tall good-looking man came out of the entrance to the building where he lived, the beggar sitting in the doorway opposite came alert without moving a centimeter. He followed the man several times now and knew where he went, but was unsuccessful at getting into the building the man entered at night. Perhaps tonight would be the night. He prayed one more time to Allah to give him strength to learn what his master wanted him to find out. His master had been patient so far, but he knew that patience would not last much longer. He had to get inside tonight.

The beggar began to trail after his target, muttering to himself and stopping here and there to examine debris on the sidewalk. He was someone that no one ever saw.

Well, no one saw him except another watcher who now also watched the beggar. His friend, the pigeon feeder, had set up this job of watching to see if anyone took an interest in the comings and goings of man in question. For months now, he and two others discreetly watched over the man. He knew the man was important to his handlers and to Israel. That much was made clear to him. He was proud he was trusted enough to do this, for he was young and fairly new to the organization.

The beggar following his charge was not even subtle. If their roles had been reversed, he could do a better job of being invisible. His charge was headed to the museum tonight, as he did on many nights. Someone should tell the professor not to take the same route every night. He wanted to tell the man himself, but his superior told him that would give away the fact that they were protecting him. The man was safer if he wasn't aware of being followed. Nothing could change about the way he acted.

The heavy mist hanging over the Seine tonight made it difficult to keep an eye on the beggar, but then it also made it harder for the beggar to keep an eye on Professor Bauer. Just as Mark came to the steps that ran down to the cellar door leading to the passages under the museum, two things happened. As he took his key from his pocket, he became aware of a presence behind him and began to turn.

A ragged beggar came at him at knee level and succeeded in pitching Mark headlong down the steps. Right behind him was another man, younger and better dressed, came after the bundle of rags. A fight broke out in the narrow space at the foot of the stairs, Mark was clipped under his chin by an elbow and had a hard time keeping his footing. Just about the time he cleared his head and managed to stand up, the ragged man launched a fist at the second man and missed, landing instead along-side Mark's head. The lights went out and Mark's inert body slumped to the ground as much as was possible in the overcrowded space.

The beggar now held a wickedly curved knife in his hand; this young punk could not keep him from his task. His adversary knew this was deadly serious, and fortunately was trained to the point where his skills were automatic. He made a motion to back up as though he was scared of the knife, and when the beggar followed, he stepped inside and turned the knife inward on the bundle of rags. There was only a sigh and a rush of hot liquid over his hands as the beggar joined Allah. It was necessary to act quickly now.

It wasn't a pleasant night, so there weren't many pedestrians, but he couldn't afford to delay. Finding the key the professor dropped took precious seconds, but soon he had it in his hand. Opening the door at the base of the stairs, he dragged Mark's unconscious body inside, relocked the latch, tossed the key in by Mark's still inert body and quickly stepped outside, closing the door behind himself.

Racing to the top of the stairs, he looked both ways. The alley was only a few feet away and there was no one on the street. Running lightly down the steps, he took off his jacket and wrapped it around the dead man. Picking the man up in a fireman's carry, he went back up the steps. No one was in sight. He swiftly made his way to the alley and deposited the remains of the beggar in the dustbin at the back of a restaurant halfway down the alley.

Retrieving his jacket, he returned to the mouth of the alley. He flew back down the stairs to the cellar landing. Listening carefully at the door, he didn't hear a sound. The professor must be still out cold. He carefully mopped up as much of the spilled blood as he could. Turning the black jacket inside out, he carried it under his arm as he walked back in the direction of the Seine. Leaning on a bench at the edge of the river, and looking cautiously in both directions, dropped the jacket into the Seine. Turning back on his path, he went back to the street beside the museum and picked out a doorway from which to watch for his charge.

***

Mark woke up on the floor. It took a while for him to get his senses about him. He knew he was on the floor in the dark, but where? He had been walking to the museum . . . it came back to him in a rush. *He had been attacked by a ragged street urchin, who was in turn attacked by someone else. Who was his unknown defender? For that matter, who was the bundle of rags? And where was he now?* He stood up carefully and began to feel around. Soon he touched a wall. It was pitch black. Feeling along a wall, he found a switch. *Oh well*, he thought as he flipped it.

Now he knew where he was. In fact he should have realized earlier, the smell of the cellars of the museum had a unique odor. *How did I get inside the hallway? I don't remember unlocking the door. For that matter, where is the key?* Looking around, he found it on the floor near where he had lain.

Guess I'll have to tell Claude about this one. But he was sure it was unrelated to what he was doing-just a bum trying to roll him. Maybe he'd take another exit when he left. After he thought about it, he decided there was no reason to tell Claude, who would just worry.

***

When the young Israeli reported to his handler the next morning, he told of the attack on the professor and what he did about it. He also reported the professor never came back out of the museum.

The old man put it all in his report when he talked to his people in Tel Aviv. "This is getting more dangerous. Someone is on to our professor. I don't think this can be ignored."

"Do you have any idea who this man was who attacked him?"

"No, and I have no good way to find out. The only clue is that the man carried a wicked curved knife according to my operative. Our friends in the Surete would be very unhappy if they got wind of us running an operation here, even if it did protect the professor."

"Keep your eyes open. Maybe we can think of a way to get the professor out of Paris for a while."

"I'll bring it up with David. He'll come up with something."

Bauer's Run

Chapter 50

The Surete was, in the person of Claude, at that very moment discussing the finding of a body in an alley just a few blocks off the Seine. He asked to be notified of anything unusual that appeared to have a Middle Eastern connection. The dead man in the alley certainly appeared to. The knife in his clothing was certainly from the Middle East, and he was certainly killed by it. He also certainly did not dispose of himself in a dustbin. He strongly suspected David's "friends" from Tel Aviv were running an operation in his city. That really irritated him.

Claude suspected they were protecting Mark while he finished his project. If Mark and David had been willing to tell him where Mark had stored the stash, he might be able to help and would not be reduced to spying on them. *I wondered if this dead body had anything to do with Mark. How could it? Damn Israelis anyway! After all, they always had their own agenda, and thought no one could protect their interests like they could.* He already figured out where Mark stored the gold. He happened to see his friend coming out of the largest Jewish-owned private bank in France. That didn't take a whole lot of deducting. Mark was not a devious person. Even when he was thinking about being careful (which Claude was convinced, was seldom), he was painfully obvious.

Something was going on and it angered him to not know what it was. David told him of the connection to the Bekka'a Valley, and this body in the dustbin only confirmed that. This was not an easy task, to protect his friend from an unknown threat, from an unknown source, without his superiors getting wind of what he was doing. Claude running a private operation in the city would anger them only slightly less than the Israelis doing the same thing. At least it was expected of the Israelis.

With his mentor, Inspector de la Croix retired; there was no one between him and some very political people over him in the Surete. If this whole project of Mark's came to light and it became known he knew about it, he would have to find a new career because he would surely be fired as well as lose his pension.

Too many people knew Mark Bauer was his best friend from childhood. No one would believe he was kept in the dark. Mark Bauer was someone who grew up secure in his own person, as big men usually do. Claude and their friend David, both being of slight build had a different outlook on life. It just would not occur to Mark to be cautious walking the streets of Paris in his own general neighborhood. Perhaps when the three met for their usual midweek meal out together, he could feel out the situation and find out how close Mark was to being done with this, if done was actually possible.

***

David was walking along the sidewalk thinking about what Isabelle said about Mark taking a trip to New York to meet Julia there, when he suddenly realized something registered in his subconscious earlier in the block. It took a supreme force of will to not go back to look at the piece of paper tacked to the lamppost. He hadn't been looking for it and it didn't register right away. It had been a long time since anyone had left an emergency signal for him. What was wrong? He had to stop and think about the message without actually stopping on the sidewalk. *What color had the paper been? Yellow. What shape? Think . . . think. You can't go back and stand in front of it you dolt.*

It was diamond shaped and pointed to the street, which was east. That meant the meet was for later tonight, in an all-night coffeehouse. He figured out the time by a simple substitution code he had been taught. As soon as he left Mark's, where he was now headed, he would call Isabelle and tell her something came up that he had to take care of and he would be home very late. Fortunately, she was used to that by now.

Mark was waiting for his friend to arrive and opened the door almost as soon as he heard the knock. He made up his mind that he would tell David at least about the incident in the stairwell. He still hadn't figured out how he got in the door, and that bothered him. It almost had to be that the good Samaritan who came to his rescue had gotten him inside, but that didn't make any sense.

When the two men were settled in over a light supper the housekeeper had left, Mark started in on his story about the previous evening. David was dumbfounded. Now he had an idea what the emergency signal was about. He, of all people, knew the shape of the watch put on Mark for his safety. They were getting very close now to getting this whole thing wrapped up. He already knew the watchers picked up on someone watching Mark's building; they saw no move toward him but decided to stay alert and find out who might be behind it. There was a nagging feeling in the group that there was a loose end out there that they weren't aware of. Their usual target, a very wealthy Syrian who was financing terrorist attacks on the West Bank, was going about his usual business, seemingly without a care. That bothered the Israelis because, in the past, the man disappeared on them several times. He was very, very good, and the fact that they could keep him in sight meant he must want them to know where he was at all times. This was not out of the kindness of his heart, rather it was an indication they were missing something or, to be more precise, someone. The presence of the gold came out in a manner they knew would, sooner or later, leak. The target had to come after it, he had to, but now they began to think he was using someone else to do the work. Until all the players could be identified, they needed to get the professor out of there for a while. If they didn't, he was going to end up very dead. Nearly everyone in the civilized world would recognize the man who picked up the telephone to set a plan in action.

"Get our friend out of the country."

"For how long?"

"At least a week. Tell me when it's done."

He hung up the phone and set to making mental lists. The professor was owed a great deal by his adopted country, and he had, over the years, returned a lot of property to Jews who resettled in Israel. Enough to have actually made a significant financial impact. They owed him. It was approved at the highest levels, both in the government and by the shadow figures that make things happen to let the professor run with this his own way. In exchange, anything that could not be returned to its owner would belong to the state, someday to hang in a national museum for all their people to see. They would let the professor run it out. Now, if they could just keep him alive.

Bauer's Run

Chapter 51

When Mark finished his story, David looked at him for a long moment before he began to speak.

"Mark, Claude and I have, in the past, tried to talk to you about your safety. You are not listening, my friend."

"It really wasn't anything."

David lost it then.

"You pig-headed idiot! People are risking their lives to keep you safe. No! Don't say a thing. Sit down and shut up. You remember Wolfe's little insurance policy, the brown leather journal? Do you recall the members of the 'council'? There was Daum, he stayed in East Germany, so did the fortune in art. We believe that was the seed money for a very large-scale operation in Russia to train 'freedom fighters'. Then there was Haussman. He went to Argentina and took the fortune with him. With the help of a very wealthy Syrian, he funded a state-of-the-art training camp for guerrillas in the Bekka'a Valley of Lebanon. There was Herter, remember we couldn't find him? He is employed in the Belgian government. He didn't do so well. It seems he has a gambling habit. Yes, he's still alive. Over the years, he lost a fortune. Now he sells information. Would you like to know the last little tidbit of information he's pedaled?"

"That you have come into the cache. It didn't mention Wolfe by name. How does he know that? I have no idea. How do we know? We intercepted the message on its way to the Bekka'a."

"How can you possibly know all this, David?"

"Just listen. He listed part of the cache as fifty million in gold. We don't really know if he meant francs, pounds, or even dollars, but who cares. If you've got it, your life isn't worth squat. The missing unnamed man? We're pretty sure he's out there somewhere. There is some string we haven't pulled on yet. Someone is following your every move, someone besides the good guys, that is."

"Are you telling me you are having me watched? Who is we?"

"Do you think you have been untouchable all these years because of your good looks and scintillating personality? You do not live in a nice world. What do I have to do to get that into your head? And by the way, should you ever mention any of this to anyone, even Claude you can add Isabelle, Sam and me to the endangered species list. The Surete is a sieve. Have you closed your mind to everything Wolfe told you in the journal? Do you not understand just the possession of the journal puts you in danger? I'm shutting you down. You are done my friend. Whatever is left to do, the governments can do. Maybe they'll give the job to the Louvre. I don't care. You're done. I don't see any way but for you to get out of town, out of the country. Take Sam, go somewhere. Give the professionals time to wrap up."

Mark sat there with all the color drained from his face. David's voice had never gone over a low whisper, which scared him more. David never shouted when he was really angry. For years he had suspected his friend worked in secretly with people within the government of Israel, but whom, he didn't know. Maybe Mossad, he didn't know all the names of those secret police bodies. Now he knew for sure. It scared him. Mark knew how far he had to have pushed his friend for him to reveal as much as he just did. He hadn't been thinking of putting others at risk, just wanted to protect Sam from the disgrace of having a war criminal for a grandfather. A pig-headed idiot indeed, more like a stupid, self-absorbed, pig-headed idiot.

"What do you want me to do?"

"Isabelle said you were planning to go to New York. Take Sam with you. Go tomorrow."

"Sam's away right now. He won't be home until the weekend."

"Where is he?"

"In Grenoble with his class."

"Can't you get him back here in the morning?"

"I don't know how, unless I went to Grenoble myself and got him."

"Not a good idea. Could you authorize me to get him from there?"

"I don't think that would be necessary, David."

"You don't have any idea what's necessary. Can you do it?"

"Yes, I know the headmaster well, I can talk to him. I'm sure it won't be a problem."

"Call him now."

"It's late. He won't be at the school. He'll

be home with his family."

"Call him now. Describe me and ask for a face-to-face meeting with me tonight."

"Oh, come on, David. Don't you think that's a bit much?"

"Losing Sam would be a bit much, don't you think? Do as I ask."

Now Mark was more frightened than he had ever been in his life. He made the phone call and put David on the line.

When he was finished, David turned to his friend and said, "Here's what's going to happen. Tonight you stay in and pack. Get on the earliest plane to New York that you can tomorrow. Give me Sam's passport."

"Which one? He has both Swiss and American."

"Both. I will put him on a plane. I expect to use his Swiss passport to buy a ticket, but he will have to have his American passport on his person. I'll route him into Kennedy in New York. When I know his arrival time, I'll call your mother. You call her tonight and tell her you're coming. When you land, call her for Sam's arrival time and flight number. He may be as much as twenty-four hours behind you. I'm going to him as soon as I finish with the headmaster."

"You're really scaring me now."

"Good, it's about damn time. Pack for Sam also and take it with you. Where do you usually stay in New York?"

"The Pierre."

"Try the Howland. I'll call for you; there will be a reservation in my name. Call me here when you and Sam are both in the hotel."

Mark sat in his chair for a long time after his friend left, berating himself, mentally trying to absorb all David had told him. He was so wrapped up in Wolfe's crimes in his own mind that he hadn't given a thought to the size of the conspiracy or the length of time it had gone on. Now he had to do what he was told for Sam's sake. He wasn't worried about Sam once David got to him, for he knew David would guard the boy with his life.

That also scared the hell out of him. He could lose them both.

Bauer's Run

Chapter 52

As David left the building, he paused briefly in the shadows of the entry hall. He knew when he went outside he would need to have all his antennae up. He took a deep breath and plunged out into the street. He walked as he would normally to go from Mark's home to his. About halfway to his own apartment, he passed a man who brushed by him closely on his right side, between him and the wall. When he arrived at his own home, he called out to Isabelle as he came through the door. He removed a small, folded up paper from his right pocket as he heard her step on the stair.

"Get what you absolutely must have for a couple of days in a small bag. You and I are going out to eat tonight, and in the middle of dinner, you're going to get mad at me, and leave the table. You are to move in the direction of the toilette but go past them and out the back door. Did I mention we would be at La Coquilles? Eli will be there to take you to Sister Michael for a few days. I will call you later tonight."

"Is this about Mark?"

"It's about all of us. I'm going to go get Sam and put him on a plane to New York. Mark will be on his way in the morning. I need you safe so I can concentrate."

"I understand. Just give me a few minutes."

David sighed with relief. His dear wife had years of experience with his succinct instructions; she knew when it was deadly serious. He would have been very astonished to find out she knew a lot about the secret work he did, much more than he told Mark tonight.

Isabelle knew very well when to follow orders without question. She trusted her husband with her life, and that included a small circle of friends who were not visible in their lives, but always close by. Eli was one of the oldest and dearest. He had been in her life since the camps. She soon came back down the stairs with a light jacket on, as well as a head scarf and carried an oversized handbag. David smiled his approval. His wife was sharp. The jacket was reversible, as was the scarf, and the bag was of a size to be one of those over stuffed things women carried all the time.

"Good girl. Let's go." She hugged him hard then, stepped aside for him to open the door. They walked to the restaurant where they ate frequently. Just after the main course was about half eaten, she looked at him and said in a perfectly normal tone, "You haven't heard a word I said."

"I did so. You were talking about your friend Corrine."

"I haven't spoken of Corrine in twenty minutes, you just don't listen," she hissed.

"Now, my dear, of course . . ."

Isabelle looked at him in disgust, threw down her napkin, picked up her purse and stalked to the back of the restaurant. David shrugged his shoulders as if to say, "What can a man do?" and went on with his meal. Five minutes passed and then ten. Soon he was glancing at his watch with an annoyed look. When the waiter came back to clear the table, he asked if one of the women would mind checking the restroom for his wife. He thought she might be sulking. Soon the woman came back to his table and said she was sorry, but there was no one in there.

David looked embarrassed, and got up to pay the check and leave. This charade may have been put on for no one at all, but he couldn't afford to take a chance. As he went out on the street, instead of turning in the direction of home, he stepped into the street and hailed a taxi going the opposite direction.

He saw just a flash of movement out of the corner of his eye as the taxi sped off. The man who was watching David's back, also saw that slight movement in the shadows.

By taking a taxi, David had broken a pattern, and done something he didn't usually do. That was as good a way as any to find out if surveillance was in place. Watchers had a tendency to get sloppy if they thought they knew what the subject was going to do. The friend stepped out on the sidewalk toward where he had seen the movement. Perhaps he could catch the person off guard. Whistling as he walked past the doorway that he was pretty sure held the culprit; he stepped left into the doorway at the last second. Leading with a brutal right punch at waist level, he knocked the wind out of the man hiding there. A quick left and then right, left the man on the ground unconscious. He rifled quickly through all the man's pockets, and checking both ways for pedestrians, stepped out into the streetlight to inspect the contents. Giving a low whistle mentally, he stepped back into the doorway and tossed the wallet down on the man, minus the money. This would go down as just another mugging if it were to be reported, which he was pretty sure it would not.

David knew he'd lost his tail as soon as the taxi turned the second corner. No car started up after them and there wasn't another taxi in sight. He grinned to himself. *Not bad for an old guy.* After taking the taxi through several twists and turns, he gave him the address of the headmaster. It didn't take long to convince the man to call the chaperone of Sam's class, for the man knew Mark well and did not question his judgment. Within the hour, David was pulling Mark's car out of the hired garage he where he kept it and turned it in the direction of Grenoble. The big Citroen took to the road like a horse that hadn't been run for a while, and was soon eating up the road.

He really hated to take Sam away from his school trip. Every year at this time, the school took the best students to the Vercor to hike and study nature. The Vercor was a magnificent area of the country, south of Grenoble, a vast wilderness of pinewoods, caves, deep gorges, and waterfalls. David knew how much Sam loved that, as he had been a chaperone on one such trip. Sam loved the great outdoors, something he didn't get a lot of in Paris. The thought reminded David of how long it was since he and Isabelle had taken a holiday. When this was over, he resolved to sit down with his wife and talk about what they wanted to do with the rest of their lives. Mark had the right idea; it was time to move on to a normal life. He owed that much to Isabelle, who had given so generously to the cause they all embraced.

Bauer's Run

Chapter 53

Sam was a bright teenager. When his teacher told him his Uncle David was coming for him, he knew something was up. His big worry was that something happened to his father. No one was saying that, but he knew both his father and his "uncle" sometimes got involved in things that could be dangerous for them. He had known for some time the nature of the work done out of his father's home office.

Everyone was so used to having him around that sometimes he heard things that were not meant for his ears. This thing about Grandfather Bauer was one of those things. He knew that his Dad was mortified by the man who was the only father he knew. Apparently Grandmother Renee had been in school in Switzerland when she became pregnant. Sam hadn't heard who the father was; just that it wasn't Wolfe. He wondered if his father and uncles still thought of him as a baby. He wasn't. The one person who talked to him like an adult was Uncle Claude.

Claude always talked to him like he was a grownup, and explained things to him when he didn't understand. If Uncle David didn't tell him what was going on, when he got home, he would call Uncle Claude. He was an adult now; did it never occur to them that he could help? That is if they ever gave him a chance. It was Claude who explained to him about the art stolen from the Jews during the war that his father worked to restore to the rightful owners. Sometimes the people who had bought them in good faith didn't want to give them up. Sometimes people had inherited artwork from people his father found were Nazis.

Last year he heard his Dad and David talking about a painting worth over a million francs that they were trying to return to its owner. The entire family of the woman it went to had been killed in the camps. His Dad could be a royal pain in the butt, (a phrase his father sometimes used about him) when he was trying to talk people into doing the right thing, but Sam was very proud of him. As he stood waiting in the foyer of the small inn, he wondered when they would let him start working with them. He was nearly grown. Surely they would let him start soon. He wanted to get some experience before he finished school and went to work with Uncle Claude. He just had to show them how grown up he was.

When David pulled to a stop at the main door to the inn where Sam was, he was startled to see the boy standing by his bags waiting just inside the door. It only took a moment to clear Sam with the chaperone, load his bags, and get on the road again. When he explained that he would be putting Sam on a plane to New York, Sam asked him quietly, "Did my Dad die?"

David was so shocked that he had to pull the car off the road to talk to Sam. What he learned was that Sam wasn't much of a kid anymore.

***

Mark left his apartment early for the taxi ride to Charles de Gaulle to catch an early flight.

Anyone who was watching would think it was just one of his usual day trips since he carried only a small bag. He was somewhat nervous about Sam, but realized David had more assets in place than he knew about. Before long, the big, wide-body jet was in the air and Mark closed his eyes for a nap.

He had been up the whole night, packing up some things he wanted David to store and thinking. Thinking over what David said, he realized he had his head in a place "designed only to keep his ears warm" as Claude was wont to say. He had gotten sloppy. It really was time for him to step down. He knew it, he didn't have to like it, but he knew it. It felt a lot better that he was stepping down to try to develop something lasting with Julia.

Several rows back in the plane, a young woman noted that her charge had settled in for a nap, and decided she might as well do the same. It wasn't like he was going anywhere. She had not spotted anyone taking an interest in the professor, but she knew there were a lot of operatives out there a whole lot more experienced than she was. She needed to rest while she could; it would be necessary to be alert in New York.

Ten hours later, Mark had checked in at the small hotel David reserved for him. Now that he was actually paying attention, he knew why this hotel had been picked.

The lobby door was locked with a doorman standing just inside. He was asked his business before the doorman buzzed him in. After he was checked in, the bellman escorted him to his room and introduced him to the elevator man and then to the housekeeper on the floor where his room was. It was obvious the staff knew each guest, and he was betting there would be few, so any non-guest who gained access would stick out like a sore thumb. Once in his room, he called his mother and Julia to let them know he was in the country. Now he had to wait for Sam.

He made some decisions on the flight. Sam would not be going back to France. Renee would be delighted to have him with her for now. He could figure out the school situation once they got to Chicago. Ordering a meal from room service, he opened his briefcase, and settled in to get some work done while he waited to hear from David.

Mark started writing. He made the decision on the plane that he was going to write down every single thing he knew about Wolfe Bauer. This was going to take some doing. He started to go back to his earliest memories of Wolfe and move forward. As he sat at the small desk by the window of his room, he filled page after page with his small neat writing, not noticing the time passing until the light began to fade in the room. He stood up then and stretched his aching back, then looked at his watch. He should be able to find out when Sam's plane was landing now. He called Renee and, as David promised, Sam was on a plane arriving at Kennedy in five hours. He'd promised David he would stay in the hotel, but he was hungry and decided to go out. When he arrived in the small but elegant lobby, the young woman at the desk greeted him at once and by his name, although he didn't remember seeing her when he checked in.

"Going out, Mr. Bauer?"

"Yes, I thought I'd go out and get some dinner. Can you recommend a restaurant nearby? It looks like a pleasant evening for a stroll."

"Actually sir, I can. Are you aware we have a small but very nice private dining room here in the hotel for our guests? We employ a five-star chef and an excellent staff. Would you like me to show you?"

He was startled, but said "Yes, that would be nice." She took him by elevator to the floor below his suite. They walked down a hall, through a small reception area where another young woman, who looked up and smiled at him, sat at a desk. She opened a door and indicated he was to precede her. To his astonishment, he found himself in a small dining room with only six tables, each in an alcove, which gave them privacy from each other. Each of the tables was set with snowy white linens, fine cream-colored china, crystal he recognized as Baccarat, silver and fresh flowers. A young waiter appeared at once with a menu in his hand and gestured.

"As you see sir, it's early, so you may have your choice of tables."

Intrigued, he decided to give it a try. Since one of his great pleasures of being in New York was an American-style steak, he ordered that and left the rest of the meal up to the chef. The wine was French and very good, the salad, crisp mixed greens in the French style, the thick steak mouth-watering and the Creme Brulee flawless. David never ceased to amaze him. How did he know these places?

Although David still taught at the Sorbonne, and had a small private school of artists as well, he had been involved over the years with a number of projects with Mark.

Whenever he was free, he did a lot of Mark's research, and many trips when they were trying to track down a particular painting. He was under no illusions about what Claude referred to as David's "friends in Tel Aviv." He was quite certain his friend was eyes and ears in the Paris art world for some very highly placed people in the government of Israel; that is, the part of the government that does not get elected, but is a part of the background.

Mark also knew that the cooperation of the museum and the bank he was using to return Wolfe's ill-gotten gains had to have come at the request of some very powerful people.

Now that he thought about it, David had come to Zurich at the drop of a hat. *Had he known or perhaps guessed what I would find in closing the estate? How could he possibly have known? Had David known before he told him about Claude not finding a Wolfe Bauer before 1945? Did David or Claude or both of them know who Wolfe had been before 1945?*

If they did, surely they would have told him, if not before then at least after they knew what he found in the house in Zurich. He was tired. The work of the trust felt good to him up until the point when he had to start finding people Wolfe stole from. It sapped his strength, almost as though he was guilty by association.

He wondered how much of his privileged lifestyle came from what was stolen from other people. He managed to keep all this from Sam and his mother, but he wasn't confident of his ability to do so in the long run. Would his mother see right through him? He hadn't seen her since closing the Zurich house. They talked on the phone and exchanged a few letters, but she never asked and he didn't volunteer. Right now he couldn't even remember if she ever asked him about closing the Swiss house.

Sam was very astute. He asked only once about the house since Mark came back from there. Even as a small boy he seemed very able to read the adults around him. Unlike some children who were completely oblivious to the adult world around them, Sam, perhaps because he had no mother, had always been like a small adult. Now he was getting to be a young man.

Mark knew he hadn't had nearly enough time with his son to make up for the loss of his mother. It was time to start. The plane was due in only two and a half-hours.

Bauer's Run

Chapter 54

As he came down the jet-way, Sam could see his father beyond the barrier to the customs area. *Dad looks tired. I wonder if he'll tell me what's going on or just expect that I will take being yanked out of school in the middle of the term, or more importantly, in the middle of the only decent trip my class had taken in the last two years. When will you stop treating me like a kid, Dad?* His Uncle David hadn't been all that forthcoming with answers. He talked a lot, but Sam realized after he boarded the plane that his uncle really hadn't said much.

Oh yes, he talked to Sam, but he knew it was just bull. On the long plane ride Sam figured out that as much as David had told him what was going on, he really didn't say much more than what Sam knew already. David talked all around the subject but he was old enough and smart enough to know the one reason they would take him out of school and out of the country was if he was in danger or his Dad was, or could be because of him. *Oh, Hell! Why couldn't they just talk to me?*

As he watched Sam move through the line in customs and presented his passport to be stamped, Mark resolved once more to make sure Sam would not be affected by who Wolfe had been or anything he had done. He would protect Sam and his mother as well. Sam was just a kid; he should be having a kid's kind of life now. His mother had taken a lot when she was married to Wolfe. The least he owed them both was to wrap this up and keep it from them. If he couldn't do that, he wasn't much of a father—son either, for that matter.

Mark swept his son up in a bear hug as he came through the customs barrier. "Look at you! Traveling all by yourself! How was the flight?"

"Fine, Dad. Of course I traveled all by myself. What did you think? I'm not a kid. I can ride a plane by myself. What am I going to do? Get off at the wrong stop?"

What did I say? "Well, that's not what I meant, Son. I'm glad you're here. We're going to have a good time. I have a great hotel suite. We can do some sight-seeing, maybe go to a ball game. Then maybe next week, we'll go to Chicago to see your grandmother."

"For Pete's sake, Dad, it's the middle of the school year! I can't be away for long. That was okay when I was a kid, but now that I'm in fourth form, there are things I must do on schedule if I'm going to get a good slot at university, I'll have to be going back in just a few days."

"You won't be going back, son. I've decided we will live in the States from now on. We'll get you in school in Chicago very soon, you won't miss anything."

Sam lost it. What was his father thinking? He was European; he wasn't going to live in the States. It was great to visit, but they didn't live here. He went to school in France; their home was in Paris! What was he thinking? At this point, the stress of the trip and being taken away from his friends and being treated like a child caught up to Sam. His bag dropped to the floor, his voice raised, his fists clenched, his face flushed and tears ran down his cheeks.

"Why can't you just be straight with me for once? I'm not a kid. Tell me what's going on, dammit."

Mark's shocked silence helped Sam get it together and settle down. He wiped his eyes and picked up his bag and started to walk down the concourse, leaving his father standing there.

When did that happen? I guess he isn't such a kid. When did he learn to swear?

Mark collected himself and caught up with his son.

"We'll talk in the hotel. I'm sorry, I didn't mean to upset you, I guess I just wasn't thinking."

"I guess you haven't been, Dad. Ever since you came back from Zurich the last time, you haven't been yourself. Something happened there. Would it be so terrible to just tell me about it? You think I don't notice when you and Uncle David send Aunt Isabelle to the convent? You think I don't know that's for her safety? Do you think I don't know it was something about your work that got my mother killed? I'm not deaf, dumb, and blind, you know. I've grown up in the middle of your work. Someday I'd like to make a difference too, like you and Uncle David and Uncle Claude. You can't protect me from the world, Dad. Why don't you just stop trying?"

Mark looked at his son in absolute shock. Then it registered, perhaps for the first time that he was looking at his son eye to eye. *When did that happen?* It was an immensely humbled man, who said, "I'm sorry. You are right. I do try to protect you from the world. We'll talk in private at the hotel. For now, just tell me about the trip I yanked you away from."

At that Sam smiled, at least he got the point. "We went hiking in the Vercors. I got to use the ropes more in one of the gorges. I even crossed a river on a rope. Some of the gorges are so deep that when you are in the bottom, by the river, you almost cannot see the sky. We were going to be white-water rafting the first of the week, but I guess I'm going to miss that."

"Some of that sounds pretty dangerous. Do you have experienced guides?"

"No Dad," he said sarcastically, "we don't use experienced guides. It's the music teacher who teaches us how to cross the gorge on a rope."

"All right, all right. I get it. It does sound very risky though."

"This is my third year for this trip, every year we learn more and go farther. Some of the younger boys along this time only get to watch the rope climbs, next year they will get a chance to try in places where they can't fall very far. The year after that, provided they feel comfortable with it, they get to cross the gorge. Even those of us who crossed the gorge this year started out at the beginning of the trip on some small crossings for practice."

By this time, Mark had hailed a cab and they were on their way to the hotel. Sam always liked New York, but today there were other things on his mind. "Dad, did you know that the Vercors was a key area for the French Resistance during the war? We saw a great museum about it the first day we got to Grenoble."

They talked about the museum and the Resistance for a few more minutes until they arrived at their hotel. They were soon settled in the suite, and after consulting with his son, Mark ordered them a meal from the kitchen. He was definitely seeing Sam in a new light. As they waited for their food, Mark cast about in his mind for a way to tell his son what was happening without telling him too much. After several false starts, Sam looked at his father and said, "Dad, I think I have figured out Grandfather Bauer was at least a Nazi sympathizer, who hated my mother because she was a Jew, and was mad at you for marrying her. How bad could the rest of it be? Besides, he wasn't even your father."

Mark just shook his head. "If only that were the worst of it. I didn't know you were aware of that much."

"Like I said, Dad, I'm not deaf, dumb, and blind. What happened in Zurich?"

With a nod, Mark started into the story. They were interrupted after a half-hour by the arrival of their meal, but when the waiter left, he went back to the story and talked all the way through the meal. When he stopped, Sam was silent for a moment and then asked, "What are you leaving out? Nothing that you've told me says why it's dangerous today."

"Why would you think it's dangerous?"

"Because we are having this conversation in a hotel room in New York, not at home. Because it was Uncle David who came to get me after you were already on your way here."

"You are right. It's dangerous because there is a lot more to this than the art. There's also a great deal of jewelry and gold. The gold is the big attraction, we believe. Someone has figured out that I have it. It amounts to millions of francs, certainly enough to kill for. It's in a safe place; the bad guys don't necessarily know that. I was mugged on the street a few days ago."

"Dad!"

"I'm fine. Thanks to a Good Samaritan, I was okay. Your Uncle David thought it would be a good idea for me to move up the New York trip and have you with me, that's all."

"That's not all. Uncle David must have thought that you, or even I, could have been held for ransom if these people are interested in the gold. What does Uncle Claude think? Do you know who the bad guys are?"

"David thinks they could be Middle Eastern terrorists. I'm sure he and Claude will get it all sorted out. We should be safe here while they do. When this project is over, I'm going to retire from this work. I'm burning out, and that could be dangerous for all of us. When Wolfe's ill-gotten gains are gone, I'm going to take a year off. I'm tired and I'm not getting any younger. Besides, I'd like to see more of you before you are off to university. I don't think I realized until today just how grown up you are."

"How are Uncle David and Uncle Claude going to 'sort this out'? They would have to have some idea who the people are, not just where they're from, and if they could be in Paris from the Middle East, couldn't they be just as easily in

New York? Wasn't there a bombing or something here in New York by terrorists last year or so?"

"I guess they could be here," he said tiredly. "We'll just have to trust that Claude in particular knows what he is doing."

Sam stood and began to pace the room. Mark sat quietly to just let his son absorb things. He was mentally exhausted. Finally Sam stood in front of him and said quietly, "Tell me about my mother."

Mark wasn't prepared for that, and made a few false starts, but Sam didn't back down. "Just tell me the whole truth."

It was nearly two hours later when Mark fell silent.

"Thank you. I have wondered a lot about her. All I've ever been given is bits and pieces. I didn't know that she, like Aunt Isabelle, had lost some of her family in the camps. I wish I had known her. Thank you for telling me."

Mark looked at his son in a new light. They discussed going to Chicago to the Harding home, where Mark wanted Sam to be from now on. Sam was not happy but agreed to do as his father wished. They left open the option of him returning to France for university. It was the very next day that they caught a flight for Chicago.

Bauer's Run

Chapter 55

The young man had been thrown out of several doorways along the street now. The population of St-Germain-des-Pres did not take kindly to an element that looked unemployed. He had been watching for the tall man for three days now. The man had not come out of the building, even though the lights had come on and gone off in the apartment where he was said to live.

There had been at least a two-day break in the surveillance, he was told. The picture he was given of the man was taken from a distance and was rather grainy, but he was pretty sure the man had not come out when he was watching. Someone came to relieve him twice, but only for an hour. This was his fourth such assignment. He was hoping if he did this well, the next time he would get something more exciting, but where was the man?

Two men sat smoking and drinking coffee as they watched the main entry of the building that housed some very expensive apartments in St-German-des-Pres. This was the third day they had been watching over the comings and goings of the building. The young man pretending to be a student begging on the street had not escaped their notice.

They actually got a picture of him with his head turned toward them. The sun had been full in the man's eyes at the time so they weren't really worried about him noticing them. The cigarette butts and coffee cups were beginning to pile up around their feet in the small car. They were under orders to report to their superior if anyone took an interest in the building or the tall man who lived there. They had his picture, but so far, they hadn't seen him. They'd sent the film in with their relief man.

The young beggar was actually a young American known to hang around Muslim students of questionable employment, although he himself was not wanted. This made them curious about the man they had not yet seen and presumably were not watching. Neither of them had any desire to question their boss too closely on the subject. Inspector Depardier was known to have a temper, and neither was willing to be the recipient of one of the sarcastic rippings he was known to hand out. The inspector was, at this very moment, sitting in his office with the door closed, talking to his very good friend, David Baruch. The very good friend was, at the moment, himself enduring one of the inspector's blisterings.

"Why didn't you tell me he was mugged? Merde! I've had people watching his building for three days now. That little piece of information would have been useful. At least we would have known why he never came out of the apartment."

"I'm sorry, I had my hands full. At least now we have some breathing room with Mark and Sam out of the country."

"They're where?"

"In New York, actually, didn't Mark call you before he left?"

"No, was he supposed to?"

"I guess I didn't make that point specifically, but I thought he would have."

"I think maybe we'd better get some things

straight here."

Claude laid it out for his friend, as David listened in amazement. He had no idea Claude was fully aware not only of what Mark was up to, but also the level of cooperation he was getting from the government to detail what he knew of David's ties to Tel Aviv.

"So, you see, my friend, it's very difficult for me to protect Mark with one hand tied behind my back and a sack over my head. I'm way off the page here with my superiors. I have no business keeping a team out there watching his back. It would have been nice to know they have been watching an empty apartment. One interesting thing has come up though. I'm not the only one who is having him watched."

"Who else is watching?"

"Take a look."

Claude opened a folder on his desk and removed a photo to hand to David.. The definition was poor, but David's quick intake of breath told Claude his friend recognized the man.

"Well, do you know him?"

"I think I may have seen a photo of him before."

"Cut the crap, you may not know his name, but you know who he hangs out with, and you know who they work for. There's a connection there, I think, to a body found in a trash bin over by the museum. Now isn't that a coincidence! You're going to have to play it straight with me, David. Nothing you tell me in confidence will leave this room, but you've got to tell me what you know. Give me some room to work here, or someone could get seriously dead, and I don't just mean the bad guys."

"Claude, I'm not just trying to stonewall you here, there are actually things you don't want to know. Trust me on this. I get your point that we should be comparing notes on a lot, but there are some things it would not help you to know. In fact, there are some things it just would not be in your best interest to know. I believe Mark has made a decision to stand down when he gets through with this project. Finding out about Wolfe and that he was probably responsible for Katya's death, even peripherally, was worse."

"Something just isn't computing here, David. There's too much reaction here. It doesn't make any sense; he's done this for years without attracting this kind of attention. What's different? What's the Middle East connection? That's what doesn't compute for me. Oh shit. Gold. How much gold was there?"

David didn't answer at once. He had hoped the razor-sharp policeman would miss the point. Claude was glaring at him now. No way around it.

"Millions, actually, billions."

"Oh my God. No wonder."

"The amount pales in comparison to its origin."   "What do you mean?"

"It's from the camps, teeth, wedding rings, etc."

"Oh my God, how could I have forgotten that? Oh,David ... "

"Just after the end of the war, when things were still pretty confused, the gold was promised to the Arabs to fight the newly forming State of Israel. A deal was struck for the future. A future where the Fourth Reich and Islam would be on the same side-temporarily at least.

Apparently when some of the paintings surfaced from Wolfe's stash, someone noticed. Someone who knew there was gold in the same cache. It's my feeling that someone is fairly highly placed today, at first blush beyond reproach. Someone with an identity like Wolfe's. Whoever he is, I think he wants to get the gold before it leaves Mark's hands. Right now, the gold has the taint of illegality about it. If Mark can get it into the hands of legitimate owners, then it's untouchable."

Claude's face was now drained of all color. This was much worse than his worst case scenario had been. He got up from behind his desk and walked to the window. Staring blindly out over the city, he failed to see his favorite view of the City of Light. Finally, he turned.

"This isn't going to be about the gold in the long run. It may be what it's about now, but the danger to Mark won't go away when the project is finished."

"What makes you think that?"

"It's not about gold, it's about knowledge. If you are right, Mark has knowledge about someone whose future would be in danger if Mark made any of this public. This person would lose everything if Mark made his name public."

"But Mark doesn't know the man's identity, any more than you and I do."

"I don't think it matters. If you are right,

and this person is highly placed, he won't be able to take the chance. He doesn't know what Wolfe may have told his son. Our mystery man could be the only one still living who knew Wolfe's identity, and would have to assume Mark was now privy to the same information about him."

Now it was David's turn to blanch.

"If that's the case, Mark will never be safe. It would be a foregone conclusion he would have to be killed."

The two men now knew their longtime friend was in very serious danger. Claude saw it was more important than ever to keep his work on Mark's behalf under wraps. Finally Claude sat back in his chair. "Here's what we need to do . . ."

Chapter 56

When Mark and Sam arrived in Chicago, Renee was so happy to see them that it took Mark several hours to catch on to the fact that his mother's health was failing. There were just small glimpses at first, but by the time his mother went upstairs to dress for dinner; he pulled aside the housekeeper who had been with the Hardings for years.

"What is going on with my mother's health?"

The housekeeper nodded her head, pleased he had caught on so fast. "She's been having some small strokes. You know her doctor is also a close friend, Mark, and he drops in often to see her. He comes at least once a week now, and his wife, who is also a friend, talks to your mother on the phone about every other day. They've all been friends for years. I'm sure she is aware they are keeping close tabs on her, but I think she doesn't mind. The little strokes have scared her I think. She used to be quite independent, but now she seldom leaves the house, and never alone."

"I'm so glad you are here with her."

"I was actually thinking of calling you in Paris when she told me you were coming." Mark patted the housekeeper's shoulder when he saw tears in the woman's eyes.

"I haven't talked to Mother about this yet, but I will tonight. Beginning now, Sam will be living here. I'll be here soon myself. I just have to wind up business and close the house in Paris."

"Oh Mark, your mother will be so happy.

She is so lonely here. She would never tell you that, but she is."

"I'm thinking I should have known that, but we're going to fix that right now. Thank you so much for your loyalty to my mother and your friendship for her."

"The Harding family has been very good to me all these years. I'm not sure you realize, but when my husband died last year, your mother asked me to move into the house here."

"No, I hadn't known that. I am sorry for your loss. It sounds like your moving here has been a good thing all around."

"I need to help cook with the dinner preparations now, if you don't need me."

"Of course, thank you again."

It was a good thing he made the decision to bring Sam here. It made even more sense now that he had seen his mother's condition.

His mind turned to Julia. He was thinking more about her, the closer he got to her. San Francisco was so much closer to Chicago than it was to Paris. He was aware she was at the back of his mind every single day. Soon he would hold her in his arms again. He put off thinking about that, because he knew that when he did, he wasn't going to be able to let her go. He closed himself off from intimate relationships when Katya died, but Julia sailed right in past his defenses somehow. He had the feeling his life would never be the same. With that thought, he picked up the phone to call her.

Julia picked up the phone with her mind somewhere else, and it was a moment before it registered who was on the other end. She had been almost afraid to think about him. There was a part of her that felt disloyal to her late husband when she thought about Mark. But it was the thought of her husband that always led her back to Mark. He would want her to live life fully; he made that quite clear when he had been dying. Her life with him was over.

Being with Mark did not take away from that. They chatted happily for a few minutes and got their timing straight for New York the following week. Mark chose not to tell her on the phone that he and Sam would be living in the States now, time enough for that later, right now he had to think of his mother.

After being in Chicago a few days, Mark was better able to see his mother's deterioration. She cried when he told her that he and Sam were going to live in the States, and when he asked if they could come to live in the big house, she was completely overjoyed.]

***

In a matter of two more days, he registered Sam in a very good private school in a nearby suburb. Sam did very well on his first visit to the school, but his father noticed he was very quiet that night at dinner. After Renee had gone upstairs, he tried to talk to his son.

"Just leave me alone, Dad. I'm doing what you want, but I don't like it much. You've turned my whole life upside down. You can't expect me to be happy about it."

Father and son talked for a while, and Mark was forced to admit his son had a point, and was behaving like an adult even though he was not happy. This surprised him somewhat as he still hadn't quite absorbed the fact yet that the boy was nearly full-grown. Certainly he wasn't that mature in his dealings with Wolfe at the same age. They agreed on the ground rules before Mark went back to New York.

Sam thought privately that this was not going to be a bad move. He had been looked after by the nanny since he was a baby and she treated him like he was still a child. At least here in his grandmother's house, he was treated like an adult; he was even called Master Sam by the household staff. Nearly all of his good friends at school in Paris did not live in Paris. He would be highly unlikely to see them any time soon once school let out for the summer in a couple months, unless some of them ended up at university. He didn't mention this fact to his father, as he didn't see any good reason to let him off too easily. His grandmother talked to him about driving one of the several cars stored in the garages; he hadn't mentioned that to his father either. Once he found out the collection contained a beautiful, bright red, fully restored 1968 Mustang, he decided his grandmother might be slipping, but not as badly as people thought. . His father still thought the only way for him to get around Paris was the Metro. This wasn't going to be so bad after all.

Chapter 57

Julia arrived in New York a bit frazzled around the edges. There was so much to do at home before she could get away, and then, at the last minute, the twins had a science fair project they needed her help with. It was then that she realized the twins had never been without at least one of their parents. They always took family vacations, and since their father died, she had not gone away without them. She was very glad to have a full day in New York ahead of Mark so she could just relax.

She was surprised at the level of luxury of the hotel suite, and the hotel itself for that matter. She came off the plane to find a young man holding a sign with her name on it. To her surprise, he said the hotel sent him. Mark may have told her about it, but it must not have registered. She was shown to the suite by the person that she understood to be the on-duty manager, which she thought was very special treatment.

The three-room suite had two bedrooms, a living area that included a desk and on-line facilities, and fresh flowers everywhere, even in the bathrooms. Mark certainly spared no expense. She was glad to hear of the small, in-house restaurant, which would save her having to search out a good place to eat before Mark arrived. Deciding to have a meal brought up from the restaurant, along with a half bottle of wine, she just relaxed for the evening and got herself organized.

She had just poured a glass of wine when

the phone rang, startling her. It was Mark, checking to make sure she had gotten in and everything was fine. They chatted for a while and, in the course of the conversation, Mark let her know he was leaving Sam in Chicago. This was a surprise to her, a pleasant one, but a surprise none-the-less. She tried to figure out why Mark would take Sam out of school in Paris, bring him to the States, and then leave him in Chicago. Oh well, she thought, not for me to figure out. After dinner, she crawled into a hot tub with a book and the last half-glass of wine.

The next day, when she arrived back at the hotel after a day of shopping, she was surprised to find Mark waiting for her in the suite. He sat in one of the big chairs in the sitting area of the suite and just stared at her.

"You look fabulous."

"I do not. I look tired and frazzled, no fair."

He came to her then, placing his hands at her waist. He looked down into her green eyes like he wanted to fall into them, and nearly did. Kissing her softly—forehead, nose, mouth, lingering there, her soft lips responding to his gentle touch—he stood back from her then and looked into her face.

"What?"

"I'm just checking to see if you are real and really here with me."

"I really am. Could you excuse me for just a moment? I need to freshen up some."

"Take your time, I'm not going anywhere."

He kissed her once more then, with

reluctance, let her go. They lingered long over dinner that night. Mark had ordered dinner from the house kitchen and the food was wonderful. They sat at a table near the window and looked out over the city and Central Park. They talked of their children and mutual friends, for the time being, staying away from the subject of the two of them. When the last of the wine was gone, he took her hand and drew her up to him, and guided her gently over to the sofa. As they sat, he wrapped his arm around her, pulling her in to rest against his shoulder, her long red hair falling over his chest.

"Hmmmm, this is so nice," he said. He knew he had avoided things long enough.

"We need to talk."

"I thought we were."

"I mean talk seriously, there are some things you need to know about me."

"I probably know more than you think. Isabelle and I have been friends for many years, and we do talk as well as write one another."

"There are things to talk about that Isabelle just doesn't know."

"Like what?"

"Like, I love you."

She laughed, "Guess what, she knows that."

He laughed with her and then turned serious. "I was not expecting this. I can't get you out of my mind and only know one thing for sure: I don't want you to slip away from me."

"I'm not planning on it. I feel the same way. I wasn't looking for someone. You sneaked up on me."

He laughed and tucked her closer to him, kissing the top of her head. "There's something I need for you to know. There are some problems with my work right now. That's the reason I came to New York ahead of schedule. David thought it would be safer for me here."

"Safer? Why?"

"Safer because I seem to have gotten the attention of some nasty people. I guess I'd better begin at the beginning. You know I had an American mother and a Swiss father."

"Yes."

"My Swiss father wasn't. He was German—Nazi to be precise."

"Oh Mark with your work that must have been very hard."

"You don't know the half of it. I didn't really find out much about him until recently, certainly long after his death."

He went on to tell her then about Wolfe, not sparing the details.

"So you see, it's not a pretty picture."

"This does not in any way reflect on you. How can you think that it would?"

"Well, I know that. At least I know that intellectually. But I wonder how much of my privileged life came from what he stole from helpless people. I know I have an obligation to find the owners, or their heirs, and give everything back. I won't be at peace with myself until that is done."

"Knowing who you are, and remembering the classes I took from you at the Sorbonne, I can understand that. It must be hard to find people after all these years though."

"Some are hard to find. Many are dead. Others can be found in the same villages they were taken from to the camps. The art is actually the easy part. It has a certain provenance, even when stolen. Money is harder to identify."

"You are trying to find the owners of money? What kind? How could you possibly?"

"I'm talking about gold. That's why I'm here in New York. There are some truly ruthless people who seem to think the gold belongs to them. I have help in high places thanks to David and my friend Claude, but the gold is still in France and still in my name. That's why I brought Sam here. Once it has moved out of my control, this should end. When it does end, it is my intention to move to America."

"But your work is in Paris, you've spent most of your life there."

"My work is about over. When I have returned everything that Wolfe stole, I'm going to hand the Trust over to Israel with David and Isabelle to guide it."

"But what will you do?"

"Asked like a true American. I may teach. I know I need to spend some time with my mother while she still lives and more time with Sam before he goes off to university. Then there's this redhead . . ."

"A redhead, I might have known . . . competition!"

"Ha! Competition is not something you have my lovely. I want to spend time with you, to find out where it leads us. I think I know, but I want to make sure you are feeling the same."

"I am, and it surprises me. My husband has not been gone that long. I didn't expect the way I feel now. I think I'm falling in love with you. I don't know where this is going but think I'm falling in love with you. We live worlds apart. Maybe we should just think about today, right here, right now, just tonight." Her voice rose a bit and contained a tremor of panic.

He moved his head back to look at her. "I didn't mean to overwhelm you. I just don't want to hide anything from you. I'm not very good at this. I am also much older than you are."

"You are just fine. I'm sorry, maybe I am overwhelmed."

She stood up then and walked over to the window and stood looking out at the dense darkness that was Central Park. After a few minutes of her silence, he got up and walked over to her. Touching her shoulder lightly, he kissed the top of her head. She turned to look up into his face, and after a moment, reached up to kiss him.

It was as though she had made a decision. He returned the kiss, but kept his distance, not wanting to crowd her now. She leaned into his shoulder and wrapped her arms around his waist. Hugging him harder now, she stepped up on her toes to reach his mouth, and when she got there, he thought he knew the answer.

"Is this goodbye?"

"No silly. It's hello."

He held her then, fiercely hungry for her. He ran his hands through her hair, the pins holding it flying out to land on the floor. He kissed her, deeply and long. It was as though he had been awakened from an age long sleep. She hesitated at first then, caught up in his ardor, she responded in kind. Picking her up in his arms, he walked to his bedroom and put her down gently on the bed. Her fingers began to open the buttons of his shirt, taking their time then, running her hands through the mat of crisp brown hair on his chest, she pulled him down to her. He let her lead him. Soon she had him completely undressed, and pushed him onto his back on the bed.

Now she stood a few feet away from him, and with an eyebrow ever so slightly arched, began to sway and strip for him. She achieved the desired result, as it was soon clear she had his undivided attention. When the last piece of silk had fallen to the floor, she advanced to the bed. Straddling him, she reached down to swing her hair across his chest before kissing him. The kiss that began at his lips ended after a few delicious minutes at that place where all feeling was focused. Groaning with pleasure, he put his hands behind his head to watch her. It took all he had not to put them on her, but he knew he wasn't going to last much longer. When she had teased him sufficiently, she lifted to lower herself over him. Her heat almost made him lose control; he bit his lip to refocus. Smiling, she began to rock slowly, in just moments he lost all pretense of control as they became one.

They lay awake together for several more hours, talking and making love twice more. He hadn't felt this way ever before, even with Katya.

Julia filled a need in him he hadn't known was there until tonight. For the next two days, they never left the suite. Finally she told him she had to think about going home. He surprised her by saying he wasn't ready to give her up just yet, so it was another day before she called to make an airline reservation.

"Julia, I love you more than I ever thought possible. When I come back, I'm going to ask you to marry me. "

"And you're telling me this now because . . ."

"Because I want you to have plenty of time to think it over."

"I love you too, Mark. I'll be ready."

Chapter 58

After Julia left, he knew he couldn't put it off any longer, so he called David. The two old friends talked freely about what was going on, both with Mark and Julia and with the progress in solving the case of the murdered attacker. David was not able to reveal that he knew the identity of the Good Samaritan, so he spoke instead of the attacker.

"We've been able to positively connect him to the Syrian, but the Syrian himself has not been seen for several days now. Claude is arranging for some protection for you when you return."

"That's hardly necessary. I'll be fine now that I know Sam will be out of the way."

"We hope. I need the address of Sam's school; of course I know your mother's is here in the file. I'll remove it, by the way. I have a friend at Interpol who has a friend in the Chicago police department. Just in case, you understand. I don't want us to be underestimating these people."

"You can't think they would reach out for Sam here in the U.S.?"

"Like every other place on earth these days, it's only a plane ride away."

"I hope you are wrong, but I guess hoping isn't enough. If I didn't know it before, I know it now. I'm getting out of this world. I want to be an old man enjoying my grandchildren one day. I never want to have to think they might not be safe because of me."

"As soon as you begin to think that way, you are right. The world is a worse place every day, and this bunch is worse than most. They'd kill their mothers and never look back. Claude and I will see you through this and then you're out to pasture. Go teach art somewhere. Call me when you have your flight number, I'll be seeing you soon."

As he deplaned in Paris, he saw his partner and good friend on the other side of the customs barrier. When he finally got through with all the formalities and came through the gate, David took his bag.

"I'm glad to see you. How did you leave Sam?"

"He's fine. More so than I thought he'd be at first. I have a suspicion that he and my mother are up to something though. Unless I miss my guess, it's probably something about a driving license. Mother's houseman did take him on a tour of the garages, and I remember myself at that age."

"You can think back that far?"

Mark laughed as they came out on the sidewalk to the taxi rank and got in the first car. As they pulled away, a man who had been standing just outside the door, moved to the edge of the pavement, and when a car stopped directly in front of him, got in the front seat.

"So far, so good. No one appeared to be interested in him."

The car held back and followed at a distance. As the taxi driver talked on, waving his hands and speaking in barely intelligible French, David sat so he could see in the side-view mirror. He saw the car with Claude's men, but no one else seemed to be interested in them.

David saw his friend into the St-Germain-des-Pres apartment, and took a walk through before settling into the sofa in the front drawing room. The housekeeper came with wine and a light meal for them, and then left the men alone.

"I've come to a decision about the gold."

"I thought maybe you would."

"I'm going to send it to Israel. Wiser heads than mine can figure out what to do with it."

"I think that is a good idea, but do you really think it will be that simple?"

"I hope so. I hope you can put me in touch with the right people."

"Are you sure this is what you want? According to Wolfe's journal, the gold came from mostly French men and women. You have the gold in a French bank. Do you think they will just move the money out of the country for you?"

"Only you and I and Isabelle, if you told her, and maybe Claude, have any idea what was in Wolfe's journal. Not the bank. Besides, it's a Jewish bank. The family who owns it has always supported Israel. If it comes down to it, I'm not afraid to enlist their help."

"You realize you have broken quite a few laws bringing it in the country like you did. How many more are you going to break to get it out? It's very hard for Claude to protect you, to say nothing of how dangerous it is for him, while you are doing something illegal. The government is going to want a piece of it for sure. The banking people are probably already running around in tight little circles trying to find out where the money came from and what you are going to do with it."

Mark was chuckling now.

"What's so funny? You could be in a very tight spot here. I don't think you're going to find it easy to get the money out of the country. Claude and I both think the likelihood of you being able to do that is very small. The government itself will keep you from moving it, which is a whole separate problem from the Syrian trying to get his hands on it, or on you, which would be the same thing."

"First they have to find it."

"What are you talking about? You have already shown where the gold is to anyone who cared to be interested in you. It's as clear as if you had taken out a newspaper advertisement. Do you think this bank is any safer than any other bank?"

"In this case, I think it is. You see, it's not gold, it's cheese."

"What in the world are you talking about?"

"There is a reason the gold is where it is. This particular bank is one of the few in France who still have cheese vaults."

"Cheese vaults?"

"Yes, it's quite common in Italy. Cheese, especially Parmigiano and Reggiano are so valuable, they are stored in bank vaults and used as collateral, even currency. Temperature-and humidity-controlled vaults keep the cheese in good shape as it ages. Temperature and humidity won't hurt the gold."

"I'm not following you at all."

"Before I had the gold moved into the

vaults of the bank, I personally packed every bit of it in cheese boxes. It took me a week. The bank thinks they have in their vaults a couple million francs in cheese. Valuable enough for them to protect it closely without burdening them with information they don't need. As long as I pay their fees, they don't care if I move my cheese. They may think I'm nuts, but they are certainly not going to try to stop me. Neither will the government, provided I pay the taxes on the cheese as it leaves the country. No one will know or care."

"The Syrian is quite capable of robbing that bank to get at the gold, if he can't get at it any other way."

"Let's say he can pull that off. He will be looking for gold, not cheese. They are not stored in the same place. The cheese vaults are two levels below the bank vaults. And there is a lot of cheese in there."

David began to see the humor in it, and soon was laughing.

"I hope you can pull this off, my friend, we've got to get you into a more normal line of work."

"You do not know about this. You will not tell Claude. You both need deniability here."

"I won't say a word to him before the fact, but you've got to let me tell him later or tell him yourself."

"We'll see. Now you can stop sweating this. It will all come together, you'll see. I'm going to need some of your Tel Aviv friends, as Claude calls them"

"I'll arrange it.   They're not going to believe this."

"You understand that, for now, they have to think it's a few million in cheese."

Chapter 59

The old man with the wine bottle in a paper bag faded back into the doorway when David walked by, lost in thought. He would have several hours to wait before it would be safe to break into the apartment. Good thing it was a fairly warm night. He could wait where he was until the man slept, and then it was just a quick in and out to pick up the tape from the recorder and leave a new one. Voice activated, it would have something interesting on it for sure, he thought, since the man was there with his business partner for so long before the other man left. He settled down to wait.

Mark took the time, now that David was gone, to call Julia in California. They talked just briefly, Mark telling her again that he loved her, and he would be out of touch for a few days. Before they hung up, he said, "Julia, darling, I love you. Know that I'll be coming back to you as soon as I can."

He went into his office then and opened his safe to look once more at Wolfe's journal. He sat by the window as the light faded alternately reading and looking out over the City of Light. He loved this place, but he loved Julia more. Both were a surprise to him, as he hadn't thought about loving anything or anyone but his mother or Sam in a long time. He just might be able to pull this off. If all went well, he could accomplish his purpose and undo some small part of the evil Wolfe had participated in. What's more, if he could pull it off, neither his mother nor Sam would ever know the whole truth. Sam thought he knew the story.

Young, idealistic Sam couldn't begin to guess at the depths of depravity his grandfather had sunk to. I will keep it from them or I don't deserve them. By the time I am finished, I can go to Julia with a clear conscience. Nothing would be tainted anymore by Wolfe's actions.

He took out a small blue book to read now. This was the one thing he kept from David . . . the book where Wolfe documented his kills.

The record began in 1938; it ended in 1969. That was the last kill. December 13, 1969. More thirty years of murder—not war, murder. The victims ranged from a Jewish shopkeeper in Munich, to a French countess during the fall of France, to a young German private in the last days of the war. There was a doctor in Switzerland, even his Tante Marie and Uncle Fritz. Mark held his head in his hands. *I worshiped him. I followed him and thought he was the greatest thing in my world. Will this be enough? Can I ever make enough restitution for what he did?* The young girl in the book, the neighbor of his in the Freidrichstrasse, the elderly Frenchwoman, the German general who befriended him.

He paced the floor now, thinking over his plan-looking for a flaw. He had to pull this off. It was his only hope. Not just for him, but for Sam, and his mother, and Julia and yes, even for his friends. He had carefully thought out his plan, and now he went over it in his head.

The "cheese" would be transferred to a truck at the back loading area of the bank. The truck would carry the shipment to Marseilles.

From there it would go onto a ship. The ship would dock at the end of its journey at the port town of Haifa.

From there, David's friends would have to take over. He would have returned everything. He would own nothing that he had not earned or inherited directly from his mother or grandfather. He could start a new life then, with a new name. He would not ever have to answer to the name of Bauer when this was done.

It was late now. He was tired; he'd almost nodded off a few minutes ago. He stood and returned the books to the safe. Turning out the light, he closed the door to the office and went down the hall to his bedroom. Tomorrow, or at least soon, he would talk to David's friends and work out the last details. The end was in sight.

As the lights went out in the apartment, the young Israeli who stood guard down the street breathed a sigh of relief. The man had gone to bed now and after waiting a while to make sure the lights didn't come back on, he'd be able to get some rest himself. He could doze in his car farther up the street and be back at his post before dawn.

The old drunk with the bottle of wine was also glad to see the lights go out in the apartment. He would wait for a while until he could reasonably be sure the man was asleep, and then would enter the apartment with the key he fashioned after several tries while the man was away. Once he retrieved the tape, and replaced it with another, he could sleep for the night. Mustafa would keep watch then. He would not have to return for a few hours.

Mark fell across his bed with his clothes still on. He hadn't realized how tired he was from the long trip. When Julia left, he flew to Chicago, spent a day with his mother and son, and then flew back to New York. Boarding the plane for France in early morning, he just got a long nap. He was very tired. Before he finished the thought, he was sound asleep.

He never heard the soft snick of a key in the lock of his front door an hour later, nor the whisper of clothing as the man moved down the hall. He didn't even hear the man stub his toe on the chair Mark left in the middle of the floor. The stranger came and went without the slightest change in Mark's snoring. A few hours later, he woke and looked around in the dim light. Amused with himself, he removed his clothing and got back into bed.

The sun was streaming into the room and the housekeeper was rattling pots in the kitchen when he next awoke. He stepped in the shower, whistling, and by the time he came out, she was shouting at him that his breakfast was ready. He must hurry unless he had fallen in love with cold eggs while he was in America. He no more than arrived in the kitchen before the telephone was ringing. His housekeeper answered it and told whoever was calling that Monsieur Bauer was unavailable at the moment, and they should call back. Mark noted that nothing had changed with her. She took over Sam's care when he was an infant and she was merely nineteen. As Sam came to need her less, she took over the care and feeding of the father. She was younger than he, but treated him like a child. He knew she genuinely cared for them all though, so he let her think he needed her to take care of him. One of the things that he needed to remember before he went on to his new life was to make some provision for her. He would call his attorney today and make arrangements.

He must not forget anything. He just finished breakfast when the telephone rang again and it was David wanting him to attend a meeting with him. Mark knew he would be meeting one of David's friends. The plan was moving along.

Bauer's Run

Chapter 60

The various watchers noted Bauer's departure from his apartment at midday. The young Israeli knew where he was going, so there was no need to follow closely. It was interesting to him though that the old wino, whose station was across from the man's door, soon came out of the doorway and began to follow Bauer at some distance. The young man only had to follow a short way to know for sure, and fortunately, there was a telephone kiosk nearby where he could report his observations.

Mark walked casually as though he had no real destination. He stopped now and then to look in a shop window along the street. As he stopped in front of a florist, he suddenly turned and entered the shop door. While the young lady was greeting him, he noted out of the corner of his eye a movement that was not quite natural. He felt he was being followed and now he knew for sure. This would be easy. He purchased a bouquet of flowers and left the shop with them.

Walking just a few more blocks, he went down into a Metro station. In his peripheral vision, he saw the same color of clothing on the man he had seen in the window of the florist. When the train came in, he boarded it and sat. Two stops later, he got off and headed whistling into the building that housed the Surete.

Once inside, he waited in the great hallway to see if the man would follow him inside. After just a few minutes, sure now his watcher was waiting for him to come out the front of the building, he took a back hallway, dropped the flowers on the desk of a lady inspector he knew as a friend of Claude's and, still whistling, made his way out the back of the building.   David   was beginning to worry when he finally saw Mark enter the opposite end of the gallery in the Louvre. Without acknowledging Mark, David slipped under a rope, which was intended to keep the public out of an area that was being renovated. Mark sauntered slowly through the gallery until he reached the rope, and with a quick glance to make sure no one was watching, slipped under to follow David. Waiting for him at the foot of the back stairway, David led him up the stairs where they found an elderly gentleman waiting for them at the top. Just a few minutes' conversation and his Haifa connection was set. The hard part was done. Just a few more days now and this would all be over.

He spent the bulk of the next several days in his home office. Cleaning up his desk and files and, in general, putting the business of the Trust in order to hand it off to David and Isabelle and Israel. He talked to Julia on the telephone once as well as his mother and Sam. It was his intention to slip out of the country quietly once the shipment safely boarded the ship in Marseilles. David tried to talk him out of even being in Marseilles when the boxes were transferred, but he felt the need to make sure the gold was on its way. His loose ends tied up now; Mark had only one more stop to make before leaving the country. It was time to say goodbye to Sister Michael.

Knowing he was being followed made the job a little tougher, but David had been helpful in teaching him how to spot surveillance and how to lose them without letting on it was being done deliberately. He left his building carrying a small briefcase. He made five stops before arriving at the church where Sister Michael was praying. He knew he'd find her there. It was the place where she had taken refuge as a child when the Nazis took her sister. She came to light a candle on the same day of the month for all these years. She was the only person to whom Mark told the whole story of Wolfe Bauer, and it was to her he turned now. She was the only person he wished to entrust with Wolfe's book of kills. Something in him would not allow him to destroy the book, but it had to be left somewhere he felt it would be completely safe.

He waited until she was done with her prayers, and then they talked quietly for a few minutes. He stood then and reached out to touch her face. "You have been a faithful friend to me. I don't know what I would have done in the darkest hours without you. I will miss you."

"I'm going to miss you too, Mark. Don't underestimate yourself. You are stronger than you realize and it is God who has given you that strength. You are a good man who has done good things for many years. You alone are not required to atone for the sins of Wolfe Bauer. Wolfe has already been called to answer for that. The small boy who followed him could not have stopped him. Forgive yourself, my dear Mark. Go on to your new life now. God keep you, my friend." Mark hugged her with tears in his eyes and then left the church.

***

Mustafa sat on a stool near a window overlooking Montmartre trying to read the transcription of the tape from the professor's apartment. *It made no sense—what was this cheese? The incompetent boob had gotten it wrong. The answer has to be here somewhere, it must be. We must find a new translator—this one I will send home to clean up after my brother's camels.*

The boy stood trembling before the Syrian. His friend Mustafa sat off to one side. So far Mustafa was not much help as the Syrian flayed him with his tongue. He was angry the boy lost the man several times over the last few days. He called curses down on the boy's mother for having spawned such an incompetent.

"We must find where he hides the gold. The gold was promised to us." He then turned to Mustafa. "This is your responsibility. If this son of camel dung cannot help you, get rid of him. You have forty-eight hours to find where the gold is kept, then you both die and I start over with someone with brains."

What did it mean? The gold was cheese or was it that the cheese was gold? He wished he could discuss it with the Syrian, but that had all the earmarks of a fatal mistake. He'd better figure it out on his own.

Chapter 61

Mark strode into the bank with a nod at the security man, walked through to the back of the building and came to a stop in front of a reception desk. This was the fourth bank he entered this morning, and there were three more to go. He was careful not to lose his watchers today. He needed to sow some seeds of confusion and he didn't know how well he was succeeding. The older, gray-haired receptionist smiled when she looked up and saw him standing there. Such a nice man, she thought, as he complimented her on the blue suit she wore today. He asked to see her superior and she went at once to the inner office. Monsieur Giscard had told her that the man was important to the bank, and if he ever came in, Giscard wanted to know of it at once. It was Giscard himself that came out to greet Mark

.   "Monsieur Bauer, come in. How can I help you today?"   Closing the door behind him, Mark laid out his wishes for the banker. An agreement was reached quickly and soon Mark left the office, stopping one last time to compliment the receptionist. A couple more hours of this and he would be finished with this charade. If his luck would hold, he only needed to lose his watchers after the last bank.

Mustafa himself was waiting in a car down the street from the man's apartment. He saw the man turn a corner and walk toward his home. Did this man never drive a car like a normal man? No wonder the boy couldn't follow him. The man was always on foot and ducking in and out of businesses and Metro stations and taxicabs. Where had he been today? Hopefully Abdul's man was able to keep up with the professor. Mustafa could not believe the man was able on his own to shake his pursuers. He just had a lifestyle that was foreign to anything they experienced before. It was hard for him to figure the man out. There were times he seemed like a professional, like when he was able to slip his watchers, and other times he did things so stupid, he could not possibly be considered a professional. He shook his head. Mustafa himself would retrieve the tape tonight. He could not afford to let many more hours go by without success in this mission. There was no doubt that the Syrian meant what he said.

***

David and Isabelle arrived at Mark's apartment in the early evening. The housekeeper prepared a scrumptious meal for them, and the old friends planned an evening to remember. Although they were sad to see Mark leave Paris after all these years, they were happy he found Julia. David also worried about his friend taking too many risks. "I, for one, will be glad when you get on that plane. It is not the same world as it was when we started out returning a small painting or two. It is a dangerous place, and the players out there now are way out of our league."

"All the arrangements have been made. The truck will make the pick up at the bank in the morning, and by evening will be at the docks to load onto the ship. When your people meet the ship in Haifa, it will be handed over to them."

He paused for a moment. "I've decided I will go on the ship myself. My job will be done then. I'll be on a plane right back here to pack up the apartment and get ready to leave for the States."

"You are not going on the ship, and not following the truck to Marseilles. That's an order. Don't even think about it. The ship is Israeli with its own security. The gold will be fine. You need to stay here. Your presence would just call attention to what you are trying to hide. Are we clear on that?"

"You said yourself the ship has good security people. What could happen to me?"

"I'm thinking mainly about the time the ship is being loaded and unloaded. It seems to me that would be the critical time. And if the wrong person saw you there, it would be like a neon sign pointing to the gold. Why else would you be on an Israeli ship?"

"All right, all right, don't worry about it, David. I'm not going to take any risks now; I have too much ahead of me."

They went on to talk of Julia and Mark's plans for a new life. Soon they talked of other things. The couple was going to miss their old friend, but they were happy for him. The doorbell rang a few minutes after they retired to the drawing room. When Mark opened it, he found his friend Claude. "This is a surprise. What brings you here?"

"A small bird told me you would be leaving on a trip soon and I thought I'd say goodbye." Mark raised an eyebrow and looked over at David who tried, without success, to look innocent. "I stopped by on the way to some art thing a friend of mine is dragging me to." They all laughed as they teased Claude. He would go wherever a beautiful woman led him. "I am, after all, French, what would you expect?"

The friends visited for a while and soon the policeman took his leave. He hugged his childhood friend and kissed his cheeks in the French tradition. Shortly after, David and Isabelle also took their leave. Mark closed the door on his friends and went to thank the housekeeper for a wonderful meal. She was just finishing in the kitchen and preparing to leave. Mark poured a glass of brandy, and turning out the light, stood in the front window of his apartment looking out at his favorite view.

Neither David nor Claude could fully appreciate what this meant to him. He was going to turn the gold over personally. Mark felt bad about misleading them, but this was something he had to do.

***

Mustafa saw the lights go out in the apartment, but as he watched, he saw a white blur appear in the darkness at the front window. The man was standing and looking out. He would have to watch carefully before entering the apartment. The man could be walking around in the dark. He had the feeling this could be an important night, as the man's best friends had visited him. It was as though something was about to happen.

The white blur of the professor's shirt

came and went in the window for the remainder of the night. As soon as the watcher thought it was safe, the man reappeared in the window. The professor did not sleep at all this night. Something important was about to happen.

***

Mark was up and moving early the next morning. He had only dozed fitfully in his big chair by the window. He was ready.

Let's get this show on the road, as Grandfather would say. He already prepared himself to leave; even told his housekeeper to take a week off as he would be away. Packing an overnight bag, he called the garage to have his big Citroen brought around for him. He walked out the door just as the car was pulling up, completely taking the watchers by surprise as he drove off.

***

Later that day the boy watched the building while Mustafa listened to the tape with the help of a friend who would translate for him. Mustafa was angry. He just finished transcribing the tape and knew the man was leaving the country. They should know more than the meager scrap of information on this tape. The cheese and the gold still made no sense to him, but the new translator insisted it was correct. With the translation in one hand and the list of the places the professor went the previous day—he knew everything was about to come together—he could feel it.

If they lost him now, Mustafa's life would be forfeit. Bauer must be found. He called his friends to aid in the search. They had a list of all the places that they knew for sure he visited recently. He sent one man to watch the airport, but he didn't think the man would be leaving the country by air if he was driving his automobile. The tape mentioned the docks, so he sent one man to Rouen and one to Marseilles. The Citroen the man drove would stand out around the docks. Allah help them!

Chapter 62

Mark arrived on the street near the bank just as a truck was pulling out from the alley. The truck driver had loaded early and was soon headed south out of the city and Mark fell in several cars back. No need to get too close, he could still see the truck well.

A small, unremarkable gray car holding two men followed the truck out of the alley and now stayed two cars back from it as it turned south. The driver kept looking in his rearview mirror until finally his partner glanced back also.

"What are you looking at?"

"The big gray Citroen back there–I think it was on the street outside the bank."

"Want to find out?"

"I think so. See if you can get the license." He began to slow almost imperceptibly until the cars behind him began, one by one to go around him. Soon, only the Citroen was behind him.

"Got it?"

"Yes, I'll call it in."

The driver pulled over to the side as though to read a map. They needed to get behind the Citroen.

"Merde!" The car belonged to one Mark Bauer. Inspector Depardier told them to follow the truck and make sure no one stopped it on its way to Marseilles. Where did Mark Bauer come into this? The policeman who was driving worked for Inspector Depardier for a long time. It probably wasn't a coincidence that the Inspector's best friend was also following the truck they were following.

"Inspector D is going to be pissed, I just know it. See if dispatch can patch me through to him." He was soon on the radio explaining in somewhat roundabout terms to the inspector what was going on. He was right, the man was pissed.

***

Claude hung up the telephone and was pounding on his desk when his friend David came through the doorway.

He yelled, "Did you know he was planning to follow the truck?"

David turned white. "I thought he understood he was not under any circumstances to do that."

"Well, he is. They are just south of Auxerre. I have to get someone else on the road without telling anyone what is really going on. The idiot! Does he never think before he jumps into things?" Shaking his head, David sat and listened while Claude pulled in some favors to get another car on the road with what was about to become a convoy.

After receiving permission from his superiors, David went to Claude about Mark's plan to move the gold out of the county. Claude responded the way he knew he would, by putting someone on the road as added protection until the shipment was transferred. Claude's job would cease to exist, to say nothing of his pension and perhaps his freedom, if anything went wrong. Even if everything went right, if his superiors got wind of this little operation, the inspector would be inspecting public toilettes for the rest of his life.

***

The truck driver stopped in Beaune to gas up and pick up some food. Mark did the same, as well as the two policemen, one of whom was thinking, "Isn't this cozy? The inspector will have my head if anything happens to this guy." As he went to return to his car, he saw a man tying his shoelaces with his foot resting on the bumper of the unmarked police car. The man stood up as he approached and said quietly, "Inspector Depardier sends his regards."

The man went past him without another word and entered an old truck parked nearby. Before long, one by one the convoy got back on the road, the police bringing up the rear. It was an uneventful drive to the docks in Marseilles.

***

The shipment was off loaded from the truck and loaded onto the ship with a crane. The truck driver, oblivious to the drama that unfolded around him the entire day, parked his truck and sought out his favorite bar near the docks.

***

Mustafa was shaking by the time the last of his men reported to him. They could not find Bauer. The Syrian would kill him—not quickly or easily. They now knew the man was in possession of the gold and was moving it to Israel. It would be impossible to steal once it got to Haifa. The boy who lost the man in the first place now lay dead in the next room. Mustafa killed him quickly and with mercy a short time before—the Syrian would have made it last. There were only a few hours left to deliver the location of the gold. The fact that it would arrive in Haifa, in Israel, at an unknown time at an unknown dock would not be an acceptable answer. His only hope was to find the ship before it left France. That meant looking in Marseilles. He caught a plane and had a car waiting when he arrived. The driver knew what he was looking for.

"There are only three possible ships leaving tonight that are going to Haifa. Only one ends its journey there, the other two merely stop in the city. Tomorrow there is one ship sailing."

"We must check them all."

The two men went from ship to ship learning nothing that could help them. None of the ships claimed a Mark Bauer as a passenger, and no one received a last minute shipment. Allah did not smile on them this night.

***

Mark drove his Citroen into the garage for hire that he located near the docks. It was not the sort of automobile that one would want to leave on the streets of Marseilles for any length of time, as in for more than about fifteen minutes. He found a café near the docks and ate a hearty meal. The ship would be sailing just after midnight and he needed to be on board by ten. Leaving the café, he walked quickly down the dock to where the ship was moored. Now in dark pants, windbreaker, and dark ball cap, he went unnoticed as he climbed the gangway. The captain showed him to a small cabin next to his own and he holed up in there until the ship sailed.

Coming up on deck just once as the lights of France faded into the mist, he spoke briefly to the captain before going below to sleep. This was much easier to accomplish than he thought. Mark was grateful for David's friends. He congratulated himself that he pulled this off without enlisting the help of his friends. The next step was to hand over the shipment to the man who was to meet him in Haifa. In the meantime, he needed to sleep.

***

Mustafa and his driver asked a lot of questions that night. Word spread fast on the docks and soon no one would talk to them. The men who worked the docks didn't like nosy people, especially foreign nosy people. He was forced to report his failure by telephone to the Syrian. He stood slumped against the pole that held the public telephone as the man gave him one last job to do. If he failed this time, he would take his own life before someone else did.

***

The trip to Haifa was uneventful for Mark. The ship was a sturdy old tub that rode low in the water. He came out on deck to watch the docking process. This was the end of the road—within the hour he would be handing over the last of Wolfe's contraband.

***

The man Bauer slipped down the gangway while most of the activity around the ship was focused on the cargo being off loaded. Mustafa stood in the shadow of some large containers. The dog dung of a captain told him he there was no one of the name of Mark Bauer on board. This time the Syrian was explicit: the man dies.

***

Mark made his way to the port authority shed where his contact was waiting for him. A short, neatly dressed young man greeted him as soon as he entered. He handed over the papers for the cargo with little comment. The man told him what a great thing he had done for Israel and her people—they would always be in his debt. Mark simply nodded and shook the man's hand. It was over. He walked out into the sunlight and took one last look around. He had to smile. Wolfe would have hated that the name of the ship carrying the gold to Israel was *The Star of Sharon*. He took the first taxicab in the line and gave the driver instructions to take him to the airport.

***

Keeping his head down and running as fast as he could back to the dilapidated car where his driver waited, Mustafa was barely able to say to follow the taxi.

***

Mark sat back in the taxi and enjoyed the sun and the warmth of the day. His driver was talking to him in the manner of taxi drivers everywhere: fast and loud. The driver stopped suddenly in mid-sentence. Mark heard a sound he didn't recognize. The driver heard a sound he knew all too well. The driver turned his head to look out the right side of the car as he was trying to steer the car off the road. The clatter of a fully automatic weapon broke the silence of the peaceful morning. Mark understood the sound at the same time that he felt something hot slam him in the chest just before the morning sun went out.

Epilogue

As he sat in the sun on the terrace of a desert house, the man closed his eyes and leaned back in the chair. A beautiful, dark-haired Sabra with the bluest of eyes sat across from him. She was beating him at chess again. The doctor demanded that they play at least twice a day, morning and evening, like taking medicine. The drug was for the brain. His needed exercise, the doctor said. They told him he was in the hospital for many weeks before being moved here. He couldn't figure out exactly where "here" was. He thought perhaps they had told him, perhaps many times and couldn't keep things in his head for very long.

This morning, when he was sitting in front of a mirror shaving, the long, jagged scar across his eye and down through his cheek triggered a small memory. One of a sunlit day and an odd sound. He tried to give flesh to that tiny glimpse of a memory, but he couldn't. The harder he tried, the more elusive the memories became, which was exactly what the doctor said would happen. He didn't tell the doctors that there was a dark-haired boy and a lovely redheaded woman flitting about in his memory also. He wasn't ready to share them just yet.

At one point they told him he was in Israel and that he was injured in a hit-and-run shooting on the coast road. He lingered between life and death for several weeks in the hospital. Every once in a while, he got just a glimmer of a hospital bed, but he couldn't be sure it wasn't something his head was making up.

He was slowly getting his strength back

now. Looking at himself in the mirror after his shower, he thought he must have been in pretty good shape at one time. Now he got tired just walking around the house.

The beautiful Sabra that was his keeper (she preferred nurse), told him that today they were going to start with some simple calisthenics to make his neglected muscles work again on their own. She was working his arms and legs as he lay on a table twice a day. Now he must begin to work them on his own.

The Sabra's name was Rebecca. She was gently teasing him that, when they started more serious exercising, he would have trouble keeping up with her. He liked to think she was wrong, but he did have a memory of her lifting him from the wheelchair to the bed when he first came here, so he kept his mouth shut.

A month had passed since he started working out with Rebecca. The pace was brutal at first but, before long, he began to get into it. It felt good. This was something he could do and get better at—not like mind exercises, which were so frustrating.

He ran on the treadmill twice a day now, not long, but he was working at it. His face was tanned from days on the terrace. As he looked in the mirror, he wondered how long his hair had been pure white. The muscles in his arms started to show some definition. He avoided all bets with Rebecca—he found out early on she could beat the pants off him in anything physical. They were now working on some landscaping around the terrace.

He taught himself some exercises for his mind. If he could make his mind as empty as the clear blue desert sky while he worked the muscles of his body, he found there were more glimpses of his past life. He knew he spoke English and French equally well, but he didn't know what that meant. There were some books in the small cottage that jogged his memory a bit, not enough for a real breakthrough, just a flicker seen through a haze.

He knew now that he was in love with the redhead. He was hoping soon to remember her name. His doctor told him his name was Mark Bauer, but it didn't seem right to him. Every time he looked in the mirror, he tried the name on, but it didn't seem to fit. He shook his head. Now that he was getting stronger, he was getting impatient about finding out more about his life. Today, Rebecca promised him a treat. They would get up before dawn, drive to the beach, and run in the sand. He suspected that she would run him into the ground. Only Rebecca would call that a treat. It would at least be a change of scene.

Pulling a knit shirt over his head, he walked out to the old car she kept in front of the house. She was leaning against it with a superior-looking grin on her face.

"This is it, big boy, today's the day you try to beat me in a run."

"Ha! I can beat a girl."

"Oh boy, you said the wrong thing. Are you going to pay for that!"

Laughing, he got into the car. "I always do."

They were doing sprints down the beach; he could

tell she was going easy on him. It was a beautiful place, white sand, blue sky, and bright sun on the water. They were running between two large black rocks that came out of the sea. Laughing as he pulled away, leaving her behind—this time he would beat her.

There came a clattering sound from up near the road, and suddenly he was face down in the sand, his arms over his head. Someone was screaming, "No, no, no!"

Rebecca ran to him and deftly turned him over on his back. His eyes were shut tight. His world exploded around him. He was the one who was screaming. Memory washed over him like the tide. Rebecca said something, but he couldn't make out the words.

"Mark! Mark, can you hear me? You're okay. You're okay. Look at me. OPEN YOUR EYES AND LOOK AT ME."

He slowly and cautiously opened his eyes. There was a halo of sunlight around her head, he couldn't really make out her face in the strong light, but he knew it was Rebecca.

"There was gunfire up on the road, Mark. Is that what you heard? You're okay, you're okay."

He sat up now to look at her. There was something in his eyes that told her.

"You just got your memory back, didn't you?"

He could only nod his head.

"Let's go home," she said.

On the way she told him, "Hearing gunfire is something we are used to here. I'm sorry I didn't warn you. Are you okay?"

"I think so, although I am suffering from too much input right now."

That evening the doctor came to see him and brought another man with him.

"Rebecca tells me you had an interesting experience this morning. How are you feeling?"

"Better than this morning."

"Good. Let's take a look at you."

The doctor stepped back after a brief check of his patient's heart, lungs, and blood pressure.

"It looks like you are none the worse for wear. How's your head feeling?"

"Only slightly less overwhelmed than this morning."

"Great. Take a couple days to rest and get your bearings, then we'll talk."

"There are some people I need to call."

"Not today. That's an order. You aren't ready. Give yourself some time."

They talked for a few more minutes and then the doctor and the other man left before Mark realized the doctor did not introduce the man.

***

The next two days and part of the nights, Mark paced the terrace. Memories came back in floods and he was having a hard time getting his head to slow down. He knew what happened to him now. The memory of leaving the Port Authority shed was clear, as was the brief taxi ride. He was anxious to call Julia. He completely ignored the doctor's orders and tried to use the telephone. It was dead. He thought ordinarily that would have worried him, but he didn't feel threatened here. Lost in thought he didn't hear the slight rustle as someone else came out on the terrace.

"It's beautiful here, isn't it?" He swung around to see the man who visited him with the doctor leaning against the wall of the house. The man advanced toward him with his hand outstretched,

"Itzak Stein, how do you do."

The men shook hands and Stein gestured to a chair and they both sat. For the next half-hour, the man explained Mark's circumstances. His taxi driver on that fateful day was an Israeli Army sergeant, and was the one to stop the bleeding and save Mark's life. There were other military men close by for his protection. The man who shot him was killed; Stein didn't go into how.

Mark was in the hospital in Haifa just two days when there was another attempt made on his life. The assassin was stopped inside Mark's hospital room. The next day, the papers were told that the French tourist shot on the coast road a few days before died of his wounds. They moved him then to another hospital, one guarded by the Army, and then to this house. Rebecca was also an Army sergeant.

"Why?"

"Why what?"

"Why the careful hiding of a French tourist?"

"Mr. Bauer, I don't know a lot about you myself, but I have been told by superiors that I respect, that Israel owes you a debt, one that can never be repaid. That is enough for me."

"I see."

"We made the assumption that with your memory back, you will be anxious to leave here."

"That is true."

"I am also told you need documents, and I am to provide them."

"Thank you. There is something else I will require."

"What is that?"

"A new name. Mark Bauer is dead. It would not be wise for him to resurface, even with an altered face."

The man smiled at him, "Now you get the picture."

***

The arrangements made, Mark spent the next two days resting and thinking. Part of him wished his memory never came back—that was the part of his head that now remembered Wolfe and his crimes. But another part of him knew he did everything in his power to make it right. The fact that he was here and so well cared for was an indication others thought so too. He realized he felt differently now than before he came so close to death; now he could let it go. He was getting used to his new name. Rebecca helped; she no longer called him Mark. The night before he was to leave, they sat on the terrace, drinking wine and watching the stars.

"I want to say 'thank you', but that hardly seems adequate."

He could hear the smile in her voice, "Thank you will do quite nicely. You've been a good patient . . . mostly."

He laughed, "I'll bet."

He stood and walked over to her chair. Reaching down to her he took her hand and drew her up to him. Wrapping his arms around her, he held her gently.

"I'll never forget."

"Nor will I."

He kissed her then. It was a kiss that spoke volumes. He hoped it would say what he couldn't. As he pulled away, he turned without a word and went back in the house to his room. The next morning she was gone. In her place was Stein. The man handed him a pile of documents. An American passport, an Israeli passport, driving license, birth certificate, and two credit cards. He looked up in astonishment.

"These look real."

"That's probably because they are. I also have airline tickets. Let's get going. They like you to check in three hours in advance of international flights, and your flight is from Lod. Taking one last look around, he picked up a small bag and followed Stein out to the car.

***

Five days later, having spent time with his mother and Sam, who were overjoyed to see him after the shock wore off, he boarded a plane for San Francisco. He thought ahead to once again seeing the woman he loved, and decided, in the end, not to call. He walked into the main entrance of the Museum and asked the young woman at the desk if he could see Julia.

"Yes sir. Is she expecting you?"

"No, and I'd like to surprise her, if that's

okay with you."

She, appearing to consider for a moment, then pointed down the hall.

Walking slowly down the softly lit hallway, he anticipated the moment. Standing in the doorway now, he watched her working at her desk. The sun from the window fell across her beautiful red hair. There were a few more lines in the lovely face. No doubt he had been responsible for them. He'd have the rest of their lives to make up for them.

"Hello."

Bauer's Run

Catherine Curtis

Made in the USA
San Bernardino, CA
18 August 2017